~U01159300

Veil of Shadows: The Case of the Order of the Eternal Flame

David L. Waters

Published by David Waters, 2024.

VEIL OF SHADOWS: THE CASE OF THE ORDER OF THE ETERNAL FLAME

First edition. October 22, 2024.

ISBN: 979-8227592163

Written by David L. Waters.

Table of Contents

Veil of Shadows: The Case of the Order of the Eternal Flame is dedicated to the tireless guardians of truth, the fearless seekers of justice, and those who walk the line between light and darkness. To every soul who believes that even the deepest shadows can be pierced by the light of knowledge and courage—this book is for you. May your determination to uncover the hidden and challenge the unknown never waver.

Veil of Shadows

Chapter 1 Introduction

As I stepped from my carriage onto Bloomsbury Street, the fog parted like a ghostly curtain. The gas lamps flickered, their feeble light barely piercing the gloom that shrouded the British Museum's grand facade. A crowd of constables and onlookers huddled near the entrance, and their hushed whispers carried on the damp night air.

"Detective Blackwood," Inspector Graves nods grimly as I approach. "I'm afraid this one's... rather unsettling."

"They always are, Inspector," I reply, my voice low. "What do we know?"

Graves hesitates, his weathered face pale in the lamplight. "It's Dr. Whitby, sir. The museum's lead historian. Found in his office not an hour ago."

A chill that has nothing to do with the fog creeps down my spine. I've known Whitby for years - a brilliant mind, if somewhat eccentric. What could have befallen him?

"Lead the way," I said, steeling myself for what lies ahead.

The museum's cavernous halls echo with our footsteps as Graves guides me to Whitby's office. The door stands ajar, lamplight spilling into the corridor. The coppery scent of blood assaults my nostrils before I even cross the threshold.

"Mother of God," I breathe, taking in the gruesome tableau.

Whitby's body is splayed across his desk, limbs twisted at unnatural angles. His wide and glassy eyes stare sightlessly at the vaulted ceiling. But the symbols carved into his flesh truly chill my blood—arcane glyphs etched in a spiral pattern across his chest and arms, still weeping crimson.

"What manner of fiend could have done this?" Graves whispers, his face ashen.

I lean closer, studying the intricate symbols. "These aren't random, Inspector. There's a pattern here, a... purpose."

"You recognize them, sir?"

I shake my head, fighting to keep my voice steady. "Not precisely. But I've seen similar markings in some occult texts I've studied. This is no ordinary murder, Graves. Someone wanted to send a message."

As I speak, my eyes fall on a scrap of parchment clutched in Whitby's lifeless hand. Carefully, I pry it free, my heart pounding as I unfold it.

"What is it, Detective?" Graves asks, peering over my shoulder.

I stare at the cryptic words scrawled in what appears to be Whitby's blood: "The veil thins. They are coming."

"I don't know, Inspector," I mutter, a sense of foreboding settling over me like a shroud. "But I fear we've stumbled onto something far darker than either of us could have imagined."

I force myself to focus, pushing away the creeping dread. My eyes scan the body methodically, cataloging every detail. The victim's fingernails are torn and bloody—he fought back. Bruising around the neck suggests strangulation, yet the cause of death appears to be exsanguination from the carved symbols.

"The killer took their time," I murmur, more to myself than Graves. "These cuts are precise, almost... ritualistic."

As I trace the air above one particularly intricate glyph, a memory flashes unbidden—another body, another time—my sister's unseeing eyes, her skin pale as moonlight. The guilt crashes over me like a tidal wave, threatening to drown me in its depths.

I clench my fist, willing the vision away. "Focus, Arthur," I scold myself under my breath.

"Did you say something, sir?" Graves inquires.

I shake my head, forcing a wry smile. "Just thinking aloud, Inspector. Old habits die hard."

But as I return to the body, the past refuses to release its grip. I see not just Whitby's corpse but a parade of victims—all those I couldn't save, their faces haunting me with silent accusations.

"Detective Blackwood?" Graves' voice seems to come from far away. "Are you alright?"

I blink, realizing I've been staring blankly at the wall. "Yes, quite," I lie smoothly. "Just... piecing things together."

But inside, I'm anything but alright. This case is stirring up ghosts I've long tried to bury, and I fear what other horrors it might unleash—both from the past and in the days to come.

I straighten up, pushing the shadows of the past to the recesses of my mind. "Inspector Graves, what's your assessment of the scene?" I ask, my voice steady despite the turmoil within.

Graves steps forward, and his brow furrowed in concentration.

"Well, sir, if you pardon my French, it's a bloody mess. But there's a... method to it if you catch my meaning."

"Go on," I encourage, curious to hear his thoughts.

"These symbols," Graves continues, gesturing to the victim's mutilated flesh, "are not random. There's a pattern, like some demented alphabet. And how the body's positioned is almost... ceremonial."

I nod, impressed by his observations. "Excellent, Graves. What else?"

Another investigator, young Constable Fletcher, pipes up. "The lack of defensive wounds, sir. It's as if the victim didn't struggle at all."

"Indeed," I muse, my mind racing. "Either Whitby knew his attacker or..."

"Or he was incapacitated somehow," Graves finishes.

As they continue their discussion, my gaze is drawn to a small, dark object partially hidden beneath the victim's left hand. I crouch down, carefully using my pen to move Whitby's stiffened fingers.

"What have you found, Detective?" Fletcher asks, peering over my shoulder.

I don't answer immediately, my heart pounding as I examine the object. It's an ancient and worn coin with unfamiliar markings that send a chill down my spine.

"Gentlemen," I say slowly, "I believe we may be dealing with something far more sinister than a simple murder." The coin's weight in my hand feels like a key, unlocking a door to mysteries I dread and long to unravel.

I rise to my feet, the ancient coin heavy in my palm. The gravity of what lies before us settles over me like a shroud. "This case demands our utmost attention and discretion," I declare, my voice steady despite the unease churning in my gut.

"But sir," Fletcher interjects, his youthful face etched with concern, "shouldn't we hand this over to Scotland Yard? It's beyond our jurisdiction, surely."

I fix him with a steely gaze. "And have them bumble through the evidence, trampling over clues they can't begin to comprehend?

No, Constable. This is our responsibility now."

Graves nods solemnly. "What's our next move, Blackwood?"

"We dig," I reply, pocketing the coin. "We uncover every scrap of information about Whitby's life, research, and associations. No stone left unturned, no shadow unexplored."

As we exit the gruesome scene, London's oppressive atmosphere envelops us. The fog has thickened, transforming familiar streets into an alien landscape. Gas lamps struggle against the gloom, their light creating eerie halos in the mist.

"Christ," Fletcher mutters, pulling his coat tighter. "It's like the city itself is trying to smother us."

I inhale deeply, tasting coal smoke and damp stone. "Perhaps it is, Fletcher. Perhaps it is."

The distant chime of Big Ben reverberates through the fog, each toll a portent of mysteries to come. As we make our way through the labyrinthine streets, I can't shake the feeling that we're being watched—not just by the shadowy figures that lurk in doorways but by the very essence of London itself.

"Keep your wits about you, gentlemen," I warn, my hand instinctively moving to the revolver at my hip. "I'm concerned that we've only made initial progress in understanding the depth of this troubling situation."

I huddle over my desk in the dimly lit study, the flickering gaslight casting long shadows across the room. Scattered papers and arcane tomes surround me, a chaotic tableau of my frantic research. My eyes burn from hours of scrutiny, but I refuse to relent.

"There must be a connection," I mutter, tracing my finger along a diagram of occult symbols. "Whitby wouldn't have died for nothing."

A gentle knock at the door breaks my concentration. "Enter," I call out, not bothering to look up.

Inspector Fletcher shuffles in, his expression a mixture of concern and exhaustion. "Any progress, Blackwood?"

I lean back, rubbing my temples. "Progress? That depends on your definition, old friend. I've uncovered enough to fill a library, yet the pieces refuse to align."

Fletcher peers at my notes. "These symbols are not just random scribbles, are they?"

"Hardly," I scoff, a wry smile tugging at my lips. "Each one is a key, Fletcher. A key to unlock secrets our fair city would rather keep buried."

"And you can decipher them?" he asks his tone a mix of awe and skepticism.

I chuckle darkly. "Decipher? I'm afraid it's not that simple. These symbols represent ancient rites, forgotten gods, and powers beyond mortal comprehension. Whitby was onto something... something that got him killed."

Fletcher's face pales. "Christ, Blackwood. Maybe we should hand this over to"

"To whom?" I interrupt sharply. "The bumbling fools at Scotland Yard? Or perhaps the Church? No, Fletcher. This is our burden to bear."

He sighs, resignation settling over him. "You're right, of course. It's just... the implications..."

I stand, placing a reassuring hand on his shoulder. "I know, old friend. But we've sworn an oath to protect this city, have we not?

Even if that means confronting horrors beyond our imagination."

Fletcher nods, a glimmer of determination returning to his eyes. "What's our next move, then?"

I turn back to my desk, rifling through the papers. "We follow Whitby's trail. These symbols... they're not just scattered across his body. They're etched into the very stones of London itself. We find them, we find our answers."

"And if we don't like what we find?" Fletcher asks, his voice barely above a whisper.

I meet his gaze, my resolve unwavering. "Then we do what we must, Fletcher. For London. For all of humanity."

As if in response, a gust of wind howls outside, rattling the windows. The gaslights flicker, plunging the room into momentary darkness. When light returns, the shadows seem more profound, more alive.

I can't help but wonder if we're already too late.

I lean closer to the parchment, my eyes narrowing as the pieces finally click into place. Once a bewildering maze, the occult symbols form a coherent pattern before me. My heart races as the implications sink in.

"Good God," I muttered, straightening up abruptly.

Fletcher looks up from his own notes. "What is it, Blackwood? You've gone pale as a ghost."

I run a hand through my hair, struggling to find the words. "These symbols, Fletcher. They're not just random occult scribblings. They're a map."

"A map?" he echoes, brow furrowed. "To what?"

"To something ancient. Something buried beneath London itself." I pause, the weight of my realization settling over me like a shroud.

"Something that should never see the light of day."

Fletcher's eyes widen. "You can't mean-"

A sharp rap at the door cuts him off. We exchange glances, tension thick in the air. I move to answer, my hand hovering over the revolver at my hip.

As I open the door, a gust of fog swirls in, bringing the acrid smell of the Thames. A figure stands silhouetted against the gas-lit street, face obscured by the brim of a hat.

"Detective Blackwood?" a raspy voice inquires.

I nod cautiously. "Who's asking?"

The figure steps forward, revealing a weathered face etched with worry lines. "Name's Hobbs, sir. I... I think I might know something about your historian's murder."

My pulse quickens. "Go on."

Hobbs glances nervously over his shoulder before continuing. "It's not safe out here. May I come in?"

I hesitate, years of caution warring with my need for answers.

Finally, I step aside, allowing him entry.

As Hobbs passes me, a folded piece of paper slips from his coat. I snatch it up, unfolding it with trembling fingers. My blood runs cold as I recognize the same arcane symbols from the murder scene arranged in a pattern I've never seen before.

"Mr. Hobbs," I begin, my voice steady despite the dread coiling in my gut. "I think you'd better start from the beginning."

The door swings shut behind us, the latch clicking with a finality that sends a shiver down my spine. Whatever Hobbs has to say, I suspect it will change the course of this investigation—and perhaps the fate of London itself.

Chapter 2 Inciting Incident

The flickering gaslight casts dancing shadows across the room, transforming the historian's study into a macabre tableau. I stand motionless, my eyes fixed on the gruesome sight before me. The victim lies sprawled across his desk, and limbs contorted at unnatural angles, his skin a canvas of arcane symbols etched in crimson.

"God," I mutter, the words escaping unbidden as I approach.

The air feels thick and oppressive, as if the very atmosphere recoils from the horror it contains.

I retrieve my notebook, its familiar weight grounding me as I begin my meticulous documentation. My pen scratches across the paper, capturing every gruesome detail. The symbols are unlike anything I've encountered—intricate whorls and jagged lines that seem to writhe beneath my gaze.

"What manner of madness is this?" I wonder aloud, my voice barely above a whisper.

As I lean closer, the coppery scent of blood assaults my nostrils, mingling with the musty odor of old books and something... else.

Something I can't quite place, an acrid tang that sets my nerves on edge.

I force myself to focus, pushing aside the growing unease. "Think, Blackwood," I scold myself. "What are you missing?"

My eyes rove over the scene, seeking any detail I might have overlooked. The desk drawer hangs slightly ajar, a faint gleam catching my attention. I carefully pull it open with gloved hands, revealing a false bottom.

"Well, well," I murmur, a grim smile tugging at my lips. "What secrets are you hiding, my friend?"

I pry open the hidden compartment, my heart quickening as I extract a folded piece of parchment. The paper feels unnaturally warm, as if imbued with some inner fire. As I unfold it, my breath catches in my throat.

The letter is written in a spidery hand, the ink seeming to shimmer in the dim light. My eyes scan the cryptic contents, a chill creeping down my spine as I decipher its meaning.

"The Order of the Eternal Flame," I whisper, the words tasting of ash and forgotten rituals. "What infernal game are you playing?"

I tuck the letter safely away, my mind racing with the implications of this discovery. The pieces fall into place, but the picture they form is of darkness and ancient malevolence.

As I straighten, a sudden wind extinguishes the gaslight, plunging the room into shadows. For a moment, I could swear I heard whispers, secrets carried on in the night air. I shake my head, dispelling the notion.

"Pull yourself together, old boy," I mutter, striking a match to relight the lamp. "There's work to be done."

With renewed determination, I return to my examination, knowing that every detail and clue brings me one step closer to unraveling this infernal mystery. And yet, as the night deepens around me, I can't shake the feeling that I've stumbled upon something far more significant and dangerous than I could have ever imagined.

I stride into my study, the floorboards creaking beneath my feet as if protesting the late hour. The shelves loom around me, their contents a testament to years of meticulous collection. My fingers trail along the spines of leather-bound tomes, searching for any mention of the Order of the Eternal Flame.

"There must be something here," I mutter, pulling out a hefty volume on occult societies. "Some thread to follow."

As I leaf through the pages, my mind races. "What connection could a centuries-old order have to our murdered historian? And those symbols..." I shudder, recalling the grotesque etchings on the victim's flesh.

Hours pass, marked only by the steady ticking of the mantle clock and the rustling of pages. My eyes burn from the strain, but I press on, driven by an insatiable need to understand.

"Blast it all!" I slam the book shut, frustration mounting. "There's nothing here but vague allusions and half-truths."

I rise to pace the room, my shadow dancing on the walls in the flickering lamplight. "Think, Blackwood. What are you missing?"

Suddenly, a chill creeps up my spine, causing me to freeze mid-step. The air grows heavy, pressing against my skin like a cold, damp cloth. The hairs on my neck stand at attention, a primal warning of unseen danger.

"What in God's name...?" I whisper, my breath visible in the suddenly frigid air.

I spin around, half-expecting to find an intruder, but the room remains empty. And yet, the feeling persists—a palpable presence that sets my nerves on edge.

"Show yourself!" I demand, my voice echoing in the silence.

No response comes save for the inexplicable sensation of being watched. I grabbed the poker by the fireplace, gripping it tightly as my eyes darted.

"I've faced worse than spectral trickery," I growl, though uncertainty gnaws at my resolve. "Whatever you are, you'll find Detective Arthur Blackwood no easy prey."

A chilling realization settles over me as I stand there, weapon raised against an invisible threat. This case has taken a turn into realms I scarcely understand. To solve it, I need to venture beyond the boundaries of rational thought.

The room begins to blur, reality rippling like a disturbed pond. My surroundings melt away, replaced by a dimly lit chamber I've never seen before. Ancient tapestries adorn stone walls, their faded scenes depicting long-forgotten battles and arcane rituals.

Flickering candlelight casts dancing shadows, creating an otherworldly ambiance that sets my heart racing.

"What sorcery is this?" I mutter, my grip tightening on the poker that has inexplicably followed me into this vision.

Before I can gather my wits, a figure materializes before me.

Ethereal and luminous, she emanates an unearthly glow that both captivates and unnerves. I recognize her immediately from the portraits I've studied—Lady Eleanor Ravenscroft, her beauty unmarred by death.

"Detective Blackwood," she speaks, her voice a sorrowful whisper that seems to come from everywhere and nowhere. "I've waited so long for one who could perceive me."

I swallow hard, forcing myself to maintain composure. "Lady Eleanor, I presume? I... I'm at a loss. How is this possible?"

Her translucent form shimmers as she glides closer. "The veil between worlds grows thin, Arthur. Dark forces stir, and the Order of the Eternal Flame threatens more than you can imagine."

My analytical mind races, struggling to reconcile the impossible scene before me with everything I know about the natural world.

And yet, I can't deny the urgency in her spectral eyes.

"My death was no accident," Lady Eleanor continues, her voice tinged with anguish. "You must uncover the truth, Detective. The Order's reach extends beyond the grave, and their ambitions could unleash horrors upon London—upon the world."

I nod, my investigative instincts kicking in despite the surreal circumstances. "Tell me what you know, my lady. Any clue, no matter how small, could be vital."

Lady Eleanor's form flickers, as if maintaining her presence requires excellent effort. "Seek the Crimson Codex in the British Museum's restricted archives. It holds forgotten histories of the Order's true purpose. But beware—they will stop at nothing to bury their secrets."

Cryptic images flash through my mind as she speaks: a blood-red book bound in strange symbols, a hidden chamber beneath London's streets, a ritual dagger glinting in candlelight.

"The key to it all lies in the past," Lady Eleanor's voice grows fainter. "My family's connection to the Order... the sacrifices made... you must..."

Her form begins to fade, and I reach out instinctively. "Wait! There's so much more I need to know!"

But she's gone, leaving me alone in the strange chamber as reality reasserts itself. My mind reels with questions, but one thing is abundantly clear. This case has taken a turn into the realm of the supernatural. I'm now embroiled in something far greater and more terrifying than I could have imagined.

My heart pounds against my ribcage as I stumble backward, knocking into the edge of my desk. The solid wood grounds me in reality, even as my mind struggles to process what I've just witnessed. Lady Eleanor's ethereal presence lingers like a ghostly perfume, her urgent pleas echoing in my ears.

"Impossible," I muttered, running a trembling hand through my hair. "And yet..."

I turn to the evidence spread across my desk—the occult symbols etched into the historian's skin and the cryptic letter mentioning the Order of the Eternal Flame. The weight of these tangible clues and the intensity of Lady Eleanor's apparition send a chill down my spine.

"There's more to this case than meets the eye," I whisper to myself, my analytical mind already piecing together connections. "The Order, Lady Eleanor, this murder—they're all intertwined."

With newfound determination, I grab my coat and hat. The British Museum's imposing Grecian structure looms in my mind, a beacon of knowledge that might hold the answers I seek.

As I step out into the fog-laden streets of London, I can't shake the feeling that I'm venturing into uncharted territory. The cobblestones beneath my feet feel solid, yet the world around me seems to shimmer with unseen possibilities.

"The Crimson Codex," I mutter, recalling Lady Eleanor's words.

"Hidden histories and forgotten truths. What secrets are you guarding, you ancient times?"

I hail a hansom cab, my mind racing with theories and questions.

As we clatter through the misty streets, I ponder the nature of reality itself. How many times have I dismissed the supernatural as mere superstition? And now, faced with undeniable evidence of forces beyond our understanding, how will this change the course of my investigation—and my life?

The British Museum's columns loom before me, shadows dancing across their surface in the flickering gaslight. I take a deep breath, steeling myself for whatever revelations await within its hallowed halls.

"Into the unknown," I whisper, ascending the steps. "For Lady Eleanor, for justice, and the truth hidden in the darkness."

The bustling streets of London envelop me as I make my way from the museum, my mind reeling from the tantalizing fragments of information I've gleaned. The fog has thickened, transforming familiar landmarks into looming specters. I can't shake the sensation of being watched, unseen eyes dull into my back from every shadowy nook and misty alleyway.

"Get a grip, Blackwood," I mutter, adjusting my collar against the chill. "Paranoia won't solve this case."

Yet even as I scold myself, the hairs on my neck stand on end. The supernatural realm that once seemed so distant now feels oppressively close, as if the surrounding air is charged with arcane energy.

I quicken my pace, my footsteps echoing off the cobblestones. The urgency of my investigation presses upon me like a physical weight. Each passing moment feels precious, as if the answers I seek slip through my fingers like wisps of fog.

"Blackwood!" A familiar voice cuts through my brooding thoughts.

I see Inspector Collins striding towards me, his face a mask of concern. His usually neat appearance is disheveled, as if he's been running through the streets.

"Inspector," I greet him, noting the tightness around his eyes.

"What brings you out on such a dreary evening?"

Collins reaches into his coat, producing a crumpled telegram. "This just came through," he says, his voice low and urgent. "There's been another murder. The details... they're unmistakable, Blackwood. It's connected to the Order."

My heart sinks as I take the telegram, its contents confirming my worst fears. The game has taken a darker turn, and I feel my resolve hardening like steel in a forge.

"We're running out of time," I say, meeting Collins' gaze.

"Whatever forces we're up against, they're moving faster than expected."

Collins nods grimly. "What's our next move, then?"

I take a deep breath, the weight of our task settling heavily upon my shoulders. "We follow the trail, no matter how dark or twisted it becomes. The truth is out there, Collins, and we'll uncover it—come hell or high water."

I scan the bustling street, my eyes narrowing as I spot a secluded alleyway between two looming buildings. "This way," I mutter, gesturing for Collins to follow.

We slip into the shadows, the unnatural fog curling around our ankles like spectral tendrils. I lean close to Collins, my voice barely above a whisper. "The telegram, Inspector. What exactly does it say?"

Collins produces the crumpled paper, his thick fingers trembling slightly as he unfolds it. "'Another lamb to the slaughter,'" he reads, his voice hoarse. "'The Eternal Flame burns brighter with each offering.'"

A chill races down my spine, colder than the damp London air.

"God," I breathe, my mind reeling. "They're escalating, Collins. This isn't just murder anymore—it's ritual sacrifice."

"Sacrifice?" Collins repeats, his skepticism evident even as fear flickers in his eyes. "Blackwood, surely you don't believe—"

"There's more at play here than mere mortal machinations," I interrupt, steeling myself for what I must reveal. "I've had... visions, Collins. Of Lady Eleanor Ravenscroft."

Collins' bushy eyebrows shoot up. "Visions? Arthur, are you well?"

"I'm perfectly sane, I assure you," I reply, though a part of me wonders if that's true. "She appeared to me, Tobias. As real as you are now. She spoke of forgotten histories, a truth that must be uncovered."

I watch as Collins processes this information, his practical nature warring with the undeniable strangeness of our case. Finally, he sighs, running a hand over his mustache. "I've known you long enough to trust your judgment, Blackwood. If you say Lady Eleanor's spirit is involved, God help us all, but I believe you."

Relief washes over me at his words. "Thank you, old friend. We'll need to explore every avenue, no matter how unconventional. The very fabric of reality seems to unravel around us."

Collins nods grimly. "Where do we start?"

I pause, considering our next move. "The British Museum," I decide. "If there are answers to be found about the Order and their ancient practices, we'll find them there."

As we step back onto the street, the fog seems to part before us as if acknowledging our renewed purpose. Whatever darkness lies ahead,

I know we'll face it together, two beacons of justice in a city shrouded in shadow.

The fog swirls around my ankles as I stride purposefully down the gaslit street, my mind a maelstrom of theories and half-formed questions. The weight of the investigation presses down upon me like a physical force, each step carrying me closer to what I hope will be a revelation. I've decided—Alastair Grey is the key to unraveling this unholy mystery.

"Hansom!" I call, raising my arm to hail a passing cab. As I settle into the worn leather seat, I can't help but ponder the enigmatic figure I'm about to confront.

"The British Museum, if you please," I instruct the driver, my voice steady despite the tumult in my chest.

As the carriage lurches forward, I close my eyes, allowing my thoughts to drift to Grey. His reputation precedes him—a man of vast knowledge and questionable allegiances. The silver-haired curator has always struck me as a riddle wrapped in an enigma, his piercing gaze seeming to penetrate the very soul.

"What secrets do you hold, Grey?" I mutter, my fingers drumming an anxious rhythm on my knee. "And will you be an ally or adversary in this infernal game?"

The cab rattles over cobblestones, each jolt mirroring the unease in my gut. Years ago, I recalled our last encounter, when Grey's cryptic words about the "veil between worlds" had seemed like mere academic posturing. Now, with Lady Eleanor's spectral visage burned into my memory, those exact words take on a chilling new significance.

As we round a corner, the imposing Grecian facade of the British Museum looms into view, its columns stretching skyward like ancient sentinels. I pay the driver and alight, my coat billowing in the damp night air.

"Detective Blackwood," a smooth, cultured voice calls out as I approach the steps. "What an unexpected glee."

I see Alastair Grey emerging from the shadows, his silver hair gleaming in the lamplight. His tailored suit and imperious bearing make him look more like an aristocrat than a curator.

"Mr. Grey," I acknowledge, studying his face for any hint of duplicity. "I find myself in need of your... unique expertise."

A smile plays at the corners of his mouth, neither warm nor cold but undeniably intriguing. "Ah, has Detective Blackwood finally stumbled upon a case that defies rational explanation?"

I meet his gaze unflinchingly. "Perhaps. What do you know of the Order of the Eternal Flame?"

Grey's eyebrows raise a fraction, showing that my words have affected him. "My, my," he murmurs, "you ask the most fascinating questions, don't you? Come, Detective. This conversation is best had away from prying eyes and curious ears."

As he leads me up the museum steps, a shiver runs down my spine that has nothing to do with the night air. I've set foot on a path from which there may be no return, and Alastair Grey, for better or worse, is now my guide into the unknown.

As Grey guides me through the cavernous halls of the British Museum, the weight of recent revelations settles upon my shoulders like a leaden cloak. The flickering gas lamps cast elongated shadows that seemed to dance and writhe, mirroring the turmoil in my mind.

"I received word of another murder," I confide, my voice barely above a whisper. "The details... they're truly abhorrent."

Grey's piercing gaze meets mine. "Do tell, Detective. What horrors has London birthed this time?"

I swallow hard, the taste of bile rising in my throat. "The victim was found in a pentagram of their blood. Symbols carved into the flesh, organs... rearranged. It bears all the hallmarks of an occult ritual."

"Fascinating," Grey murmurs, his eyes glinting with an unsettling hunger for knowledge. "And you believe this connects to the Order?"

"I'm certain of it," I reply, clenching my fists. "But the implications... they're almost too terrible to contemplate."

As we enter Grey's private office, cluttered with arcane tomes and peculiar artifacts, I can't shake the feeling that I'm descending into a world of darkness from which there may be no escape. The air feels thick and oppressive, as if the walls are closing around us.

"You must understand, Detective," Grey says, his cultured voice tinged with gravity, "that in pursuing this path, you risk more than just your life. There are forces at play that defy mortal comprehension."

I meet his gaze, steeling myself against the fear that threatens to overwhelm me. "I've come too far to turn back now. Whatever the cost, I must see this through to its end."

Grey nods solemnly, reaching for an ancient, leather-bound volume. "Then let us begin. The Order of the Eternal Flame has roots stretching back centuries, intertwined with the fabric of London's dark history."

As he speaks, I brace myself for the unhallowed challenges ahead, knowing that each revelation will plunge me deeper into a world of unspeakable horror and ancient evil.

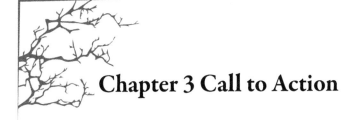

Chapter 3 Call to Action

The gaslight flickers, casting elongated shadows across my study as I pore over ancient tomes. A sharp rap at the door jolts me from my reverie. My housekeeper enters, her face etched with concern.

"A telegram for you, Mr. Blackwood. Marked urgent."

I take the folded paper, my fingers trembling slightly as I open it. Inspector Collins' familiar scrawl leaps from the page:

"Another body. Whitechapel. Same markings. Come at once."

My breath catches in my throat. The Order has struck again.

"Thank you, Mrs. Finch," I manage, my voice steadier than I feel. "I'll be going out."

As she retreats, I slump into my chair, the weight of this recent development settling on my shoulders like a leaden cloak. My mind whirs, connecting invisible threads between this latest atrocity and the mounting pile of evidence we've gathered.

The fog outside seems to seep through the windows, carrying the whispers of dark forces at work. I can almost hear the city's pulse-quickening and feel the shadows lengthening as night descends upon London's labyrinthine streets.

I rise, my resolve hardening with each passing moment. "What game are you playing?" I murmur to the unseen architects of this madness. The question hangs in the air, unanswered but laden with portent.

My gaze falls upon the map of London spread across my desk, each pinprick marking a murder site. Another will soon join their ranks. The pattern eludes me still, but I can sense its edges like a shape glimpsed through frosted glass.

"The Order," I mutter, tasting the bitterness of the word. "What unholy ritual are you performing, painting the streets with innocent blood?"

As if in answer, a chill wind whistles through the cracks in the window frame, extinguishing the gaslight and plunging the room into darkness. For a moment, I stand frozen, my heart thundering in my chest.

Then, with practiced ease, I strike a match, reigniting the lamp. Its warm glow chases away the shadows, but the unease lingers.

"No time to waste," I tell myself, gathering my coat and notebook.

"Collins is waiting, and so are the dead."

With one last glance at the room—my sanctuary amid the storm of this investigation—I step out into the fog-shrouded night, ready to confront whatever horrors await in Whitechapel's twisted alleys.

The weight of my coat settles on my shoulders as I slip it on, a familiar armor against the chill of the night and the darkness that awaits. My fingers brush the worn leather of my notebook, its pages filled with the whispers of the dead and the secrets of the living.

"Time is not our ally," I muttered, tucking the notebook into my pocket. The ticking of the mantel clock seems to grow louder, a relentless reminder of the urgency at hand.

I pause at the mirror, meeting my gaze. The man who stares back is etched with the lines of countless sleepless nights and haunted by memories of cases past. But in his eyes, a fire refuses to be extinguished.

"For Sarah," I whisper the name, a prayer and a promise. My hand instinctively reaches for the locket hidden beneath my shirt, a tangible reminder of why I push myself to the brink of sanity with each fresh case.

As I leave, my eyes fall on the framed photograph of my grandfather, the first Blackwood to don the detective's mantle. "I won't let you down, old man. Not this time."

With a deep breath, I stride towards the door, my mind already racing ahead to the gruesome scene that awaits. "The Order thinks they can outsmart us, Collins," I say to the empty room as if my colleague could hear me. "But they've never faced a Blackwood before."

I pause, hand on the doorknob, steeling myself for what's to come.

The weight of duty and personal vendetta presses down on me, a familiar burden that drives and haunts me.

"Into the abyss we go," I murmur, stepping out into the fog-shrouded night, ready to confront the darkness that threatens to engulf London—and my soul.

As I step onto the cobblestones, the fog engulfs me, a thick, spectral veil that muffles the city's nocturnal chorus. My footsteps echo hollowly, each one carrying me deeper into the labyrinth of London's underbelly. The gas lamps struggle against the murk, their sickly light barely penetrating the gloom.

"Blasted weather," I mutter, pulling my coat tighter. "Perfect for murderers and monsters alike."

As I navigate the winding alleys, my mind races, piecing together the fragments of information I've gathered. The Order's involvement adds a sinister depth to this case, sending a chill down my spine despite my years of experience.

I round a corner, the acrid stench of fear and death assaulting my nostrils. Constables mill about, their faces pale in the flickering lamplight. Inspector Collins materializes from the fog, his expression grim.

"Blackwood," he nods, "I wish I could say I'm glad to see you, but..."

"Save the pleasantries, Collins," I interrupt, eyes scanning the scene. "What have we got?"

As Collins briefs me, I approach the body. It lies twisted on the cobblestones, limbs contorted in an unnatural pose. Blood seeps between the stones, forming intricate patterns that make my skin crawl.

"Dear God," I breathe, crouching beside the corpse. My trained eye picks out details others might miss—the precise angle of the cuts, the strange symbols carved into the flesh. "This is no ordinary murder."

I pull out my notebook, sketching rapidly. "Collins, see these markings? They're consistent with the rituals described in the Grimoire of Shadows. The Order's fingerprints are all over this."

My mind whirls, connecting dots and forming theories. Each new piece of evidence paints a darker picture that threatens to consume not just me but the entire city.

"What game are you playing?" I mutter, more to myself than to the corpse or Collins. "And more importantly, how do we stop you before it's too late?"

I rise from my crouched position, the weight of the investigation bearing down on my shoulders. The victim's vacant eyes seem to plead for justice, and I can't shake the feeling that their silent cry echoes those of countless others who may fall victim to the Order's machinations.

"Collins," I call out, my voice steady despite the turmoil. "We need to speak with any witnesses. Immediately."

As if on cue, a trembling figure emerges from the shadows. A young woman, her face ashen, steps forward. "I... I saw something, sir," she stammers.

I approach her, softening my expression. "What's your name, miss?"

"Elizabeth, sir. Elizabeth Hartley."

"Miss Hartley," I say gently, "anything you can tell us could be crucial. Take your time."

She nods, wringing her hands. "I was walking home from my shift at the factory when I heard... chanting. It was coming from that alley there." She points with a shaking finger. "I saw hooded figures, at least three of them. They were standing around something... someone. I couldn't see clearly, but there was a flash of metal, and then... and then..."

"It's alright," I assure her, my mind already racing with the implications of her account. "You've been fearless. Can you remember anything else? Any distinguishing features of the figures, perhaps?"

Elizabeth furrows her brow in concentration. "One of them... the tallest one... I glimpsed his hand when he raised the... the knife. He had a ring, I think. It glinted in the moonlight. It looked like a serpent eating its own tail."

My breath catches in my throat. The Ouroboros is a symbol I've encountered in my research on the Order. "Thank you, Miss Hartley. You've been immensely helpful."

As I turn back to the crime scene, the full gravity of the situation crashes over me. The Order is growing bolder, their rituals more frequent and brazen. If we don't stop them soon, how many more innocent lives will be sacrificed in their quest for power?

I clench my fists, a renewed determination coursing through my veins. "Collins," I call out, "we need to expand our investigation. The Order is escalating their activities, and we're running out of time."

The fog swirls around my ankles as I stride through the darkened streets, my mind a maelstrom of theories and half-formed connections. The Ouroboros ring, the timing of the murders, the precise locations—it's all starting to form a pattern, a sinister tapestry woven through London's underbelly.

"It can't be coincidence," I mutter, my breath visible in the cold night air. "The Order is retracing steps, recreating ancient rituals. But to what end?"

I find myself at the threshold of St. Dunstan's Church, its weathered stone facade looming before me. Inside, I know, lives Father Malcolm—a man whose knowledge of occult history rivals my own.

The heavy wooden door creaks as I push it open, the scent of incense and old books enveloping me. Father Malcolm emerges from the shadows, his lined face etched with concern.

"Detective Blackwood," he greets me, his voice barely above a whisper. "I feared you might come."

I arch an eyebrow. "You know why I'm here, then?"

He nods gravely. "The murders. They follow a pattern from centuries past. A dark time in our city's history."

"Tell me everything," I urge, leaning forward.

Father Malcolm's eyes dart nervously. "It's said that in the 1600s, a sect of the Order attempted to harness an ancient power. They believed that sacrificing souls at specific points in the city could open a gateway to... something beyond our world."

My mind reels with the implications. "And you believe the current murders mirror those sacrifices?"

"The locations match perfectly," he confirms, his voice trembling. "If they complete the ritual..."

I finish his thought, a chill running down my spine. "Then whatever was almost unleashed centuries ago could be set free now."

As I leave the church, the puzzle pieces start to click into place.

The Order isn't just killing—they're following a centuries-old blueprint for something far more catastrophic.

My next stop takes me to a dingy tavern in Whitechapel. Inside, I find Maggie, a street-wise informant who's always had her ear to the ground.

"Blackwood," she hisses, pulling me into a shadowy corner. "You shouldn't be here. They're watching."

"Who's watching, Maggie?" I press, keeping my voice low.

Her eyes are wide with fear. "The ones in the black cloaks. They've been asking questions, looking for something. An artifact, I think. Something old and powerful."

I lean in closer. "Did you hear anything specific?"

Maggie hesitates, then nods. "They mentioned a dagger. Said it was the key to completing their 'grand work.' Whatever that means."

As I step back into the fog-shrouded streets, my mind races. A dagger, ancient sacrifices, a gateway to another realm—the pieces are falling into place, revealing a picture more terrifying than I could have imagined. The Order isn't just committing murders; they're on the brink of unleashing something that could plunge all of London—perhaps the entire world—into darkness.

I pull my coat tighter, the chill of realization seeping into my bones. The fog thickens around me, as if the city is trying to conceal the horrors lurking within its shadowy recesses.

As I turn down a narrow alley, the hairs on my neck stand on end. I'm being followed.

"Show yourself," I command, my hand instinctively moving to the revolver concealed beneath my coat.

A figure materializes from the mist, cloaked in black. "Detective Blackwood," a raspy voice intones. "You're treading dangerous waters."

I stand my ground, meeting the stranger's gaze. "I've faced danger before. It doesn't deter me from seeking the truth."

The figure chuckles, a sound devoid of mirth. "The truth? You do not know what forces you're meddling with."

"Then enlighten me," I challenge, my mind racing to catalog every detail of this encounter.

Instead of answering, the figure lunges forward. I dodge, but not quickly enough. A searing pain erupts across my arm as a blade slices through my coat.

Gritting my teeth, I retaliate, landing a solid punch that sends my assailant reeling. But as I move to apprehend them, they melt back into the fog with unnatural speed.

I lean against a wall, breathing heavily. The cut on my arm throbs, a stark reminder of the actual dangers I face. Yet even as I inspect the wound, my resolve hardens.

"They're getting desperate," I mutter, tearing a strip from my shirt to bind the injury. "Which means I'm getting close."

The encounter only fuels my determination. Each obstacle and threat brings me one step closer to unraveling this infernal conspiracy. The darkness may be creeping, but I'll be damned if I let it consume this city without a fight.

I push off the wall with renewed purpose and continue my journey through London's treacherous underbelly. The night is far from over, and I feel this is merely the beginning of the challenges ahead.

I stride through the fog-laden streets, my footsteps echoing off the cobblestones. The gaslights flicker, casting long shadows that seem to dance and twist with a life of their own. My mind races, piecing together the fragments of information I've gathered.

"The Order's reach is far greater than I initially surmised," I mutter, ducking into a narrow alley. "But why? What's their goal?"

As I emerge onto a wider street, I spot a familiar figure hunched over a street-corner newspaper stand. It's one of my informants, a grizzled old beggar named Jeremiah.

"Evening, Jeremiah," I say, approaching cautiously. "Any whispers on the wind tonight?"

Jeremiah's rheumy eyes dart around before settling on me. "Aye, Detective. Dark whispers indeed. They say the Order's tendrils reach even into Parliament itself."

My breath catches. "Are you certain?"

"As certain as the fog is thick, sir," he nods solemnly. "There's talk of a meeting tonight. In the old Blackfriar's Abbey."

I press a coin into his palm, my mind already racing ahead.

"You've been invaluable, Jeremiah. Stay safe."

As I hurry towards Blackfriar's, the pieces fall into place. The murders, the occult symbols, the reach of the conspiracy - it's all connected to something far more insidious than I'd imagined.

I pause in the abbey's shadow's crumbling walls, my heart pounding. "What unholy alliance have you forged, gentlemen?" I whisper to the night. "And at what cost to the soul of this city?"

Taking a deep breath, I steel myself for what lies ahead. Time is running out, but with each step, I draw closer to the heart of this darkness. And I swear by all that's holy, I will drag it into the light.

The wind whispers through the ancient stones of Blackfriar's Abbey, carrying with it the weight of centuries and the promise of revelation. I press myself against the cold wall, straining to catch any sound from within. My fingers brush the reassuring weight of my revolver, a talisman against the horrors I've glimpsed in this investigation.

"Come now, Arthur," I mutter, "steel your nerves. The abyss gazes back, but you've stared it down before."

With practiced stealth, I edge towards a shattered stained-glass window, its jagged edges glinting in the moonlight like teeth.

Through the gap, flickering candlelight paints grotesque shadows on the abbey's interior walls. Voices drift out, hushed but fervent.

"The next full moon must complete the ritual," a cultured voice insists. "Our benefactors grow impatient."

"And the sacrifices?" another asks, his tone dripping with anticipation.

I clench my jaw, disgust, and determination warring within me.

How many more innocents must fall before I can end this madness?

Suddenly, a hand clamps down on my shoulder. I whirl, my heart leaping to my throat, only to find Inspector Collins' weathered face inches from mine.

"Blackwood," he whispers urgently, "you shouldn't be here alone. This goes deeper than either of us imagined."

I nod, grateful for his presence despite the shock. "We're on the precipice, Collins. Whatever's happening in there, it's the key to everything."

As we crouch in the shadows, planning our next move, I feel a surge of resolve coursing through me. The Order may have its tendrils in the fabric of London, but we are the city's defenders, its last line against the encroaching darkness.

"Ready?" Collins asks to have his hand on his weapon.

I meet his gaze, seeing my determination reflected there. "Always. Let's end this, once and for all."

Together, we step from the shadows, prepared to confront whatever eldritch horrors or all-too-human monsters await us within those hallowed walls. The battle for London's soul has only begun, but by God, we'll see it through to the bitter end.

Chapter 4 Meeting the Mentor

The flickering candlelight casts grotesque shadows across the faded wallpaper, transforming the small parlor into shifting darkness. I drum my fingers against the worn leather armrest, my mind racing with possibilities as I await the enigmatic Alastair Grey. The air hangs thick with anticipation, mingling with the ever-present London fog that seeps through the cracks in the windowpane.

A floorboard creaks outside the door, and I straighten in my chair, my pulse quickening. The door swings open with an ominous groan, revealing a figure silhouetted against the dim hallway light.

As he steps into the room, I find myself transfixed.

Alastair Grey's silver hair catches the candlelight, creating an ethereal halo around his sharp features. But his eyes truly captivate me—penetrating, ancient, and filled with secrets that seem to span centuries. I've faced hardened criminals and cunning masterminds, yet something about Grey's gaze sends a chill down my spine.

"Detective Blackwood," he says, his voice smooth as aged whiskey. "I've been expecting you."

I rise to my feet, the urgency of the situation pressing on me. "Mr. Grey, thank you for agreeing to meet with me on such short notice.

Lives are at stake, and we need to act swiftly."

He moves further into the room with a fluid grace that belies his years. "Time is a curious thing, Detective. What seems urgent to some may be but a blink of an eye to others."

His cryptic response leaves me momentarily speechless. I clear my throat, gesturing to the chair across from mine. "Please, have a seat. I have some questions regarding the recent... occurrences at the British Museum."

Grey settles into the chair, his piercing gaze never leaving my face.

"Ah yes, the whispers in the halls of antiquity. Tell me, Detective, do you believe in forces beyond our mortal understanding?"

I hesitate, torn between my rational mind and the inexplicable events I've witnessed. "I believe in following the evidence, Mr. Grey. And right now, the evidence points to something... extraordinary."

A slight smile plays at the corners of Grey's mouth. "Evidence can be deceiving, Detective. Sometimes, the truth lies in the spaces between what we can see and touch."

As Grey speaks, I can't shake the feeling that I'm standing on the precipice of something vast and unfathomable. The weight of unseen forces presses upon me, and I wonder if I've ventured too far into the realm of shadows and secrets.

I lean forward, my curiosity piqued by Grey's enigmatic words.

"Mr. Grey, I'm afraid I don't have time for riddles. Lives are at stake."

Grey's smile widens, a glimmer of something ancient and knowing in his eyes. "Ah, but Detective, riddles are the very essence of your predicament. The veil between worlds is thin, and the answers you seek are woven into the fabric of time itself."

His words send a chill down my spine, but I press on. "What do you know about the artifacts that have gone missing from the museum?"

Grey leans back, steepling his fingers. "Consider, if you will, the nature of possession. Are these objects truly missing, or have they returned to their rightful place in the cosmic order?"

I furrow my brow, frustration warring with intrigue. "And where might that place be, Mr. Grey?"

"In the shadows of history, Detective," he replies, his voice dropping to a whisper. "Where the echoes of forgotten rituals still resonate, and the boundaries of our reality grow thin."

As I process his words, I can't help but feel that Grey is leading me down a path I may not be prepared to tread. Yet, the pull of the mystery is undeniable, and I find myself drawn deeper into the web of secrets he's weaving.

I lean forward, my gaze locked on Grey's penetrating eyes. His cryptic words hang in the air, heavy with hidden meaning. The flickering candlelight casts dancing shadows across his face, accentuating the sharp angles of his features.

"The shadows of history," I mutter, my mind racing. "You're suggesting these artifacts have some... supernatural significance?"

Grey's lips curl into an enigmatic smile. "The veil between worlds, Detective Blackwood, is not as impenetrable as most believe.

These objects, imbued with centuries of ritual and belief, serve as conduits."

I feel a chill run down my spine, my analytical mind grappling with the implications. Could there truly be forces at work beyond our mortal understanding? The very notion challenges everything I've built my career upon.

"Conduits for what, exactly?" I press, my voice barely above a whisper.

Grey leans in, his silver hair gleaming in the dim light. "For power, Detective. For entities that hunger for a foothold in our realm."

As his words sink in, puzzle pieces align in my mind. The random pattern of thefts and the inexplicable phenomena at the crime scenes all make a twisted sense.

I lean back in my chair, a spark of realization igniting in my eyes.

"The curator's suicide," I breathe, "it wasn't suicide at all, was it?"

Grey's expression remains impassive, but there's a glimmer of approval in his gaze. "You begin to see, Detective. The threads of this mystery stretch far beyond the confines of your mortal laws."

A surge of determination courses through me. Whatever dark forces are at play, they pose a more significant threat than I'd initially imagined. The weight of responsibility settles heavily on my shoulders, but with it comes a renewed sense of purpose.

"Mr. Grey," I say, my voice steady despite the turmoil in my mind, "I believe I'm going to need your expertise on this case."

I lean forward, my elbows resting as I fix Grey with an intense gaze. "What are the intentions of these entities you speak of? What do they hope to gain by manipulating artifacts?"

Grey's lips curl into an enigmatic smile. "Ah, Detective, you ask the right questions, but perhaps not in the right order." He pauses, his eyes gleaming with hidden knowledge. "Consider this: what if the artifacts themselves are not the true conduits but merely vessels for something far more... potent?"

My mind races, trying to decipher his cryptic response. "You mean there's something else? Something we're overlooking?"

"Indeed," Grey nods, his voice dropping to a near-whisper. "The key lies not in what is seen, but in what remains unseen."

I furrow my brow, frustration gnawing at me. "Mr. Grey, I appreciate your insights but need more concrete information. Lives are at stake."

Grey leans back, regarding me with an unreadable expression.

"Patience, Detective. The veil between worlds is thin, and hasty actions could tear it irreparably."

A strange sensation washes over me as I listen to Grey's words.

The room seems to darken, the shadows deepening in the corners.

For a fleeting moment, I could swear I heard whispers, unintelligible yet somehow urgent.

"Do you feel it, Detective?" Grey asks, his voice cutting through my reverie. "The pulse of the unseen world, beating just beneath the surface of our reality?"

I swallow hard, my skepticism wavering in the face of this inexplicable experience. "I... I'm not sure what I feel," I admit, a mixture of awe and unease settling in my chest.

Grey nods, a knowing look in his eyes. "That uncertainty, Detective Blackwood, is the first step towards proper understanding.

The rigid logic of our world does not bind the supernatural realm.

To unravel this mystery, you must embrace the impossible."

As his words sink in, I feel a shift within myself. The Detective in me, so long anchored in facts and evidence, begins to yield to a new perspective. The air around us feels charged, alive with possibilities I'd never considered.

"Tell me more," I hear myself say, my voice barely above a whisper. "I need to know everything to hope to stop whatever's coming."

Grey leans in closer, his silver hair catching the flickering candlelight. His voice drops to a whisper, sending a shiver down my spine. "Listen carefully, Detective. The key lies in the convergence of the celestial and the terrestrial. The veil between worlds grows thin when the moon's shadow kisses the earth. Seek the place where stone whispers and water remembers."

My heart races, pounding against my ribs as if trying to escape. I'm on the precipice of something monumental; I can feel it. The cryptic words dance in my mind, each one a piece of a puzzle I'm only beginning to comprehend.

"Stone whispers... water remembers," I murmur, my brow furrowing. Could it be..." The thought crystallizes, igniting a spark of realization in my mind.

Grey's penetrating gaze meets mine, and there is a flicker of approval in his eyes. "You begin to see, Detective. Trust your instincts. They will guide you through the darkness that lies ahead."

With a nod of understanding, I rise from my seat, my legs slightly unsteady. My mind buzzes with newfound purpose, the weight of this revelation settling on my shoulders. "Mr. Grey, I... thank you. Your guidance has been invaluable."

Our eyes lock briefly, a silent understanding passing between us. In that instant, I feel I've been started into a world with few ever glimpses, a world of shadows and secrets that lurk beyond our perception.

"Remember, Detective Blackwood," Grey says softly, "nothing is as it seems in this realm. Trust your instincts, but guard your heart. The path ahead is treacherous."

I nod, my resolve hardening. "I won't forget. Whatever comes, I'll face it head-on."

I step out into the bustling streets of Victorian London, my footsteps quickening as the cool night air hits my face. The gas lamps flicker, casting long shadows that seem to dance and whisper, echoing the supernatural forces I now know I must confront.

"Stone whispers, water remembers," I mutter under my breath, weaving through the crowd of late-night revelers and workers. The cobblestones beneath my feet seem to pulse with hidden meaning, each step bringing me closer to... what?

A passing constable tips his hat. "Evening, Detective Blackwood. All well?"

I nod distractedly. "As well as expected, Johnson. Keep your eyes open tonight."

Grey's words replied as I continued down the fog-laden street. Each cryptic phrase, each pregnant pause, takes on new significance. I analyze them, turning them over like puzzle pieces.

"The veil thins where the ancients sleep," I whisper, recalling Grey's intense gaze as he spoke those words. "Could he mean... the British Museum?"

A chill runs down my spine, not entirely because of the damp night air. The pieces begin to fall into place, a picture forming that both exhilarates and terrifies me.

"By God," I breathe, my pace quickening further. "It's all connected. The missing artifacts, the strange sightings, the unexplained deaths..."

A surge of confidence courses through me. I might solve it for the first time since this baffling case began. But with that confidence comes a sobering realization of the dangers.

I pause at a crossroads, the fog swirling around my legs. To my left, the safe confines of Scotland Yard. To my right, the unknown perils that await at the British Museum.

Taking a deep breath, I turn right. "Into the belly of the beast," I mutter, steeling myself for whatever supernatural forces I encounter. "May God have mercy on my soul."

The weight of my revolver presses against my hip as I stride purposefully toward the British Museum, its Grecian columns looming like ancient sentinels through the mist. My heart pounds with a mixture of trepidation and exhilaration.

"Time is of the essence," I remind myself, quickening my pace. "If Grey's warnings hold, the very fabric of our world may be at stake."

As I approach the museum's grand entrance, a figure emerges from the shadows. It's Constable Jenkins, his youthful face etched with concern.

"Detective Blackwood!" he calls out. "I've been waiting for you. There's been another incident inside."

I clench my jaw, steeling myself. "What kind of incident, Jenkins?"

He lowers his voice, glancing nervously over his shoulder. "A guard, sir. Found unconscious in the Egyptian wing. Babbling about 'eyes in the darkness' when he came to."

"Bloody hell," I mutter. "Any sign of forced entry?"

Jenkins shakes his head. "None, sir. It's as if... well, as if whatever did this materialized inside."

I nod grimly, recalling Grey's cryptic words about veils and ancient slumbers. "Right then. Let's not waste another moment. Lead the way, Constable."

As we ascend the steps, I can't shake the feeling that we're crossing a threshold into a realm where the laws of nature no longer apply.

But I've come too far to turn back now. Whatever otherworldly forces await us inside, I'm determined to face them head-on.

"Stay close, Jenkins," I warn, drawing my revolver. "And for God's sake, keep your wits about you. We're treading on unhallowed ground tonight."

As we descend the museum steps, the fog swallows us, Jenkins' footsteps fading behind me. I pause at the edge of the pavement, my mind racing with the implications of what we've uncovered.

The chill of the night seeps through my coat, but it's nothing compared to the icy dread coiling in my gut.

"Ancient slumbers stirring," I mutter, recalling Grey's haunting words. "What have we awakened?"

A distant clock chimes the hour, its sonorous tones barely penetrating the thick mist. I deeply breathe, tasting coal smoke and damp stone on my tongue. The weight of my revolver is reassuring against my hip, though I wonder if mere lead will be enough against the forces we're facing.

As I stepped into the street, the fog parted momentarily, revealing a shadowy figure at the far end of the block. My heart leaped into my throat—is it Grey? Or something far more sinister? But as quickly as it appeared, the silhouette vanished, swallowed by the encroaching darkness.

"No time for spectral fancies, Blackwood," I scold myself. "Focus on the facts, on what you can prove."

Yet as I stride forward, my footsteps echoing hollowly on the cobblestones, I can't shake the feeling that I'm being watched. The fog seems to press in around me, alive with whispers beyond the edge of hearing. I quicken my pace, my hand instinctively moving to rest on the grip of my revolver.

"Whatever you are," I mutter into the mist, "whatever dark design you have for this city, know that I will not rest until I've unraveled your mystery and brought you to justice."

The fog swirls in response, tendrils curling around my legs as if trying to hold me back. But I press on, my resolve hardening with each step. The shadows may claim this night, but I am Arthur Blackwood and will not falter in the unknown's face.

As I disappear into the murk, London's gas lamps flicker behind me, their light struggling against the encroaching darkness—the next phase of my investigation beckons, fraught with danger and otherworldly peril. But armed with Grey's cryptic wisdom and determination, I'm ready to confront whatever horrors await in the depths of this fog-shrouded night.

Chapter 5 Backstory

The acrid smell of gunpowder assaults my nostrils as I bolt upright, gasping for breath. My heart pounds against my ribs, a frantic drumbeat echoing the chaos of that fateful night. I'm no longer in my bed at 221B Baker Street but back in the shadowy halls of the British Museum, surrounded by ancient artifacts that appear to loom in the flickering gaslight.

"Get down!" I shout, my voice hoarse with panic as I dive behind a display case. The shattering of glass rings out, followed by the loud crack of gunfire. I taste copper on my tongue - have I bitten my lip, or is it solely the memory of blood?

Smoke curls through the air, obscuring my vision and burning my lungs. I strain through the haze, desperately trying to make sense of the commotion. Screams pierce the air, mingling with the thunderous report of pistols and wood splintering.

"This way!" I call out, gesturing frantically to a group of terrified museum-goers cowering behind a fallen statue. "Quickly now, to the east wing!"

As they scramble past me, I glimpse my reflection in a shattered display case. My face is pale, my eyes wide doggedly, and I barely contain terror. Is this truly me? Detective Arthur Blackwood, renowned for his calm demeanor, now trembling like a green constable on his first beat?

I shake my head, forcing myself to focus. "Stay calm," I mutter under my breath. "Observe. Deduce. Act."

The taste of adrenaline is bitter on my tongue as I survey the scene before me. Priceless artifacts lie shattered on the floor, their histories lost in an instant of senseless violence. The air is thick with tension, fear, and something else - something otherworldly that sends a chill down my spine.

"Blackwood!" a voice calls out, barely audible over the din. "We need to secure the Egyptian wing!"

I nod grimly, steeling myself for what's to come. As I move to join my colleagues, a stray bullet whistles past my ear, leaving a burning trail across my brow. I stumble, momentarily disoriented, and in that instant, I glimpse a figure moving through the smoke - a silhouette that defies description, seeming to shift and warp before my very eyes.

"What in God's name?" I whisper, my analytical mind struggling to process what I'm seeing. But there's no time for contemplation. The gunfire intensifies, and I'm plunged back into the heart of the fray, the taste of fear and determination mingling on my tongue.

I push forward, my heart pounding as I weave through the chaos.

The smoke stings my eyes, but I force myself to keep them open, scanning for any sign of the ethereal figure I glimpsed moments ago.

"This way!" I shout to my fellow officers, gesturing towards the Egyptian wing. "We must protect the artifacts!"

As we advance, I can't shake the feeling that we're being watched, hunted even. The hairs on my neck stand on end, and I fight the urge to look over my shoulder.

Suddenly, a bone-chilling laugh echoes through the museum halls, seeming to come from everywhere and nowhere. I freeze, my blood turning to ice in my veins.

"Do you think you can stop us, Detective Blackwood?" a voice hisses, its otherworldly timbre sending shivers down my spine.

I swallow hard, forcing my voice to remain steady. "Show yourself!"

In response, the shadows in the room's corner merge, forming a shape that defies logic and reason. It's as if the darkness has come alive, writhing and twisting in a vaguely humanoid form.

"God," I whisper, my mind reeling. "What manner of creature is this?"

The shadow entity seems to grow, looming over us all. Its presence is suffocating, filling the air with a palpable dread.

"We are the guardians of forgotten truths," it intones, its voice a cacophony of whispers. "And you, Arthur Blackwood, are meddling in affairs beyond your comprehension."

I stand my ground, even as every instinct screams to run. "I will uncover the truth," I declare, my voice more assertive than I feel.

"Whatever the cost."

The entity's laughter fills the air once more, and I brace myself for what's to come, knowing that this night will change everything.

The shadowy entity lunges forward, its form rippling like smoke. I dodge, my heart pounding against my ribs, the taste of fear bitter on my tongue.

"You cannot elude us, Blackwood," it hisses, its voice a symphony of malice.

I grit my teeth, anger flaring hot in my chest. "I've faced worse than you," I spit, though my voice quivers.

My hand flies to my coat pocket, fingers closing around the cold metal of my revolver. Its weight is reassuring, grounding me in this moment of madness.

"Have you now?" The entity seems to smirk if such a thing were possible for a being of pure darkness. "Let's put that to the test, shall we?"

Tendrils of shadow lash out, whipping past my face. I fire, the muzzle flash illuminating the room for a split second. The entity recoils but doesn't dissipate.

"Fool," it growls. "Mortal weapons cannot harm us."

Fear and frustration war within me. "Then what can?" I demand, desperately searching for a weakness.

The entity's laughter echoes once more. "Nothing in your pitiful world, Detective. We are eternal, we are—"

Its words were cut off as I drove for the nearest gas lamp, smashing it to the ground. The flame spreads quickly, pushing back the darkness.

The entity shrieks, a sound that sets my teeth on edge. "This isn't over, Blackwood," it hisses as it retreats. "The truth will destroy you."

I stand there, panting, as the flames lick at my heels. "Not if I destroy it first," I vow, my voice barely above a whisper.

The acrid smoke fills my lungs as I stumble out of the burning building, coughing and gasping for air. My coat is singed, and I can feel a warm trickle of blood running down my face from where the entity's shadows lashed out. The night air contrasts vividly with the inferno behind me, and I shiver despite the heat still radiating from my skin.

As the adrenaline begins to fade, the total weight of what I've just experienced crashes over me. My legs buckle, and I find myself on my knees on the cold cobblestones, retching forcefully.

"Steady on, sir," a concerned voice breaks through my haze. I see a constable approaching, his face etched with worry. "Are you alright? What happened here?"

I wipe my mouth with a trembling hand, struggling to find words that won't make me sound completely mad. "There was... an intruder," I manage. "Dangerous. I had to... to set the fire to drive them out."

The constable's eyebrows shoot up. "An intruder? In the old Blackwood Manor? But it's been abandoned for years!"

I compel myself to my feet, swaying faintly. "Not abandoned enough, it seems," I mutter, more to myself than to him.

"Sir, you're injured," the constable says, reaching to steady me.

"Let me call for a doctor."

I shake my head, wincing at the movement. "No, no doctors. I'll be fine." I straighten my posture, trying to regain some semblance of authority. "I need you to cordon off this area. No one is to enter until I've investigated."

The constable hesitates. "But sir, the fire—"

"Will burn itself out," I interrupt. "There's nothing of value left in there, anyway. ... just make sure it doesn't spread to neighboring buildings."

As the constable hurries to follow my orders, I lean against a nearby lamppost, my mind racing. The entity's words echo: "The truth will destroy you." But what truth? And why me?

I gingerly touch the cut on my forehead, feeling the warm stickiness of blood. It'll scar, I'm sure of it. This is another reminder of the night that changed everything.

"No," I whisper fiercely to myself. "I won't let this break me. I'll find the truth, no matter what it takes."

With renewed determination, I push myself off the lamppost and start walking. The streets of London stretch before me, dark and full of secrets. But I'm a detective and do my best to uncover secrets.

"Whatever you are," I vow to the shadows, "whatever game you're playing, I will stop you. For the sake of this city and my family's memory, I will not rest until I've brought you to justice."

The fog swirls around my feet as I disappear into the night, the burning ruins of Blackwood Manor casting an eerie glow behind me. The hunt has just begun.

I stand at the edge of Blackstone Bridge, gazing into the murky waters of the Thames—the city's reflection ripples beneath, distorted and dreamlike. My fingers absently trace the newly formed scar above my brow, a constant reminder of that fateful night.

"What does it all mean?" I mutter, my words lost in the cacophony of London's nocturnal symphony.

A passerby gives me a curious glance. "You alright there, guv'nor?"

I nod, forcing a tight smile. "Just fine, thank you."

As the man shuffles away, I return to the river. The weight of recent events presses down on me, threatening to pull me under like the current below.

"I've seen things," I whisper to the night, "things that defy explanation. But I can't let that stop me. I won't."

The scar tingles as if in response to my thoughts. I run my fingers over it once more, feeling its raised edge. It's a badge of sorts—a mark of my extraordinary path—or perhaps the path that's chosen me.

A nearby clock tower chimes midnight, jolting me from my reverie. I straightened my coat and adjusted my hat, ready to face whatever the shadowy streets of London had in store for me.

"Right then," I say to myself, my resolve hardening. "Time to get back to work. The truth won't uncover itself."

As I turn away from the bridge, the fog seems to part before me, revealing the gas-lit cobblestones stretching into the distance. The city beckons, its secrets waiting to be unraveled. And I, Detective Arthur Blackwood, am more than ready for the challenge.

The taste of determination settles on my tongue as I walk confidently down the moonlit street. The rhythmic tap of my shoes against cobblestones echoes my racing thoughts.

"The Whitechapel case," I mutter, my breath misting in the chill air. "It's all connected. It has to be."

I pause at the corner of Dorset Street, the shadows of decrepit buildings looming over me. A flicker of movement catches my eye—a ragged figure darting between alleyways. My hand instinctively moves to the pocket where I keep my revolver.

"You are there!" I call out, my voice sharp in the night. "Show yourself!"

Silence answers, broken only by the distant howl of a stray dog. I take a deep breath, steadying my nerves. The phantom pain from my scar throbs, a reminder of past dangers and future risks.

"Come now, Blackwood," I scold myself. "Your imagination's getting the better of you."

A gust of wind whips around me, carrying the acrid scent of smoke and something else—something hauntingly familiar. My mind races back to that fateful night, the chaos, the gunshots, the...

No. I vigorously shake my head. "Focus on the present," I remind myself. "The answers are here, waiting to be found."

I pull out my notebook, flipping through pages of meticulous notes in the dim light of a nearby gas lamp. Names, dates, locations—all pieces of a puzzle I'm determined to solve.

"What am I missing?" I mutter, tapping my pencil against the page. "What's the connection?"

A soft chuckle behind me sends a chill down my spine. I whirl around, heart pounding, to find a woman leaning against a doorway. Her eyes glitter with amusement—or is it malice?

"Lost something, detective?" she purrs, her voice hinting at danger.

I straighten, meeting her gaze firmly. "Perhaps. And you are?"

She smiles, revealing teeth that seem too sharp in the shadows.

"Someone who might have answers... for the right price."

My grip tightens on my notebook. This could be the breakthrough I've sought, but at what cost? The memory of my past trauma wars with my desire for the truth.

"I'm listening," I say cautiously, my resolve strengthening with each word. "But know this—I'll stop at nothing to uncover what's happening in Whitechapel. Whatever it takes."

The woman's smile widens, and I swear her eyes flash an unnatural color momentarily. "Oh, detective," she whispers, "I'm counting on it."

As she steps forward, the fog swirling around her feet, I know with certainty that my hunt for justice has turned into the realm of the extraordinary. But I'm ready. Whatever secrets lurk in London's shadows, I'll drag them into the light—no matter the personal cost.

Chapter 6 Exploration

As Inspector Collins and I approach the looming, decrepit mansion, the skeletal fingers of barren trees claw at the night sky, creating an eerie backdrop. The once-grand facade now crumbles beneath a suffocating blanket of ivy, nature reclaiming what man has abandoned. The fog swirls around our ankles, a sinister presence dragging us into the earth.

"Blackwood," Collins mutters, his voice tight with apprehension, "are you certain this is the place?"

I nod, my eyes never leaving the mansion's darkened windows.

"The evidence points here, old friend. Whatever secrets the Order hides, I'm convinced we'll find answers within these walls."

The wind picks up as we near the entrance, carrying the faint whisper of something. A chill runs down my spine, and I can't shake the feeling we're being watched. The uncertainty of our situation only adds to the suspense of our exploration.

"Stay alert," I caution Collins as I reach for the tarnished door handle. "We don't know what awaits us inside."

The door creaks open with a bone-chilling groan, revealing a cavernous foyer shrouded in shadows. Our footsteps echo ominously as we cross the threshold, the floorboards protesting beneath our weight. The air is heavy with the musty scent of decay and something else I can't quite place.

"We should split up," Collins suggests, his hand resting on the butt of his revolver. "Cover more ground."

I shake my head, my instincts screaming against the idea. "No, we stay together. There's safety in numbers, especially in a place like this."

As we move deeper into the mansion, my eyes scan every nook and cranny, searching for hidden passages or rooms. The wallpaper peels away in long strips, revealing glimpses of faded frescoes underneath—scenes of arcane rituals and otherworldly entities that make my skin crawl.

"Look here, Blackwood," Collins calls, gesturing to a series of strange markings carved into a doorframe. "These symbols are similar to the ones we found at Ravenscroft Manor."

I lean in for a closer look, my mind racing. "Indeed, they are. It seems our suspicions were correct—there is a connection between this place and the Order."

A sudden gust of wind extinguishes our lantern, plunging us into darkness. In the following silence, I hear Collins's ragged breathing beside me.

"Stay calm," I whisper, fumbling for matches in my coat pocket. "It's just the wind."

But even as I speak the words, doubt gnaws at me. Is it the wind, or is something more sinister at play? As I strike a match, casting a feeble light around us, I can't shake the feeling that we've stumbled into something far beyond our understanding. This mystery threatens to consume us both.

The match flickers, casting dancing shadows across the peeling walls. A glimmer catches my eye as I relight our lantern—a faint shimmer of light emanating from behind a dusty bookshelf.

"Collins," I murmur, my voice barely above a whisper. "Do you see that?"

He nods, his eyes widening. "What do you think it could be, Blackwood?"

I approach the bookshelf cautiously, my fingers tracing the spines of long-forgotten tomes. "There's only one way to find out."

With a deep breath, I push against the shelf. It gives way with a groan, revealing a narrow passage beyond. The air that rushes out is stale and carries the scent of secrets long buried, adding to the mansion's mystery.

"Should we proceed?" Collins asks, his voice tinged with apprehension.

I hesitate for a moment, weighing the risks. The rational part of my mind screams caution, but my insatiable curiosity wins out. "We must. The answers we seek could lie just beyond."

The bookshelf swings shut behind us as we enter the hidden passage with an ominous thud. The narrow corridor leads us down a winding path, the walls closing around us. My heart pounds in my chest, each beat echoing in the confined space.

Finally, the passage opens into a chamber that takes my breath away—dim light filters through grimy stained-glass windows, illuminating a room that seems to exist outside of time. The sense of discovery is palpable as we step into this hidden sanctuary.

"God," Collins gasps beside me.

The chamber is a treasure trove of the arcane and forbidden. Shelves lined with ancient tomes stretch to the ceiling, their leather bindings cracked and worn. Bizarre artifacts clutter every surface—crystal balls, ornate daggers, and objects I can't begin to identify.

"What is this place?" Collins whispers, his eyes darting from one corner to another.

I run my fingers along a nearby table, feeling the weight of centuries beneath my touch. "If I had to guess, we've stumbled upon the heart of the Order's operations. A sanctum where they conducted their darkest rituals."

The air feels heavy, charged with an energy that makes the hairs on the back of my neck stand on end. It's as if the very walls are watching us, judging our intrusion into this forbidden realm.

"We should document everything," I say, trying to keep my voice steady despite the growing unease in my gut. "Every artifact, every book could be crucial to our investigation."

A chill runs down my spine as I move deeper into the room. What secrets are hidden within these walls? More importantly, what price will we pay to uncover them?

I approach a pedestal in the center of the room, upon which an intricately carved stone tablet rests. My eyes narrow as I study the symbols etched into its surface, their familiarity tugging at the recesses of my mind.

"Collins," I call softly, "bring that lantern closer."

As the flickering light illuminates the tablet, my breath catches.

"These markings... I've seen them before."

"Where?" Collins asks, his voice tinged with apprehension.

"In my research on the Order," I reply, tracing a finger along a spiraling glyph. "This one represents spiritual transcendence. And here," I point to a series of interconnected triangles, "a gateway between worlds."

My mind races, piecing together fragments of lore and whispered rumors. "They were attempting to bridge the gap between our reality and... something else."

Collins shifts uneasily beside me. "Blackwood, I don't like the sound of that."

I'm about to respond when a faint sound catches my attention. "Did you hear that?"

Collins tenses, his hand instinctively moving to his service revolver. "Hear what?"

"Shh," I hush him, straining my ears. There it is again—a soft, barely perceptible whisper from the far corner.

"This way," I murmur, moving cautiously toward the source of the sound.

The whispering grows more distinct as we approach, though the words remain indecipherable. Collins's face is a mask of concern, but his steps are steady as he follows me.

In the corner, we find an ornate wooden panel, its surface adorned with the same symbols as the tablet. I run my hands along its edges, feeling any irregularities.

"There must be a mechanism," I mutter, more to myself than to Collins.

Suddenly, my fingers catch on a hidden latch. With a soft click, the panel swings open, revealing a small compartment.

Inside, nestled among velvet cushions, lies a collection of aged letters and leather-bound diaries. The whispers emanate from these weathered pages as if the words are alive.

"My God," I breathe, carefully lifting one diary. "Collins, do you realize what we've found?"

I open the diary with trembling hands, the ancient leather creaking under my touch. The musty scent of aged paper fills my nostrils as I begin to read, my eyes darting across the faded ink.

"Blackwood?" Collins's voice is tight with apprehension. "What does it say?"

I swallowed hard, and my throat suddenly dried. "It's... it's a record of the Order's activities. Dating back nearly a century." My voice drops as I continue, "Dark rituals, Collins. Blood sacrifices. And Ravenscroft Manor... it's mentioned repeatedly."

Collins leans in, his face pale in the flickering candlelight. "What's the connection?"

"It seems the Manor was a focal point for their ceremonies. A nexus of supernatural energy, they believed." I flip through more pages, my heart racing. "There are accounts of summoning otherworldly entities, of bargains struck with forces beyond our comprehension."

"Surely you don't believe—" Collins starts, but I cut him off.

"I'm not sure what to believe anymore, old friend. But these records are too detailed, too consistent to be mere fabrication."

A chill creeps up my spine as I delve deeper into the diary's grim contents. The room seems to darken, the air growing heavy and oppressive. I glance up, meeting Collins's worried gaze.

"Do you feel that?" I ask, my breath visible in the suddenly frigid air.

Collins nods, his eyes darting around the chamber. "It's as if... as if we're not alone anymore."

The candle flames flicker violently, casting grotesque shadows that seem to writhe on the walls. A sense of otherworldly presence presses in on us, invisible yet palpable.

I clutch the diary tighter, my mind racing. Have we disturbed something by uncovering these secrets? Or is this merely a manifestation of our fears?

"We should leave," Collins whispers urgently. Still, I am rooted to the spot, torn between terror and an insatiable need to uncover the truth.

The shadows dance around us, and I can't shake the feeling that we've stumbled upon something far more sinister than we ever imagined. Whatever darkness the Order unleashed, it seems to linger still, waiting in the shadows of London's foggy streets.

A whisper, soft as a dying breath, drifts through the air. "Arthur... Tobias..." It caresses my ears, sending a shiver down my spine.

"Did you hear that?" I ask, my voice barely audible.

Collins nods, his face ashen. "Names... our names."

The ethereal voice beckons again, drawing me toward the chamber's far end. My feet move of their own accord, curiosity overriding caution.

"Blackwood, wait!" Collins hisses, grabbing my arm. "We don't know what we're dealing with here."

I pause, torn between heeding his warning and pursuing the truth.

"We can't turn back now, Tobias. Whatever this is, it might be the key to unraveling the mystery."

"Or it could be a trap," he counters, eyes darting nervously around the room.

The whispers grow more insistent, pulling at the edges of my consciousness. I gently remove Collins's hand from my arm. "I have to know."

As I approach the far wall, my keen eyes catch a slight irregularity in the stonework. I run my fingers along the rough surface, feeling for any hidden mechanism.

"Ah!" I exclaim as a section of the wall gives way beneath my touch. A hidden door swings open, revealing a narrow staircase descending into impenetrable darkness.

I hesitate at the threshold, peering into the abyss. The whispers emanate from below, growing stronger with each passing moment.

"Arthur," Collins warns, his voice tight and concerned. "Think this through."

I turn to my loyal friend, seeing the fear and worry etched on his face. "I must, Tobias. Whatever lies below might hold the answers we seek."

With a deep breath, I place my foot on the first step, the darkness swallowing me as I descend into the unknown.

The staircase spirals downward, each step creaking ominously beneath my feet. The air grows thick, almost oppressive, as if the atmosphere is trying to force me back. But I press on, driven by an insatiable need to uncover the truth.

"Blackwood," the whispers caress my ears, growing more distinct with each step. "Come closer..."

My heart pounds in my chest, a mix of excitement and trepidation coursing through my veins. The darkness is almost complete now, except for a faint, otherworldly glow from below.

As I reach the bottom, the chamber steals my breath away. Ancient relics line the walls, their surfaces etched with arcane symbols that seem to writhe in the dim light. The air is heavy with the scent of decay and something older and far more sinister.

"God," I whisper, my eyes wide as I take the scene. "What is this place?"

The sound of footsteps behind me announces Collins's arrival. I turn to see his usually composed face now slack with shock.

"Arthur," he breathes, "I've seen nothing like this. It's... it's..."

"The heart of it all," I finish for him, my mind racing. "The Order's inner sanctum."

As we step into the chamber, the whispers crescendo into a cacophony of voices, each vying for our attention. I force myself to focus, scanning the room for any clue that might shed light on the murders plaguing London.

"Look at these markings," I say, gesturing to a nearby altar. "They match the symbols we found at the crime scenes."

Collins nods grimly. "Aye, and those over there," he points to a far corner, "I recognize from the victim's bodies."

A chill runs down my spine as the full implications hit me. "This is where they performed their rituals," I murmur, my voice barely audible over the supernatural whispers. "Whatever dark power they were trying to harness, it all started here."

"We need to leave," Collins urges, his hand instinctively moving toward his revolver. "This place... it's not right, Arthur. We're not meant to be here."

I turn to him, seeing the fear in his eyes and the unwavering loyalty that has made him my most trusted ally. "Just a few more minutes, Tobias. We may never get another chance like this."

As I move deeper into the chamber, the whispers merge, forming words I can almost understand. I strain to listen, knowing the key to unraveling this mystery might lie within their ethereal chorus.

My fingers trace the cold stone of an ornate pillar, feeling for any irregularities. Suddenly, a section gives way under my touch, sliding inward with a soft click. The whispers intensify, as if urging me on.

"Blackwood, what have you found?" Collins asks, his voice tight and apprehensive.

"A hidden compartment," I reply, my heart racing. "Help me with this."

Together, we pry open the concealed drawer. Inside lies a weathered parchment, its edges crumbling beneath my trembling fingers. As I unfurl it, my breath catches in my throat.

"It's a map," I whisper, eyes wide. "Collins, look at this. It shows secret rooms all across London."

Collins leans in, his mustache twitching as he frowns. "God, Arthur. The Order's reach... it's far greater than we imagined."

I nod, my mind already racing with possibilities. "This is it, Tobias. Our key to unraveling their entire network."

"And our way out of this godforsaken place, I hope," Collins mutters, glancing over his shoulder.

"Indeed," I agree, carefully folding the map and tucking it into my coat. "Let's make haste. We've much to discuss, and I'd prefer to do it somewhere less... occupied."

I can't shake the feeling we're being watched as we retrace our steps through the hidden passages. The walls seem to pulse with otherworldly energy, and the whispers follow us, growing more insistent with each step.

"Tell me, Tobias," I say, desperate to distract myself from the oppressive atmosphere, "what do you make of all this? The Order, the murders, these secret chambers..."

Collins lets out a heavy sigh. "I've seen many dark things in my years on the force, Arthur, but this... this is beyond anything I could have imagined. It's as if we've stumbled into a nightmare."

"A nightmare we must see through to its end," I reply, my voice filled with grim determination. "Whatever the cost."

As we emerge from the final hidden door, the familiar musty air of the mansion's main floor greets us. I pause, taking a moment to collect my thoughts.

"We have a long night ahead of us, my friend," I tell Collins. "The map may be our guide, but I fear the path it leads us down will be fraught with dangers we've yet to comprehend."

Collins nods, his eyes reflecting the same mix of fear and resolve I feel churning within me. "Where you go, I follow, Arthur. God help us both."

With one last glance at the secrets we've left behind, we step forward into the unknown, the weight of our discovery heavy upon our shoulders.

As we step out of the dilapidated mansion, the fog-laden air of Victorian London envelops us like a shroud. The gas lamps flicker weakly, their light barely penetrating the oppressive darkness that seems to have followed us from the depths of that accursed chamber.

I pause on the crumbling steps, my mind reeling from our uncovered revelations. The map in my coat pocket feels like a lead weight; each location marked a potential gateway to further horrors.

"Arthur," Collins' voice breaks through my reverie, "what's our next move?"

I turn to face him, noting the worry etched across his features. "We follow the trail, Tobias. Each location," I tap my pocket, "holds a puzzle piece. We must uncover them all to stop whatever dark design the Order has set in motion."

As we go down the overgrown path, the whispers that haunted us in the chamber seem to have followed, carried on the night wind. I can't shake the feeling that we're being watched, observed by unseen eyes from every shadow.

"Do you hear that?" I ask, my voice barely above a whisper.

Collins strains, listening. "I hear nothing but the wind, Arthur."

I nod, unsure whether to be relieved or more concerned. "Perhaps it's just my imagination, then. This case... it's affecting me more than I care to admit."

We reach the wrought-iron gates, their rusted hinges groaning in protest as we push through. The streets of London stretch before us, a maze of potential dangers and revelations.

"I can't help but feel," I say, my eyes scanning the fog-shrouded streets, "that with each step closer to the truth, we're inviting something... darker into our lives. The Order's influence seems to seep into the very stones of this city."

Collins places a reassuring hand on my shoulder. "We've faced darkness before, Arthur. We'll face it again together."

I manage a grim smile, grateful for his unwavering support.

"Indeed, we shall, old friend. Indeed, we shall."

As we set off into the night, Big Ben's chime echoes in the distance, a reminder of the world we're fighting to protect. Yet with each toll, the shadows seem to grow longer, the whispers more insistent. We're on the precipice of something monumental—I can feel it in my bones. And I fear we'll be forced to confront horrors beyond our wildest imaginings before this case ends.

Chapter 7 First Challenge

The heavy oak door creaks open, revealing a chamber shrouded in darkness. I pause at the threshold, my eyes straining to pierce the gloom. The flickering light of my lantern casts long shadows that dance across the walls, hinting at secrets hidden in the murky depths.

"Steady now, Collins," I murmur, my voice barely above a whisper. "We don't know what awaits us."

Inspector Collins nods, his weathered face etched with tension.

"Right, you are, Blackwood. I've got a queer feeling about this place."

We step inside, our footfalls echoing in the oppressive silence. The floorboards groan beneath our weight as if protesting our intrusion.

I sweep my lantern in a slow arc, illuminating the room's contents.

My breath catches in my throat. The walls are adorned with arcane symbols, their sinister forms seeming to writhe in the flickering light. Pentagrams, inverted crosses, and esoteric runes cover every surface, a tapestry of the occult that makes my skin crawl.

"Lord," Collins breathes, his mustache twitching. "What manner of deviltry is this?"

I don't answer immediately, my mind racing to catalog every detail.

The air is thick with the scent of melted wax and something else—a cloying, metallic odor that sets my teeth on edge. Candles of varying sizes are scattered throughout the room, flames guttering in an unfelt breeze.

"This is far beyond our usual fare, my friend," I finally respond, my voice tight. "We've stumbled upon something truly sinister."

As I speak, a chill runs down my spine. The shadows seem to deepen, pressing around us almost palpably. I can't shake the feeling that we're being watched, observed by unseen eyes that peer out from the darkness.

Collins moves closer, his shoulder brushing mine. "What's our next move, Arthur? This is well outside my area of expertise."

I take a deep breath, centering myself. "We proceed with caution. Document everything, but touch nothing. These symbols are not mere decoration. They have power, Collins. Actual power."

"You don't mean to say you believe in all this mumbo-jumbo?" Collins asks, skepticism warring with unease in his voice.

I turn to face him, my expression grim. "After what we've seen these past months, can we afford not to? The world is changing, old friend. The veil between what we know and fear is growing thin."

As if in response to my words, the candles flicker violently.

Shadows leap and twist across the walls, forming grotesque shapes that vanish as quickly as they appear. My heart pounds in my chest, adrenaline surging through my veins.

"Stay close," I warn Collins, my hand instinctively moving towards the revolver at my hip. "And be ready for anything."

The words barely left my lips when a sudden chill permeated the air, causing the hairs on my neck to stand on end. The temperature plummeted, and I could see my breath misting before me. A low, otherworldly moan echoed through the room, seeming to come from everywhere and nowhere.

"Blackwood," Collins whispers, his voice tight with fear, "what in God's name is that?"

I don't answer, my eyes fixed on the far corner of the room where the shadows are coalescing, twisting, and writhing into a vaguely humanoid shape. As we watch, a spectral figure emerges from the darkness, frozen in place. Its form is translucent, shimmering like a heat haze, but its eyes glow with an unearthly, piercing light that seems to bore into my soul. It's a being from a realm beyond our own, a creature of nightmares and ancient lore.

"Steady, Collins," I murmur, trying to keep the tremor from my voice. My hand moves of its own accord, fingers closing around the grip of my revolver. The cold metal offers a fleeting comfort, a connection to the rational world I know. But as I draw the weapon, a chilling realization washes over me.

What use is lead and gunpowder against a being that defies the very laws of nature?

The entity drifts towards us; its movements are fluid and unnatural.

The surrounding air seems to ripple and distort, and I can feel an oppressive weight settling over my mind, threatening to crush my resolve.

"This can't be real," I think, even as my analytical mind races to understand what I'm seeing. "There must be an explanation, a trick of the light, a hidden mechanism..."

But deep down, I know the truth. We've stumbled into something far beyond our understanding, where the impossible becomes terrifyingly real.

"Arthur," Collins's voice breaks through my internal struggle, "what do we do?"

I swallow hard, my mouth dry as parchment. "I... I don't know, Tobias. But we can't back down now. Whatever this thing is, it holds the key to our investigation. We must communicate, to understand..."

The entity continues its inexorable approach, and I steel myself for whatever comes next, knowing that this encounter will change everything.

As the spectral figure looms closer, a familiar voice resonates within my mind, cutting through the fog of fear and uncertainty.

"Blackwood," Grey's silky tone echoes, "the entity feeds on fear. Its weakness lies in the ancient symbols surrounding you. Use them."

I blink, momentarily disoriented by the intrusion. "Grey? How—"

"No time," his voice interrupts. "The dagger on the altar. It's your key."

My eyes dart around the room, taking in the occult symbols etched into the walls. My analytical mind whirs into action, connecting the cryptic guidance to our dire situation.

"Collins," I whisper urgently, not taking my eyes off the approaching entity. "I need you to create a diversion. Anything to draw its attention."

Tobias's eyes widen, but he nods firmly. "Right, then. I suppose it's time for some of that famous Collins charm," he says, straightening his tie and flashing a nervous smile that does little to hide his fear.

As my partner moves to the left, voice raised in a mixture of taunts and nervous laughter, I edge towards the altar. My heart pounds in my ears, each beat a countdown to what? Salvation or damnation?

The entity's glowing eyes follow Collins, its form shimmering like a heat haze. I force myself to breathe and think. How do the symbols, the dagger, and the entity's nature connect?

"Fear," I mutter to myself. "It feeds on fear, but fear is just another emotion. And emotions can be manipulated."

My fingers close around the hilt of the ceremonial dagger, its weight both comforting and terrifying. As I turn to face our otherworldly foe, a plan crystallizes in my mind.

"Tobias," I call out, my voice steadier than I feel, "whatever happens, remember why we're here. Remember what we fight for."

The entity's attention snaps back to me, and I raise the dagger, its blade glinting in the flickering candlelight. "Now," I think, steeling myself, "let's see what you're truly made of."

I lunge forward, the dagger's ancient symbols gleaming as I slash through the air. The entity howls a sound that reverberates through my bones and dodges with inhuman speed.

"Bloody hell, Blackwood!" Tobias shouts, his voice strained. "What in God's name are you doing?"

"Testing a theory," I grunt, pivoting to face the creature again. My eyes dart around the room, cataloging potential advantages. The flickering candles, the occult symbols etched into the floor—all pieces of a puzzle I'm desperately trying to solve.

The entity strikes, its ethereal form coalescing into razor-sharp tendrils. I duck and roll, feeling the rush of air as it passes inches from my face. The dagger hums in my hand, almost alive with energy.

"It's tied to this place," I call out to Tobias, my breath coming in brief gasps. "The symbols, the ritual items, are anchoring it here."

As I speak, I'm moving again, using the altar as a barrier between myself and the entity. Its eyes, pits of swirling darkness, lock onto mine. For a moment, I feel a crushing weight of despair and hopelessness.

"No," I growl, gritting my teeth. "You don't control me."

I thrust the dagger forward, aiming for the center of its mass.

There's a moment of resistance, then a feeling like plunging my hand into ice-cold water—the entity shrieks, a sound that threatens to shatter my sanity.

"Arthur!" Tobias yells, concern evident in his voice. "Are you alright?"

I can't answer him. Every fiber of my being is focused on maintaining my grip on the dagger, on pushing through the overwhelming sensations assaulting my mind. Memories flash before my eyes—triumphs, failures, moments of joy, and crushing sorrow.

"You want to know me?" I think, directing my thoughts at the entity. "Then know this—I will not yield. Not to you, not to anyone."

The entity's form flickers like a candle in a gust of wind, its edges blurring and dissipating where the dagger pierces its ethereal body.

A high-pitched keening fills the air, setting my teeth on edge. I twist the blade, feeling a surge of triumph as the spectral figure recoils, retreating into the shadows cast by the flickering candlelight.

"It's weakening," I shout to Tobias, my voice hoarse. "We've found its vulnerability!"

I don't wait for a response, my feet already moving, propelling me after the retreating entity. The secret room seems to warp and shift around us, shadows dancing in impossible ways. My analytical mind races, recalling every scrap of occult knowledge I've accumulated.

"The pentagram," I mutter, noting the intricate design etched into the floor. "It's using the points to move."

I pivot sharply, anticipating the entity's next position. As it materializes, I'm there, dagger at the ready.

"You're predictable," I growl, slashing at its form again. "And that will be your undoing."

The entity howls, a sound of rage and frustration that makes the candles gutter. It darts away again, but I'm in pursuit, my coat billowing behind me like wings.

"Arthur," Tobias calls out, his voice strained. "Be careful! We don't know what else it's capable of!"

I glance in his direction, noting the worry etched on his face. "Trust me, old friend. I've got this bastard's number now."

A cold dread settles in my stomach as I return to the chase. What if I'm mistaken? What if this thing is merely toying with us? I push the doubts aside, focusing on the task at hand. There's no room for hesitation now.

The entity materializes again near a shelf laden with arcane tomes.

I lunge forward, my free hand grabbing a book bound in what looks suspiciously like human skin. "Let's see how you like this," I mutter, hurling the tome at the specter.

To my surprise, the book passes through its form but leaves a visible disturbance. The entity shudders, its outline becoming even more indistinct.

A grim smile tugs at my lips. "So, you're not invulnerable after all," I say, advancing with renewed determination. "Come on then, let's finish this dance."

The entity's form coalesces again, its glowing eyes fixed upon me with evil intent. I grip the ceremonial dagger tighter, my knuckles white against the ornate hilt. This is it - the last confrontation.

"You've nowhere left to run," I declare, my voice steady despite the rapid pounding of my heart. "Your reign of terror ends here."

The spectral being lets out an unearthly screech that sends shivers down my spine. It lunges forward, elongated fingers reaching for my throat. I dodge, pivoting on my heel, and strike out with the dagger. The blade slices through its ethereal form, leaving a trail of silvery mist in its wake.

"Arthur!" Collins shouts from across the room. "The sigil on the floor - I think it's binding the entity here!"

I glance down, noticing the intricate pattern etched into the stone beneath our feet for the first time. Of course - how could I have missed it? "Brilliant observation, Tobias," I call back, my mind racing. "Keep it distracted!"

I move as Collins chants in Latin, drawing the entity's attention.

With practiced precision, I use the dagger to scrape away at the sigil's lines, feeling a surge of energy with each mark I destroy.

The entity whirls back towards me, its form writhing in apparent agony. "It's working!" I shout, redoubling my efforts.

With a final, decisive slash, I complete my task. The sigil shatters, and a blinding light erupts from the floor. The entity lets out one last bone-chilling shriek before imploding in on itself, vanishing into the ether.

Silence descends upon the room, broken only by the soft hiss of guttering candles. I stand motionless, chest heaving, as the reality of what just transpired washes over me. My limbs feel leaden, the adrenaline slowly ebbing away.

"Is it... is it truly gone?" Collins asks, his voice barely above a whisper.

I nod slowly, my gaze fixed on where the entity disappeared. "I believe so, old friend. Though I suspect our troubles are far from over."

As my racing pulse begins to slow, I realize the oppressive stillness that has settled over the secret room. The dancing shadows cast by the flickering candles mock us, hinting at other secrets yet to be unveiled.

"What do we do now, Arthur?" Collins inquires, breaking the eerie muted.

I take a deep breath, steadying myself. "Now, Tobias, we dig deeper. This entity was but a guardian - a test, perhaps. Whatever it was protecting, I intend to uncover."

As I speak these words, a chill runs down my spine. I can't stop thinking that we have barely begun to understand a mystery that is much bigger and scarier than we could have ever imagined.

My hands tremble as I lower the ceremonial dagger, its ancient symbols now etched with an otherworldly glow. I stare at my quivering fingers, a stark reminder of my mortality in the face of forces beyond comprehension.

"I've seen many things in my years, Tobias," I murmur, my voice hoarse. "But this... this defies all logic, all reason."

Inspector Collins steps closer, his sturdy presence a welcome anchor in the sea of uncertainty we now navigate. "You handled yourself admirably, Arthur. I've seen nothing quite like it."

I turn to face him, searching his weathered features for any sign of doubt or fear. "How does one prepare for such encounters? Our training and experiences seem woefully inadequate in the face of such supernatural malevolence."

Collins places a reassuring hand on my shoulder, his grip firm and grounding. "Perhaps we're not meant to be prepared, old friend. But we adapt, we persevere. It's what we've always done."

I nod, grateful for his unwavering support. "Indeed. Though I can't help but wonder what other horrors await us as we delve deeper into this case."

"Whatever they may be," Collins says, his voice low and determined, "we'll face them together. Remember why we're here, Arthur. The truth we seek is bigger than our fears and these supernatural terrors."

I take a deep breath, steeling myself. "You're right, of course. We mustn't lose sight of our purpose. The answers we seek are here, Tobias. I can feel it in my bones."

As I speak, I can't shake the feeling that we're standing on the precipice of something monumental that will change the fabric of our understanding. The weight of our mission settles heavily upon my shoulders, but with it comes a renewed sense of determination.

With a last glance at the haunting symbols etched into the walls, I turn towards the door. "Come, Tobias. We've lingered here long enough."

We step out of the secret room, the floorboards creaking beneath our feet as if reluctant to release us. After the eerie glow of the occult chamber, the corridor beyond feels impossibly dark. I fumble for my matchbox, striking a flame that casts dancing shadows on the peeling wallpaper.

"What do you make of it all, Arthur?" Collins whispers, his voice barely audible above the pounding of my heart.

I pause, considering. "We've stumbled upon something far more sinister than we initially expected. The entity we encountered is merely a symptom of a greater darkness lurking beneath London's streets."

As we navigate the winding passages, my mind races with possibilities. The encounter has shaken me, yet I feel an odd exhilaration coursing through my veins. "We must redouble our efforts, Tobias. The answers we seek are out there, hidden in plain sight. We just need to look closer, dig deeper."

Collins nods, his face a mask of determination in the flickering light. "I'm with you, old friend. To the bitter end, if need be."

We emerge from the building into the fog-laden streets of London.

The city seems different now, as if the veil between our world and the supernatural has been irrevocably torn. Every shadow holds the potential for danger, and every whisper of wind could be a spectral warning.

"Where to now?" Collins asks, his hand resting instinctively on his service revolver.

I take a deep breath of the damp night air, feeling my resolve harden like steel. "To tell the truth, my friend. Whatever the cost."

Chapter 8 Gathering Allies

The flicker of gaslight dances across Lady Evelyn Worthington's pale features as I enter her opulent drawing room. She sits poised in a high-backed armchair, her elegant fingers curled around the edges of a leather-bound tome. The air is thick with the scent of aging paper and lavender, mingling with the ever-present London fog that seeps through the ornate windows.

I clear my throat, and her eyes dart up, a mix of curiosity and caution in their depths. "Lady Worthington, I presume? I am Detective Arthur Blackwood."

She sets the book aside, her movements graceful yet guarded. "Detective Blackwood, your reputation precedes you. To what do I owe the glee of this unexpected visit?"

I take a measured step forward, my coat rustling in the silence. The weight of my purpose settles heavily upon my shoulders. "I'm afraid glee has little to do with it, my lady. I've come on a matter of utmost urgency."

Lady Evelyn's brow furrows, a flicker of concern passing across her face. "Urgency, you say? What could be so pressing as to bring London's finest Detective to my doorstep at this hour?"

I pause, choosing my words carefully. The gravity of the situation demands precision. "A series of inexplicable events have transpired that defy rational explanation. I believe your unique perspective may prove invaluable in unraveling this mystery."

Her eyes widen, a spark of intrigue igniting within them.

"Inexplicable, you say? How utterly fascinating." She leans forward, her voice dropping to a hushed whisper. "Go on, Detective."

As I delve into the details of the case, I can't help but notice the subtle changes in Lady Evelyn's demeanor. Her initial wariness melts away, replaced by a keen interest that radiates from her very being. It's as if the promise of intellectual stimulation has awakened something within her, something long dormant.

"I must admit, Detective Blackwood, your proposition is most enticing," she says, a hint of excitement coloring her refined tones.

"To contribute to such an investigation... it's an opportunity I find difficult to refuse."

I feel a surge of relief tempered by the knowledge of the dangers that lie ahead. "Your help would be invaluable, Lady Worthington.

But I must warn you, this is no trivial matter. The path we tread is fraught with peril."

She rises from her chair, her posture straight and unwavering. "I am no stranger to adversity, Detective. If my intellect and analytical skills can aid in uncovering the truth, then I shall gladly lend them to your cause."

As I gaze at Lady Evelyn, I'm struck by the transformation. The guarded socialite has given way to a woman of purpose, her eyes alight doggedly. At this moment, I realize I've gained an ally and a formidable partner in our quest for answers.

"Then let us begin, Lady Worthington," I say, extending my hand.

"Together, we shall pierce the veil of this mystery and bring the truth to light."

As our hands meet, a chill runs down my spine. Whether from anticipation or foreboding, I cannot say. But one thing is sure: the game is afoot, and the shadows of London hold secrets yet to be revealed.

The fog swirls around my ankles as I make my way through the winding streets of Bloomsbury. My destination looms ahead: a modest townhouse, its windows aglow with the warm light of gas lamps in Dr. Amelia Lancaster's residence.

I rap my knuckles against the door, echoing in the muted street. Moments later, it swings open, revealing a small, fiery-haired woman whose piercing gaze seems to cut right through me.

"Detective Blackwood, I presume?" she asks, her voice sharp and precise.

I nod, studying her face. "Dr. Lancaster. Might I have a word?"

She steps aside, ushering me into a cluttered study. Books and papers cover every surface, and the air is thick with the scent of ink and old parchment. Dr. Lancaster returns to her desk, where an open tome lies waiting.

"I apologize for the mess," she says, not sounding sorry. "I was amid research. What brings London's finest Detective to my humble abode?"

I clear my throat, choosing my words carefully. "I find myself in need of your expertise, Doctor. A case has come to my attention that defies conventional explanation. It requires a mind as brilliant as yours to unravel its supernatural elements."

Dr. Lancaster's eyebrow arches, a spark of interest igniting in her eyes. "Supernatural, you say? How intriguing. Please elaborate."

As I detail the peculiarities of the case, I watch her expression shift from curiosity to fascination. Her fingers drum against the desk, her mind racing with possibilities.

"This is unlike anything I've encountered in my medical practice," she muses. "Yet, the challenge it presents... it's exhilarating."

I lean forward, sensing her eagerness. "Your knowledge of science and the inexplicable would be invaluable to this investigation. Will you join us, Dr. Lancaster?"

She stands in her petite frame, somehow filling the room doggedly.

"Detective Blackwood, how could I possibly refuse? This is an opportunity to apply my skills in ways I've only dreamed of. To help others by venturing into the unknown—that's precisely why I became a doctor."

Relief washes over me, tempered by a twinge of concern for the dangers ahead. "Your dedication is admirable, Doctor. But I must warn you—"

"Of the risks?" she interrupts, a wry smile on her lips. "I assure you, Detective, I'm no stranger to adversity. My entire career has been a battle against those who would dismiss me for my gender.

This investigation? It's simply another challenge to overcome."

Her confidence is infectious, and I return her smile. "Then welcome aboard, Dr. Lancaster. I believe your insights will prove crucial in unraveling this mystery."

As we shake hands, sealing our alliance, I can't help but wonder what forces we've set in motion. The fog outside seems to press against the windows as if the city is holding its breath, waiting to see what secrets we'll uncover in the shadows of London.

The drawing room of Lady Evelyn Worthington's townhouse is a study of elegance. Its rich tapestries and gleaming mahogany contrast with the gloom clinging to London's streets. As I settle into a high-backed chair, the weight of our task settles upon my shoulders.

"Now then," I begin, my gaze moving between Lady Evelyn and Dr. Lancaster, "I believe it's time we lay our cards on the table. What drives each of us to pursue this dangerous mystery?"

Lady Evelyn's fingers trace the delicate embroidery of her sleeve as she speaks. "For me, it's a matter of justice. Whispers of involvement with dark forces tarnished my late husband's reputation. I aim to clear his name and, perhaps, find closure."

Dr. Lancaster leans forward, her eyes bright doggedly. "As a physician, I've sworn not to harm. But I've realized that sometimes, to help truly, one must confront the detrimental things. If supernatural forces are at play, I want to understand them to protect others from their influence."

I nod, feeling a kinship with these women and their noble intentions. "And I," I admit, my voice dropping low, "Carry the weight of a personal failure. Years ago, I couldn't save someone dear to me from a fate worse than death. This investigation offers a chance at redemption."

The room falls silent, the gravity of our confessions hanging heavy in the air. Then, unbidden, a wry chuckle escapes my lips. "Well, we're quite the band of merry misfits, right? A widow seeking justice, a doctor chasing the unknown, and a detective haunted by ghosts of his own making."

To my surprise, Lady Evelyn's lips curve into a smile. "Misfits we may be, Detective Blackwood, but perhaps that's precisely what this mystery requires."

Dr. Lancaster's laughter, bright and unexpected, join in. "Indeed! Who better to unravel the impossible than those who defied expectations?"

As their joy washes over me, I feel the tension in my shoulders ease. For a moment, the shadows that have dogged my steps seem to retreat, and I hope that together, we might just be equal to the task ahead.

The laughter fades, and I lean forward, my palms pressed against the polished mahogany of Lady Evelyn's writing desk. "Now, ladies," I say, my voice low and purposeful, "we must chart our course."

Lady Evelyn nods, her red hair catching the flickering lamplight. "Where do we begin, Detective?"

I pull a crumpled map of London from my coat pocket and spread it across the desk. "We revisit the scenes of each murder," I declare, finger tracing a path through the city's veins.

"There may be clues we've overlooked, patterns yet to emerge."

Dr. Lancaster leans in, her keen eyes scanning the marked locations. "And what of the Order of the Eternal Flame?" she asks, her voice tinged with curiosity and caution. "Their involvement cannot be coincidental."

"Precisely," I agree. We'll need to delve deeper into their history and rituals. Lady Evelyn, your social connections might prove invaluable here."

She straightens, a determined glint in her eye. "I'll discreetly make inquiries among the upper echelons. Surely someone knows more than they're letting on."

As we discuss, my mind races ahead, piecing together the puzzle.

"And Lady Eleanor Ravenscroft," I muse aloud. "Her name keeps surfacing. We must uncover her role in all this."

Dr. Lancaster nods thoughtfully. "I can research any medical records and see if there's a connection we're missing."

I feel a swell of admiration for my newfound allies. "Ladies," I say, meeting each of their gazes, "I want you to know that your contributions are not just valued but essential. This case is unlike anything I've encountered before. We're venturing into uncharted waters, and I need your unique perspectives and expertise."

I pause, choosing my following words carefully. "Trust between us is paramount. We must be open, honest, and united. The dangers we face are not just physical. There are forces at work here that defy explanation and could shatter one's sanity if faced alone."

Lady Evelyn reaches out, her gloved hand resting lightly on my arm. "We stand with you, Detective Blackwood. Together, we shall shine a light into the darkness."

Dr. Lancaster's voice rings with conviction. "Indeed. Our diverse skills are our strength. Where one falters, the others shall support."

Looking at these remarkable women, I feel a warmth in my chest, a sensation I haven't experienced in years. It's hope, I realize. I hope we might unravel this infernal mystery together and emerge unscathed.

Lady Evelyn's melodic voice breaks the momentary silence.

"Gentlemen, I must express my deepest gratitude for including me in this most extraordinary endeavor." Her auburn hair catches the flickering gaslight as she inclines her head, eyes shimmering with excitement and determination. "I believe, with every fiber of my being, that our collaboration holds the key to unraveling this enigma that plagues our fair city."

I watch as she gracefully rises from her seat, her richly embroidered gown rustling softly. She paces towards the window, gazing out at the fog-shrouded streets of London. "Together, we possess a formidable array of talents and perspectives. I sincerely hope that through our combined efforts, we may solve this mystery and bring solace to those affected by these dark occurrences."

Her words perhaps stir something within me—a renewed sense of purpose. I nod in agreement, her eloquence strengthening my resolve.

Dr. Lancaster leans forward, her fiery hair in stark contrast to the somber tones of the drawing room. "I concur wholeheartedly with Lady Evelyn," she states, her tone crisp and direct. "Mr. Blackwood, Lady Evelyn, I want to assure you of my unwavering commitment to this investigation."

Her keen eyes dart between us, a glint of determination visible in their depths. "We must approach this methodically, relying on concrete evidence wherever possible. Yet," she pauses, a slight furrow appearing on her brow, "I also believe we must trust our instincts. In matters that defy conventional explanation, intuition may prove to be our most valuable tool."

I consider her words carefully. "You're right, Dr. Lancaster. We're treading a fine line between the rational and the inexplicable. Your analytical mind will be crucial in maintaining that balance."

As I speak, I can't help but feel a sense of unease creeping up my spine. What horrors await us in the shadows of this investigation?

Will our combined strengths be enough to face the darkness that looms ahead?

I rise from my seat, sensing the weight of our shared purpose settling upon us. Lady Evelyn and Dr. Lancaster follow suit, their movements mirroring my own. We stand together, a trio forged by circumstance and united by determination.

"Well then," I say, my voice low and steady, "it seems we've formed quite a formidable alliance."

Lady Evelyn's eyes meet mine, a mixture of trepidation and resolve swirling in their depths. "Indeed, Mr. Blackwood. Though I confess, the path ahead appears treacherous."

Dr. Lancaster nods, her posture straight and unyielding.

"Treacherous, yes, but not impossible. Together, we stand a far greater chance of unraveling this mystery."

I feel a slight smile tugging at the corners of my mouth despite the gravity of our situation. "Quite right, Doctor. United we stand, divided we fall—isn't that how the saying goes?"

As we exchange determined glances, I can't help but marvel at the strange twist of fate that has brought us together. Despite our so-different backgrounds and approaches, each of us is now linked by this dark enigma that threatens to consume London.

The air in the room seems to thicken, charged with anticipation and a hint of foreboding. Outside, a distant clock chimes, its somber tones a reminder of the relentless march of time. We have precious little of it to waste.

"Come," I say, gesturing towards the door. "The night grows long, and our investigation awaits. Shall we venture into the unknown?"

As we move to leave, the flickering gaslight casts long shadows across the room, dancing and twisting like spectral fingers reaching out to grasp us. A chill runs down my spine, and I can't shake the feeling that we're about to enter a world far darker and more dangerous than any of us could have imagined.

The door creaks open, revealing the fog-shrouded streets of London beyond. Together, we step out into the night, ready to face whatever challenges come our way. Little do we know, the rising tension that awaits us will test our skills and resolve and the fabric of our newfound alliance.

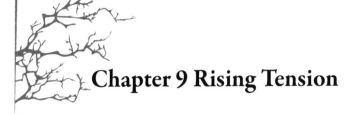

Chapter 9 Rising Tension

The gaslight flickers, casting serpentine shadows across the wall as I pore over the scattered documents before me. My eyes burn from hours of scrutiny, but I cannot look away. Each fragment of evidence is a thread in a tapestry of horror that grows more intricate with every passing moment.

"Blackwood," Evelyn's voice cuts through my concentration. "I think I've found something."

I rise, my joints protesting after hours of stillness, and reach her side. She holds a faded parchment, its edges crumbling with age.

"Look here," she points to a series of dates scrawled in faded ink.

"These correspond with the murders we've been investigating, but they're from over a century ago."

My mind races, connecting disparate pieces of information. "It can't be a coincidence," I mutter, more to myself than to her. "The Order's been orchestrating these killings for generations."

Lancaster's voice carries from across the room, tight with tension.

"But to what end? What could justify such a prolonged campaign of terror?"

I turn to face him, the weight of our discoveries pressing upon me like a physical force. "Power," I say, the word tasting bitter on my tongue. "The power that can only be gained through blood and sacrifice."

A chill runs down my spine as I speak the words aloud, making them real. The Order's reach seems to extend far beyond what we'd initially imagined, its tendrils burrowing deep into the very foundations of our city.

Suddenly, a crash echoes from the hallway outside. We freeze, exchanging glances of alarm. Have we been discovered?

"Quick," I hiss, gathering the most crucial documents. "We need to move."

As we hurry towards the back exit, the door splinters inward.

Masked figures pour into the room, their eyes glinting with malice behind ornate facades.

"Run!" I shout, drawing my revolver. The acrid smell of gunpowder fills the air as I fire, buying precious seconds for my team to escape.

We flee through winding corridors, the pounding of feet behind us growing ever closer—my heart races, not just from exertion but from the realization that we've struck a nerve. The Order is frightened, and a frightened enemy is the most dangerous.

As we venture into the foggy streets, I can't shake the feeling that we've only just begun to unravel the mystery of this conspiracy.

The genuine horrors still lie ahead, waiting to be unearthed. And I, Arthur Blackwood, will not rest until I've dragged them into the light, no matter the cost.

The fog swirls around us as we duck into a narrow alley, our breaths coming in ragged gasps. I press my back against the damp brick, eyes scanning the murky darkness for any sign of pursuit.

The distant chime of Big Ben cuts through the eerie silence, reminding me that time is not on our side.

"Everyone alright?" I whisper, my gaze darting between Evelyn, Lancaster, and Collins. They nod, their faces pale in the dim light of a nearby gas lamp.

We gather in a tight circle, the tension palpable. Evelyn's auburn hair is disheveled, her eyes wide with fear and determination.

Lancaster's slight frame is taut, her analytical mind racing to process our narrow escape. Ever the steady presence, Collins watches the alley's entrance, his mustache twitching with each measured breath.

"We need a safe place to regroup," I murmur, my mind whirling with possibilities. "Somewhere the Order wouldn't think to look."

As if in answer to my unspoken question, a street urchin materializes from the shadows, clutching a crumpled piece of paper. "Message for you, gov," he squeaks, thrusting the note into my hand before vanishing into the night.

I unfold the paper with trembling fingers, a chill running down my spine as I read the cryptic words scrawled in an unfamiliar hand:

"The truth lies where the forgotten sleep. Seek the stone angel's tears at midnight."

"What does it mean?" Evelyn whispers, peering over my shoulder.

I meet her gaze, seeing my hope and trepidation reflected in her eyes. "It's a lead," I reply, my voice low and urgent. Perhaps this is our only chance to uncover the evidence we need."

LANCASTER STEPS FORWARD, her red hair gleaming in the lamplight.

"The stone angel... could it be referring to a cemetery?"

Collins nods grimly. "Highgate, most likely. It's old enough to have secrets."

I clench my fist around the note, feeling the weight of our next move pressing down upon me. "It's risky," I admit, "but we have no choice. Time is running out, and this might be our only opportunity to get ahead of the Order."

As we prepare to venture into the unknown, I can't shake the feeling that we're being watched. The city seems to hold its breath, waiting to see what dark revelations the night will bring.

"Stay close," I warn my companions, drawing my revolver again.

"Whatever we find at Highgate, I doubt the Order will let us claim it without a fight."

With a shared nod of determination, we slip back into the foggy streets, our footsteps echoing softly on the cobblestones as we race against time and shadows.

The fog thickens as we navigate the labyrinthine alleys of London's underbelly, our breath coming in short, misty puffs. I lead our small group, my senses heightened, every nerve crackling with anticipation. The gas lamps cast sickly halos in the murk, barely penetrating the gloom that seems to close in around us.

"Arthur," Evelyn whispers, her fingers brushing my sleeve, "I think we're being followed."

I nod imperceptibly, having noticed the furtive movements in the shadows myself. "Keep moving," I murmur, my hand resting on the cold metal of my revolver. "We can't afford to be waylaid now."

We duck into a narrow passage, the damp walls pressing in on either side. The stench of rotting refuse and stagnant water assails our nostrils, a grim reminder of the city's fetid undercurrent.

"Bloody hell," Collins hisses as he stumbles over an unseen obstacle. "This place is a maze."

I pause, listening intently. The distant clop of hooves and rattle of carriage wheels mingles with something more sinister—the soft scuff of boots on stone, too close for comfort.

"We're nearly there," I assure them, though doubt gnaws at the edges of my conviction. The warehouse should be ahead, but nothing is certain in this haze of shadows and secrecy.

Suddenly, a figure looms out of the fog. I raise my revolver, heart pounding, only to lower it as I recognize the weathered face of one of my informants.

"Mr. Blackwood," he wheezes, eyes darting nervously. "You shouldn't be here. They're watching, they are. Eyes everywhere."

"Who's watching, Tom?" I press, urgency coloring my tone.

He shakes his head, terror etched in every line of his face. "Can't say. But the warehouse... it isn't natural, what's in there. Be careful, sir."

With that cryptic warning, he melts back into the fog, leaving us to press on towards our destination. The weight of unseen eyes bears down upon us, the city itself seeming to constrict around our small party as we approach the truth hidden within the abandoned warehouse.

The warehouse looms before us, a hulking silhouette against the night sky. Dr. Lancaster's sharp intake of breath echoes my unease as we approach the rusted door.

"Arthur," she whispers, her nimble fingers brushing my sleeve, "whatever we find in there..."

"I know, Amelia," I murmur, meeting her concerned gaze. "We must be prepared for anything."

Inside, the air is thick with dust and secrets. Our lanterns cast dancing shadows across walls lined with ancient tomes and peculiar artifacts. As we spread out to investigate, I can't shake the feeling that we're disturbing something long dormant.

Lancaster's eager gasp cuts through the silence. "Over here! There's something..."

I hurry to her side, watching her run her hands along an ornate wooden panel. With a soft click, a hidden compartment springs open, revealing a yellowed parchment.

"God," I breathe, unrolling the map with trembling fingers. "It's their entire plan, laid bare."

The design's intricacy is staggering—a web of locations, dates, and cryptic symbols spanning centuries. My mind reels as I begin to grasp the implications.

"They mean to alter the very fabric of history," Lancaster whispers, her face pale in the flickering lamplight. "If they succeed..."

The magnitude of the threat crashes over me like a tidal wave.

"Then everything we know, everything we are, could be erased."

A sudden crash from the entrance shatters our revelation. Masked figures pour into the warehouse, weapons glinting in the dim light.

"Ambush!" I roar, drawing my revolver as chaos erupts around us.

The air fills with the acrid smell of gunpowder and the clash of steel on steel. I duck behind a stack of crates, heart pounding as bullets whiz past.

"Lancaster!" I call out, desperate to ensure her safety amidst the melee.

"Here!" Her voice rises above the din, steely doggedly. "I won't let them take the map!"

As I return fire, my mind races. We've stumbled upon something far more significant than we ever imagined, and now the Order wants us silenced. But I'll be damned if I let them succeed. Too much hangs in the balance—the past, the present, and the very future itself.

A piercing scream cuts through the chaos, freezing my blood. I whip around to see Evelyn, her auburn hair disheveled, struggling in the iron grip of a masked assailant. Their blade glints at her throat, a silent threat that echoes louder than any gunshot.

"Blackwood!" she cries, her eyes wide with terror but burning with defiance.

I take a step forward, my gun raised, but the assailant presses the blade closer. "One more move, detective, and she bleeds."

My mind races, desperation clawing at my chest. "Let her go," I growl, fury and fear warring within me. "Your quarrel is with me."

The masked figure chuckles, a sound devoid of mirth. "Oh, but she's our leverage now. Lower your weapon, or watch her die."

I hesitate, my grip on the revolver tightening. Evelyn's gaze meets mine, and a silent communication passes between us. At that moment, I saw not just fear but trust in me to make the right choice.

"Arthur," she whispers, her voice steady despite the blade at her throat, "don't you dare give up."

Her words ignite a fire within me. I won't let them take her or let the Order win. As I slowly lower my gun, my mind is already planning a plan. Time is slipping away like sand through an hourglass, but failure is not an option. Not when Evelyn's life hangs in the balance. Not when the very fabric of history is at stake.

"You want me?" I say, my voice low and dangerous. "Then let's negotiate. But know this—if any harm comes to her, there won't be a place in the past, present, or future where you can hide from me."

The cloying scent of incense mingles with the musty air as I inch forward, every nerve in my body on high alert. Lancaster's words echo: "The Order's stronghold will be riddled with traps. Watch for pressure plates, tripwires, anything out of place."

I pause, my eyes scanning the dimly lit corridor. A faint glint catches my attention—moonlight reflecting off a nearly invisible wire stretched across the passage. Carefully, I step over it, my heart pounding in my chest.

"Well spotted, Blackwood," I mutter to myself, Collins' gruff voice seeming to reply in my head. "But don't get cocky. These bastards are clever."

As if on cue, the floor beneath my feet shifts slightly. I freeze, holding my breath. A memory surfaces—Collins hunched over a map of London's underground, finger tracing a path. "This route should get you close, but be wary. The Order's lair is likely built atop old Roman ruins. Unstable ground."

Slowly, I distribute my weight, easing forward until I'm on solid stone again. The passage gradually widens, opening into a vast chamber. And there, at its center, stands Evelyn, her auburn hair gleaming in the flickering torchlight. Relief floods through me, quickly followed by icy dread as I notice the figure looming behind her.

"Detective Blackwood," the man's voice rings out, smooth as silk and twice as deadly. "How kind of you to join us."

I step forward, my hand hovering near my concealed weapon. "I believe you have something that belongs to me."

The leader of the Order chuckles, pressing a blade closer to Evelyn's throat. "Oh? And what might that be?"

"My partner," I growl, locking eyes with Evelyn. Her gaze is steady, defiant even in the face of danger. "Let her go. This is between you and me."

"Ah, but where's the fun in that?" The man's eyes glitter with malice. "No, I think we'll play a little game. Your wits against mine, Detective. After all, isn't that what you excel at? Solving puzzles, unraveling mysteries?"

I feel my jaw clench, knowing I'm being baited but unable to resist. "And what are the stakes of this... game?"

The leader's smile widens, a predator sensing weakness. "Simple. You win; she goes free. You lose..." He trails off, the implication clear.

Evelyn's voice cuts through the tension. "Don't you dare, Arthur? Whatever he's planning-"

"Silence!" The man hisses, pressing the blade harder. A thin line of red appears on Evelyn's pale skin.

Rage boils within me, barely contained. "I accept," I spit out, praying my voice doesn't betray the fear gnawing at my insides.

"Name your challenge."

As the leader begins to speak, I desperately search for a way out of this deadly game. The fate of Evelyn—and perhaps all of London—hangs in the balance, and I cannot afford to lose.

The leader's eyes gleam with malevolent delight as he produces a small, ornate box from his coat. "Inside this box lies your salvation... or your doom, Detective. A simple riddle, really. Solve it, and Lady Worthington goes free. Fail, and, well..." He trails off, the unspoken threat hanging heavy in the air.

I study the box, my mind racing. The intricate carvings on its surface seem to shift and writhe in the flickering candlelight. "And what guarantee do I have that you'll keep your word?"

A dry chuckle escapes his lips. "Why, my man, you have none. But what choice do you have?"

Evelyn's eyes meet mine, and a silent communication passes between us. I see fear there, yes, but also trust. Unwavering faith in my abilities. It steels my resolve.

"Very well," I say, reaching for the box. "Let's begin."

As my fingers brush the cold metal, a jolt of energy courses through me. The room seems to tilt and spin, reality blurring at the edges. I hear Evelyn gasp, but it sounds distant, muffled.

Focus, Blackwood, I commend myself. This is no ordinary puzzle.

With trembling hands, I unlatch the box. Inside lies a single piece of parchment covered in arcane symbols. As I unfold it, the writing begins to glow, rearranging before my eyes.

"Speak the name that binds us all," I read aloud, "The force that shapes both successful and small. In darkness found, yet light it brings, The key to past and future things."

My mind whirls, possibilities flashing by in rapid succession. What force could...

And then it hits me. The answer is so simple, yet so profound.

"Time," I whisper, the word barely audible.

The effect is instantaneous. The leader's face contorts shock and fury. His grip on Evelyn loosens just enough for her to wrench free, driving her elbow into his solar plexus.

I lunge forward, my fist connecting with his jaw. He crumples to the ground, unconscious.

"Evelyn!" I cry, rushing to her side. "Are you alright?"

She nods, her composure returning even as she trembles slightly.

"I'm fine, Arthur. Thanks to you."

As the adrenaline fades, I hear footsteps approaching. Lancaster and Collins burst into the room, weapons drawn.

"Impeccable timing, as always," I say dryly, relief flooding through me at the sight of our companions.

While Lancaster secures our captive, I notice a leather-bound book protruding from the man's coat. Curiosity piqued, I retrieve it, flipping it open to reveal pages of cramped handwriting.

"What is it?" Evelyn asks, peering over my shoulder.

I scan the first few lines, and my blood is running cold. "It's a journal," I murmur, "detailing the Order's true plans. And it's far worse than we imagined."

As I continue reading, the gravity of our situation becomes painfully clear. The Order isn't just trying to change history—they're attempting to unravel the fabric of time itself.

I look up at my team, their faces mirroring my burning determination. "We have work to do," I say grimly. "The actual battle is just beginning."

The fog swirls around our feet as we emerge from the Order's stronghold, the weight of our newfound knowledge pressing upon us like a physical burden. I clutch the journal tightly, its secrets burning in my mind.

"We're making for the British Museum," I announce, my voice cutting through the oppressive silence. "The last piece we need is there."

Evelyn falls into step beside me, her face set with grim determination. "Arthur, are you certain about this? The risks—"

"Are immeasurable," I finish for her, a wry smile tugging at my lips. "But so are the consequences if we fail."

As we navigate the labyrinthine streets of London, I can't shake the feeling that we're being watched. Shadows seem to move of their own accord, and whispers echo from darkened alleys.

"Keep close," I murmur to my companions. "The Order's agents could be anywhere."

We round a corner, and the imposing facade of the British Museum looms before us, its Grecian columns stark against the night sky. I pause, my mind racing.

"How do we proceed?" Lancaster asks, his hand resting on the hilt of his concealed weapon.

I take a deep breath, the pieces of our plan falling into place.

"Collins, you'll create a distraction at the main entrance. Lancaster, secure our escape route. Evelyn and I will retrieve the artifact."

As we prepare to split up, I catch Evelyn's eye. "Ready to make history? Or rather, preserve it?"

She nods a fierce light in her eyes. "Always."

With a final shared glance, we disperse into the night. As Evelyn and I slip around to the museum's side entrance, I can't help but marvel at the strange turns my life has taken. From solving mundane crimes to preventing the unraveling of time itself—it's a far cry from what I once imagined for myself.

"Arthur," Evelyn whispers, pulling me from my reverie. "The door."

I focus on the lock, my fingers working deftly. With a soft click, it yields, and we step into the museum's peaceful darkness.

"Remember," I breathe, "we're looking for the Chronos Stone. According to the journal, it's the key to their entire plan."

As we move through the shadowy halls, surrounded by relics of the past, I can't shake the feeling that we're walking a knife's edge between salvation and catastrophe. One misstep and all of history could unravel.

But with Evelyn by my side and the rest of my team in place, I allow myself a glimmer of hope. We've come too far to fail now.

Chapter 10 Midpoint Reveal

T he air grows thick with foreboding as I ease open the heavy oak
door, its ancient hinges groaning in protest. My fingers tighten
instinctively around the cold metal of my revolver, a comforting weight
against the unknown that awaits.

I pause at the threshold, every nerve alight with anticipation.

"Steady on, Blackwood," I muttered, drawing a deep breath of
musty air. "What secrets do you guard, I wonder?"

The chamber before me is awash in flickering shadows cast by a
dozen sputtering candles scattered about the room. Their wavering
light dances across the stone walls, creating phantasmal shapes that
seem to writhe and twist with their lives. I force myself to look away,
focusing instead on the tangible threats that may lurk in the gloom.

My eyes dart from corner to corner, seeking any sign of movement
or danger. The room appears empty of life, yet I cannot shake the
feeling of being watched. Perhaps it is merely the weight of history
pressing upon me, for this chamber is a veritable treasure trove of
antiquity.

Slowly, I step further into the room, my footfalls muffled by a thick
layer of dust. Ancient artifacts line the walls and crowd ornate tables,
each a silent sentinel to bygone eras. A tarnished suit of armor stands
guard in one corner. Delicate pottery and age-darkened paintings vie
for space on crowded shelves.

"God," I breathe, my analytical mind racing to catalog the wealth of historical significance surrounding me. "What I wouldn't give for a fortnight to examine this collection properly."

But time is not a luxury I can afford. Somewhere in this labyrinth of relics lies the key to unraveling the mystery that has brought me here and, with it, the power to prevent an unspeakable evil from being unleashed upon London.

I move deeper into the chamber, my senses straining for any hint of danger. The flickering candlelight casts my shadow upon the wall, a dark doppelgänger that seems to mock my caution. I push aside the fanciful notion, focusing instead on the task.

"Now, if I were a nefarious villain bent on rewriting history," I muse aloud, my voice barely above a whisper, "where would I hide the means to do so?"

My gaze falls upon an ornate writing desk, its surface cluttered with yellowed parchments and leather-bound tomes. Could the answers I seek be hidden within those weathered pages? Or perhaps...

A sudden chill runs down my spine, causing me to whirl around, revolver at the ready. But the chamber remains as still and silent as a tomb. I shake my head, chiding myself for succumbing to nerves.

"Pull yourself together, man," I growl, forcing my racing heart to slow. "You've faced far worse than shadows and dust." My determination is unwavering, a beacon of strength in this chamber of secrets.

Yet, as I return to my investigation, I cannot shake the feeling that I am no longer alone in this chamber of secrets. Something watches from the darkness, patient and calculating. And I fear that before this night is through, I shall face the evil I have sworn to stop.

As my eyes sweep the chamber again, they narrow upon a figure standing near a mahogany table. My breath catches in my throat.

Quentin Thorne. The tension in the room is palpable, a thick fog of dread threatening to suffocate me.

The flickering candlelight dances across his gaunt features, casting sinister shadows that seem to writhe with a life of their own. He cradles an ancient tome in his bony hands, its pages open. A smile plays upon his thin lips, a grotesque parody of mirth that sends a shiver down my spine. His presence exudes malevolence, a darkness threatening to consume everything in its path.

"I should have known you'd be here, Thorne," I say, my voice steady despite the thundering of my heart. "Always one step ahead, aren't you?"

Thorne's piercing eyes lock onto mine, a mix of amusement and malice swirling in their depths. He turns to face me fully, closing the book with a soft thud that echoes in the chamber.

"Ah, Detective Blackwood," he purrs, his voice as smooth as silk and twice as deadly. "How kind of you to join us. I do so enjoy an audience for my work."

I feel my resolve hardening, steeling myself for the confrontation to come. My fingers twitch, itching to reach for my revolver, but I resist the urge. Not yet. I need answers first.

"And what work might that be?" I ask, taking a careful step forward. "Rewriting history? Tampering with forces beyond your comprehension?"

Thorne's lips curl into a sneer. "Oh, Arthur. Quick to judge, yet slow to grasp. But then, that's why I'm here, and you're always playing catch-up, right?"

His words sting, but I refuse to let it show. Instead, I focus on the tome in his hands, my mind racing to identify it. What secrets does it hold? What power has Thorne unleashed?

"Why don't you enlighten me, then?" I challenge, my eyes never leaving his. "Surely a man of your... talents... would relish the opportunity to gloat."

Thorne's laughter, cold and mirthless, fills the chamber. "All in time, Detective. All in time."

Thorne's piercing gaze seems to bore into my soul, his voice dropping to a menacing whisper. "But first, let's talk about you, Arthur. About the ghosts that haunt your every step."

My blood runs cold as he continues, "Poor Elizabeth. Such a tragic end, wasn't it? And you, powerless to save her."

The mention of my late wife's name sends a jolt through me. My grip tightens on the revolver at my side, knuckles whitening. "You know nothing of Elizabeth," I growl, fighting to keep my composure.

"Oh, but I do," Thorne counters, his eyes glinting with malice. "I know how her screams still echo in your nightmares. How you blame yourself for not being there that fateful night."

I struggle to maintain my stoic facade, but inside, my heart races.

How could he possibly know these intimate details of my past?

Thorne's lips curl into a cruel smile as he gestures to the tome before him. "You see, Arthur, this isn't just about rewriting history. It's about mastering it. With the power in these pages, I can reshape reality itself."

"You're mad," I breathe, my mind reeling at the implications.

"Mad?" Thorne laughs. "No, my dear Detective. I'm a visionary. Imagine a world where the past, present, and future are malleable. Where one man can hold the strings of fate in his hands."

As he speaks, I notice a faint glow from the book, pulsing like a heartbeat. The air grows thick with otherworldly energy, making the hairs on my neck stand on end.

"And what of the consequences?" I demand, fighting to keep my voice steady. "The lives you'll destroy in your pursuit of power?"

Thorne waves a dismissive hand. "Mere casualties in the grand tapestry of time. A small price to pay for ultimate control."

I feel my resolve hardening, my determination to stop this madman growing with each passing second. No matter the cost, I cannot allow Thorne to succeed in his diabolical plan.

My mind races, analyzing every detail of the chamber, seeking any weakness in Thorne's defenses. The flickering candlelight casts shifting shadows across ancient artifacts, and I glimpse a familiar symbol etched into the stone floor—a protective ward I've encountered in my studies of the occult.

"You've overlooked something crucial, Thorne," I say, carefully stepping closer to the runic circle. "The very forces you seek to control have safeguards against such hubris."

Thorne's eyes narrow, a flicker of doubt crossing his face before it's masked by arrogance. "Your parlor tricks won't save you now, Blackwood. You're out of your depth."

"Am I?" I counter, my hand inching towards a small vial concealed in my coat pocket. "Then why does the air crackle with unease? The spirits you've summoned sense your lack of true understanding."

Thorne's laugh is sharp and mocking. "You think your paltry knowledge can match centuries of arcane wisdom? I've delved into depths of magic you can't even fathom."

"Perhaps," I concede, my fingers closing around the vial. "But there's one thing you've forgotten, Thorne. Something that gives me an advantage you'll never have."

"And what's that?" he sneers, his voice dripping with disdain.

I meet his gaze unflinchingly. "A conscience. The willingness to sacrifice everything to protect the innocent. Can you say the same?"

I see a flicker of uncertainty in Thorne's eyes and know I've struck a nerve. It's not much, but it's a start—a crack in his impenetrable armor of self-assurance. And in that moment, I vow to exploit it, no matter the cost to myself.

As Thorne's momentary uncertainty fades, his features harden into a mask of cold determination. I seize upon the opening, racing to exploit this newfound weakness.

"Your ambition blinds you, Thorne," I press, taking a calculated step forward. "The Order of the Eternal Flame may have groomed you since childhood, but they've also shackled you. You're nothing more than a pawn in their grand design."

His eyes flash with a mixture of anger. Is that fear? "You know nothing of my role, Blackwood," he hisses, his fingers tightening around the ancient tome.

I allow a grim smile to play across my lips. "Don't I? Your family's legacy, the weight of expectations... I recognize the burden of destiny when I see it. But unlike you, I chose my path."

Thorne's composure slips further, his voice rising. "I chose this! The power, the knowledge—it's all within my grasp!"

"Is it?" I count, inching closer. "Or are you simply dancing to the tune of forces beyond your comprehension?"

As I speak, my eyes dart around the chamber, searching for an advantage. The flickering candlelight catches on a peculiar symbol etched into the floor—one I recognize from my research into the arcane.

"You speak of power," I continue, my voice low and measured, "but true power comes from understanding. Tell me, Thorne, do you even know the sigil's meaning beneath your feet?"

His hesitation is all the confirmation I need. In that split second of doubt, I lunge forward, and my hand outstretched towards the tome. Thorne reacts, but a heartbeat is too slow. My fingers close around the ancient leather binding, and I wrench it from his grasp with a sharp twist.

The book tumbles to the floor, pages fluttering open, the carefully arranged ritual disrupted instantly. Thorne's eyes widen in horror as he realizes what I've done.

"No!" he roars, lunging for the fallen tome, but it's too late. The delicate balance of power he'd been maintaining shatters, and I brace myself for whatever chaos may follow.

A blinding flash erupts from the tome, and a loud crack splits the air. The chamber shudders, ancient stone groaning under the strain of unleashed mystical energies. My skin prickles and my hair stands on end as the air crackles with otherworldly electricity.

"What have you done?" Thorne bellows, his face contorted with rage and fear.

I have no time to answer. Tendrils of spectral energy whip around us, lashing out at random. One slices past my cheek, leaving a trail of numbing cold in its wake. I must act quickly, or we'll both be torn apart by the unraveling ritual.

"The containment runes!" I shout over the cacophony. "We need to activate them!"

Thorne's eyes narrow, torn between his hatred for me and the imminent danger. "And why should I trust you, Blackwood?"

A ghostly tendril wraps around his arm, eliciting a cry of pain. I lunge forward, grabbing his shoulder. "Because if we don't work together, neither of us will leave this chamber alive!"

For a moment, I think he'll refuse. Then, with a grudging nod, he moves towards one corner of the room. I sprint to the opposite side, my mind racing through the chants I've studied.

As I begin to chant, Thorne mirrors my actions. With our combined efforts, the air thrums, pushing back against the chaotic energies.

But it's not enough. The storm of power intensifies, and I feel my strength waning.

Thorne notices, too. With a snarl, he abandons his post and charges at me. "If I'm to fall, I'm taking you with me, detective!"

I barely have time to brace myself before his body slams into mine. We tumble to the floor, grappling in a desperate struggle. His hands find my throat, squeezing with manic strength. I gasp for air, spots dancing before my eyes.

"You've ruined everything!" Thorne hisses, his face inches from mine. "Years of planning, all for naught!"

I drive my knee up, catching him in the stomach. His grip loosens just enough for me to gulp in a breath and rasp, "Your ambition... was always... your weakness, Thorne."

With a surge of strength born of desperation, I flip our positions. Now, I pin his arms atop him, but I know I can't hold him for long. The chamber continues to shake around us, debris raining down from the ceiling.

"We can still contain this," I plead, even as I struggle to keep him subdued. "But we must act now, or all of London may pay the price for your hubris!"

I see a flicker of doubt in Thorne's eyes, a momentary crack in his resolve. It's all I need. My analytical mind races, recalling every detail of the arcane tomes I've studied, every whispered secret of the supernatural world I've encountered. In that split second, I made a plan.

"The ritual's energy," I pant, "it's seeking a vessel. We can redirect it!"

Thorne's eyes narrow. "You're bluffing, Blackwood. You don't have the power—"

I cut him off, my voice steady despite the strain. "No, but you do. And I know. Together, we might just save ourselves and this blasted city."

As I speak, I subtly shift my weight, preparing for what I know must come next. Thorne's lips curl into a sneer, his voice dripping with contempt. "You fool. I'd rather see London burn than—"

I don't let him finish. With every ounce of strength, I drive my forehead into his nose. The sickening crunch is lost in the howling of the supernatural wind, but the effect is immediate. Thorne's eyes roll back, his body going limp beneath me.

Breathing heavily, I scramble to my feet. "I'm afraid I can't oblige you on that, old chap," I mutter, my mind already racing to the next steps. I drag Thorne's unconscious form to the center of the chamber, positioning him precisely where I believe the ritual's focus to be.

As I work, I can't help but reflect on the path that led us here. "You were right about one thing, Quentin," I say to his unhearing form.

"My past haunts me. But it also drives me. And today, it's saved us both."

With a final, decisive movement, I complete the improvised containment circle. The chamber falls eerily silent, the air heavy with spent power and the acrid scent of ozone. I slump against a nearby pillar, exhaustion washing over me in waves.

"Well," I breathe, grimly smiling, "I daresay this will make for an interesting report to the Yard."

My chest heaves as I struggle to catch my breath, eyes fixed on Thorne's crumpled form. The flickering candlelight casts grotesque shadows across his face, distorting his features into a macabre mask. A trickle of blood seeps from his broken nose, a stark crimson on his pallid skin.

"It's over," I whisper, more to steady myself than for any other reason. But even as the words leave my lips, a chill runs down my spine. The air still crackles with an unseen energy, and the hairs on my neck stand on end.

I force myself to look away from Thorne, surveying the chamber with newfound wariness. Ancient artifacts line the walls, their surfaces seeming to writhe in the dancing candlelight. The tome Thorne had been studying lies open on the floor, its pages rustling without a breeze.

"Temporary victory," I muttered, running a hand through my sweat-dampened hair. "But at what cost?"

As if in response, a low moan escapes Thorne's lips. I tense, hand instinctively moving to my revolver. But he remains unconscious, trapped within whatever dark dreams plague him.

"You've opened a door that won't easily be closed, haven't you?" I address his prone form. "And now, I fear, we must all face what comes through."

The weight of the situation settles heavily upon my shoulders. With its arcane secrets and lingering supernatural presence, this chamber is the first piece of a far greater puzzle that threatens not just London but perhaps the very fabric of reality itself.

I steel myself, squaring my shoulders. "Well, Blackwood," I say aloud, my voice echoing in the chamber, "it seems your work is far from done."

The acrid stench of sulfur hangs heavy in the air, mingling with the iron tang of blood. My chest heaves as I stand over Thorne's crumpled form, his once-immaculate suit now torn and stained.

The candlelight flickers, casting grotesque shadows across his face—a face I've pursued through the darkest corners of London.

"It's over, Thorne," I rasp, my voice hoarse from exertion. "Your ritual has failed."

A chuckle, wet with blood, escapes his lips. "Oh, Blackwood," he gasps, "you naïve fool. This is merely the beginning."

I grip my revolver tighter, its weight comforting in my trembling hand. "What do you mean?"

Thorne's eyes, usually cold and calculating, now sparkle with a fevered light. "The Order of the Eternal Flame cannot be extinguished so easily. We are legion, Blackwood. Cut off one head, and two more shall rise."

Despite the oppressive heat of the chamber, a chill runs down my spine. I scan the room, taking in the ancient artifacts and arcane symbols etched into the stone walls. The air seems to pulse with otherworldly energy, a reminder that the veil between our world and the supernatural remains perilously thin.

"You've lost, Thorne," I say, forcing conviction into my words.

"Whatever dark forces you've awakened, I'll stop them."

He laughs again, a sound that sets my teeth on edge. "You? A man of logic and reason? You're out of your depth, Detective. The mysteries that await you... they'll shatter that analytical mind of yours."

I kneel beside him, my face inches from his. "Then I'll piece it together as many times as it takes. I've faced my demons, Thorne. I'm not afraid of yours."

As if in response to my declaration, a gust of wind sweeps through the chamber, extinguishing half the candles. Shadows leap and dance across the walls, and for a moment, I swear I see shapes moving within them—grotesque, twisted forms that defy description.

I stand, my eyes darting from corner to corner. "What have you unleashed, Thorne?"

But when I look down, his eyes have rolled back in his head, unconsciousness finally claiming him. The following silence is deafening, broken only by the pounding of my heart.

I holster my revolver, my mind racing with Thorne's words' implications. The Order of the Eternal Flame. A cult, perhaps? Or something far more sinister? Whatever the truth, I know my work is far from over.

As I move to secure Thorne, a whisper seems to echo from the stones beneath my feet. "Beware, Arthur Blackwood," it hisses, "for in seeking the truth, you may lose yourself to the shadows."

I straighten my back, squaring my shoulders against the unseen threat. "Then let the shadows come," I mutter, more to myself than any unseen listener. "I'll shine a light so bright, lopsided the darkest corners of London will hide their secrets."

Chapter 11 Crisis Point

The flickering gas lamp casts grotesque shadows across the room, its meager light barely penetrating the gloom. I strain against the coarse ropes binding my wrists, the rough fibers biting into my flesh. My chest heaves with each labored breath, the cloth gag muffling my desperate attempts to cry out. How did I come to be in this wretched place? The last thing I remember is...

The creak of rusted hinges sends a chill down my spine. Footsteps approach, slow and deliberate. A tall figure emerges from the shadows, and my blood runs cold as I recognize the gaunt features of Quentin Thorne.

"Ah, Lady Evelyn. I trust you're finding your accommodations... adequate?" His thin lips curl into a cruel smile as he looms over me.

I glare at him, mustering all the defiance I can in my helpless state. If only I could speak, demand answers, and plead for release. But the gag renders me mute, leaving me at the mercy of this monster.

Thorne begins to pace, his footsteps echoing in the cramped space. "I'm sure you're wondering why you're here., it's nothing personal.

Well, not against you, at least." He pauses, fixing me with a penetrating stare. "Your dear friend Blackwood..."

My eyes widen at the mention of Blackwood's name. What could Thorne want with him? And how am I to be used as a pawn in this vile game?

"You see, Lady Evelyn, Blackwood possesses something I require.

Something of success, value, and power." Thorne's voice drops to a menacing whisper. "And you, my dear, are the key to ensuring his cooperation."

I shake my head vehemently, silently willing Blackwood not to agree to this madman's demands, whatever they may be. But a nagging doubt gnaws at me—would he sacrifice whatever Thorne seeks to ensure my safety?

"Oh, don't fret," Thorne continues, misinterpreting my gesture. "I have no intention of harming you. Not yet, at least. You're far too valuable as a bargaining chip." He reaches out, running a cold finger along my cheek. I recoil from his touch, my skin crawling.

"Such spirit," he muses, withdrawing his hand. "I can see why Blackwood is so fond of you. It will make his inevitable capitulation all the sweeter."

As Thorne continues to gloat, revealing snippets of his nefarious plan, my mind races. There must be a way out of this, some weakness I can exploit. But bound and gagged as I am, what hope do I have? The weight of my predicament threatens to crush me, but I refuse to succumb to despair. I am Lady Evelyn Worthington, and the likes of Quentin Thorne will not break me.

My eyes dart frantically around the dimly lit room, searching for any escape. The flickering gaslight casts elongated shadows across the peeling wallpaper, transforming innocuous objects into looming specters. A heavy wooden desk, its surface cluttered with papers and curious artifacts, dominates one corner. Perhaps a letter opener or other potential weapon is hidden amongst the detritus?

"Your mind is working overtime, isn't it, Lady Evelyn?" Thorne's silky voice cuts through my desperate thoughts. "I can almost hear the gears turning. But I assure you, there's no way out."

I glare at him defiantly, wishing I could spit out the gag and tell him exactly what I think of his assurances. Instead, I focus on the window behind him. Through the grimy panes, I catch glimpses of fog-shrouded rooftops. If I could just get to that window...

"You're wondering where we are, no doubt," Thorne continues, pacing slowly around me. "Let's just say we're in a part of London.

Your dear Arthur Blackwood would never think to look. The City of Shadows has many secrets, my lady, and I know them all."

My heart races at the mention of Arthur. Where is he now? Is he searching for me? I picture him striding through the fog-laden streets, his piercing blue eyes scanning every shadow, that familiar crease of concentration furrowing his brow. Hold on, Arthur. Find me.

"I wonder," Thorne muses, leaning in close, his breath hot against my ear, "what Blackwood would do if he knew the true nature of what I seek. Would he still come charging to your rescue if he understood the power at stake?"

I turn my head away, fighting the urge to shudder. What is this power Thorne speaks of? And how is Arthur involved? My mind whirls with possibilities, each more terrifying than the last.

I steady my breath, forcing myself to meet Thorne's cold gaze. His eyes glitter with malice, but I detect something else—a flicker of uncertainty, perhaps? I seize upon this, my voice steadier than I feel as I speak around the gag.

"Mmph... mmm..."

Thorne pauses, a cruel smile playing on his thin lips. "What's that, my lady? Do you have something to contribute to our little tête-à-tête?"

With an exaggerated sigh, he reaches forward and roughly yanks the cloth from my mouth. I gasp, tasting the metallic tang of fear on my tongue, but I push forward.

"You speak of power, Mr. Thorne," I say, my words measured and careful, "but true power lies in knowledge. And it seems you're lacking more of that."

Thorne's eyes narrow dangerously. "Oh? And what knowledge might that be, Lady Evelyn?"

I allow a hint of a smile to touch my lips, channeling every ounce of aristocratic disdain I can muster. "Why, the knowledge of Arthur Blackwood's capabilities, of course. You underestimate him at your peril."

As I speak, I catch a flicker of movement outside the grimy window. A shadow, perhaps? Or is it just my desperate imagination? I press on, keeping Thorne's attention fixed on me.

"Arthur isn't just relentless, Mr. Thorne. He's brilliant. Your traps and diversions? They'll only challenge him, to sharpen his resolve.

Every obstacle you place in his path is another clue, another piece of the puzzle he'll use to find me."

Thorne's confidence wavers momentarily, his gaunt face tightening with doubt. "You place too much faith in your detective, my lady. Even now, he wanders through a labyrinth of my design, chasing phantoms and false leads."

I lean forward as much as my bindings allow, my voice dropping to a whisper. "Are you certain of that, Mr. Thorne? Or is that just what you need to believe?"

Thorne's face contorts, anger and uncertainty flashing across his sharp features. He paces the room, his footsteps echoing ominously in the confined space. I watch him, my heart pounding, hoping I've planted a seed of doubt in his mind.

"Your detective," Thorne spits, his composure cracking, "is nothing but a mortal man fumbling in the dark. He cannot comprehend the forces at play here."

I keep my voice steady, even as a chill runs down my spine. "What forces might those be, Mr. Thorne?"

He whirls to face me, and for a moment, I glimpse something inhuman in his eyes—a swirling darkness that seems to consume the surrounding light. "Forces beyond your comprehension, Lady Evelyn. Ancient powers that have slumbered beneath London's streets for centuries."

My breath catches in my throat. Is this madness, or something far more terrifying?

Thorne's voice drops to a menacing whisper. "I serve entities older than time itself. They whisper secrets of the universe and grant powers beyond mortal reckoning. Your precious detective? He's an ant scurrying before a storm."

I struggle to keep my voice from trembling. "And what do these... entities... want with me?"

A cruel smile twists Thorne's thin lips. "You, my lady, are to be a vessel. A conduit for their return to this world."

Terror grips me, but I force myself to think of Arthur. He's out there, I know it. I have to buy him more time.

"You speak of power," I say, fighting to keep my voice level, "but true power doesn't hide in shadows. It doesn't need to resort to kidnapping and threats."

Thorne's eyes flash dangerously. "You do not know the true nature of power, Lady Evelyn. But soon... soon... you will."

I pace the dimly lit study, my mind racing as I piece together the fragments of information I've gathered. Thorne's secret location is no ordinary hideout; it's a nexus of dark energies, where the veil between our world and something far more sinister grows thin. My fingers trace the outline of an old map of London, focusing on a district known for its abandoned tunnels and forgotten catacombs.

"If I were to harness eldritch forces," I mutter, "I'd need a place steeped in history and hidden from prying eyes."

I grab my coat and hat, checking the revolver concealed within my waistcoat. Its weight is comforting and a stark reminder of the dangers ahead. As I step out into the fog-shrouded streets, I can't shake the feeling that unseen eyes are watching my every move.

"Caution, Arthur," I remind myself. "Lady Evelyn's life depends on your wits as much as your courage."

I go through winding alleys, avoiding the major thoroughfares where Thorne might have eyes and ears. The cobblestones beneath my feet whisper secrets with each step. I listen for any hint of supernatural interference.

Meanwhile, Lady Evelyn seizes a moment in her dimly lit prison when Thorne's attention wavers. Her fingers work frantically at the knots, numb from the tight bindings. A surge of hope courses through her as she feels the ropes give way ever so slightly.

"Just a little more," she thinks, her heart pounding. "Arthur will come, but I must be ready when he does."

The dank air of the hidden catacombs assaults my senses as I descend into the depths beneath London's streets. My footsteps echo ominously off the ancient stone walls; each sounds a potential betrayal of my presence. I pause, listening intently for any sign of Thorne or his accomplices.

"Steady on, Blackwood," I mutter, my voice barely a whisper. "Lady Evelyn needs you."

As I round a corner, I'm confronted by an intricate network of tunnels branching off in every direction. The flickering light from my lantern casts dancing shadows that mock my indecision. I close my eyes, drawing upon years of deductive reasoning to guide my choice.

"The leftmost passage," I decide, my intuition prickling. "It bears the faintest trace of recent disturbance."

No sooner have I taken three steps down the chosen path than a hidden mechanism triggers. The ground beneath my feet gives way, and I plummet into darkness. My hands scrabble for purchase on the slick walls as I slide down a steep, winding chute.

"Blast it all!" I curse, my mind racing to calculate my trajectory and potential landing.

Meanwhile, Lady Evelyn works tirelessly at her bonds, each minor victory bringing a mixture of hope and trepidation. The ropes around her wrists loosen incrementally, but the process is agonizingly slow.

"Come on, come on," she urges herself silently, her fingers raw from the effort. "I must be ready when Arthur arrives. I won't be a helpless damsel."

A noise from beyond the door causes her to freeze momentarily.

Has Thorne returned? Or could it be...? She redoubles her efforts, knowing that her window of opportunity may be rapidly closing.

"Arthur," she thinks fiercely, "wherever you are, whatever obstacles you face, know that I'm fighting too. We'll overcome this together."

The chute spits me onto cold, damp flagstones, and I roll to absorb the impact. As I spring to my feet, my eyes lock with Thorne's icy gaze. The room is cavernous, lit by guttering torches that cast writhing shadows on the walls—the air thrums with otherworldly energy that sets my teeth on edge.

"Ah, Detective Blackwood," Thorne drawls, a cruel smile on his thin lips. "How kind of you to drop in."

I straighten, brushing off my coat with affected nonchalance.

"Thorne. I'd say it's a pleasure, but we both know that would be a lie."

My eyes dart around the chamber, cataloging every detail. Ancient symbols are carved into the floor, forming a complex pattern that pulses with an eerie violet light. At the far end, I spot a heavy oak door—could Evelyn be behind it?

Thorne's voice cuts through my observations. "Your persistence is admirable, if futile. You're far out of your depth, Blackwood. This game is where the stakes transcend your meager understanding of reality."

I force a sarcastic chuckle. "Enlighten me then, Thorne. What grand design justifies your crimes?"

As Thorne launches into a pontificating monologue, I subtly shift my weight, inching towards the oak door. Every fiber of my being screams to rush to Evelyn's aid, but I know I must play this carefully. One wrong move could spell disaster for us both.

Behind that door, Evelyn feels the last of her bonds give way. She suppresses a gasp of triumph, her heart pounding a frantic rhythm against her ribs. Voices filter through the thick wood—one unmistakably Arthur's. Hope surges through her veins like lightning.

"Now or never," she thinks, rising on unsteady legs. Her fingers fumble with the door's latch, praying it isn't locked from the outside. She takes a deep breath as it yields, steeling herself for whatever lies beyond.

I lock eyes with Thorne, my gaze is unwavering as I process his words. His monologue has revealed more than he intended—the Order's vulnerabilities and the true nature of their rituals—and my mind races, piecing together the puzzle even as I maintain an outward facade of skepticism.

"Impressive, Thorne," I drawl, injecting a note of boredom into my voice. "But you've overlooked one crucial detail."

His eyes narrow. "And what might that be, detective?"

The door behind him creaks open, and I see a flash of Evelyn's pale face. My heart leaps, but I force myself to remain focused. This is our chance.

That your precious ritual requires absolute precision," I say, taking a deliberate step forward. "One misplaced symbol, one mispronounced word, and the whole thing unravels."

Thorne's confidence wavers for a fraction of a second—all I need to confirm my suspicion. I lunge forward, my hand darting out to smear the intricate chalk lines on the floor. The violet light flickers and dies.

"No!" Thorne roars, his composure shattering. He reaches for me, but I'm ready.

In one fluid motion, I sidestep his grasp and produce the amulet I'd pocketed earlier—the one I'd seen him use to channel his dark energies. I hold it aloft, reciting the incantation I'd committed to memory from the Order's stolen texts.

The effect is instantaneous. Thorne's face contorts in agony as an invisible force seems to grip him. "How..." he gasps, sinking to his knees.

"You're not the only one who's done his homework," I reply grimly, maintaining the magic.

As Thorne writhes on the floor, I see Evelyn emerge fully from the room, her eyes wide with relief and shock. "Arthur," she breathes, stumbling towards me.

I long to embrace her, to ensure she's truly safe, but I can't let my guard down yet. "It's over, Evelyn," I say softly, my free hand steadying her. "But we need to leave. Now."

The building around us groans ominously as if the foundations rebelled against the disrupted ritual. I tighten my grip on the amulet, knowing our escape is far from guaranteed. But with Evelyn by my side and Thorne incapacitated, I allow myself a flicker of hope. We've turned the tables, but the night's dangers are far from over.

Chapter 12 All Is Lost

The flickering light of a lone gas lamp casts grotesque shadows across the chamber walls, transforming ancient artifacts into leering faces. My heart pounds as I take it in our dire circumstances.

Evelyn's fingers dig into my arm, her breath coming in short, panicked gasps.

"Blackwood," she whispers, trembling, "what is this place?"

I scan the room, my detective's instincts kicking into overdrive.

Dusty shelves line the walls, laden with crumbling scrolls and ominous relics. Arcane symbols etched into the stone floor seem to writhe in the dim light as if alive and hungry.

"Some sort of occult sanctuary," I murmur, my mind racing. "Thorne's trap has sprung, and we're the unfortunate mice."

I stride to the heavy stone door through which we entered, running my hands along its unyielding surface. There is no handle or visible mechanism, so we're tightly sealed.

"Damn it all," I growl, slamming my fist against the door in frustration. The dull thud echoes through the chamber, mocking our predicament.

Evelyn's eyes dart around the room, her usual poise cracking under the weight of our imprisonment. "There must be another way out," she says, strained but determined.

I nod, forcing myself to think rationally despite the creeping tendrils of panic threatening to cloud my judgment. "We need to stay calm and assess our options," I say, as much to steady myself as to reassure Evelyn.

My gaze sweeps the chamber once more, cataloging every detail—the eerie symbols, the ancient artifacts, the oppressive darkness pressing in from all sides—each element a piece of Thorne's sinister puzzle.

"What do you think he wants with us?" Evelyn asks, her fingers absently tracing one symbol etched into a nearby pillar.

I shake my head, a chill running down my spine. "Nothing good, I'm certain. Thorne's ambitions have always been dangerous, but this..." I gesture to our surroundings, "This speaks of something far more nefarious than we ever imagined."

As I speak, my mind races through possibilities, each more disturbing than the last. What dark forces has Thorne allied himself with? And to what end?

"We can't let him succeed," I say, my voice low and fierce. "Whatever his plan, we must stop it."

Evelyn nods, her resolve visibly strengthening. "Then we'd best start looking for a way out of this cursed place," she says, her eyes gleaming doggedly in the flickering lamplight. Our determination to find a way out is unwavering, giving the audience hope we will overcome this predicament.

I admire her courage even as the weight of our predicament settles heavily upon my shoulders. We're trapped at the mercy of a madman's machinations, with no apparent means of escape. And yet, surrender is not an option. Our resilience in the face of danger is a testament to our strength, inspiring the audience and fostering a sense of connection.

"Indeed," I reply, squaring my shoulders. "Let's get to work."

I scan the chamber, my eyes straining in the dim light. The walls seem to pulse with otherworldly energy, ancient symbols casting long shadows that dance in the flickering lamplight. Evelyn's suggestion cuts through the oppressive silence.

"Arthur," she says, her voice steady despite our dire circumstances, "there must be some hidden mechanism. A secret passage, perhaps? These chambers were built for a purpose, after all."

I nod, impressed by her astute observation. "Brilliant thinking, Lady Evelyn. We mustn't overlook any possibility, no matter how small."

Without hesitation, we begin our frantic search. My hands glide over the cold, damp stone, feeling for any irregularity that might betray a hidden switch or lever. The rough surface scrapes against my palms, but I push the discomfort aside, focusing solely on our desperate task. Our resourcefulness in this dire situation keeps the audience engaged and intrigued.

"Do you feel anything?" I call out to Evelyn, who's examining the opposite wall.

She shakes her head, auburn curls swaying in the dim light.

"Nothing yet. But we can't give up."

As I continue my methodical search, my mind races. What if we can't find a way out? What horrors await us if Thorne returns? The weight of our predicament threatens to crush me, but I force the panic down. I must remain clearheaded if we're to have any chance of escape.

"Wait!" Evelyn's eager exclamation cuts through my brooding thoughts. "I think I've found something!"

I rush to her side, my heart pounding. "What is it?" We're in this together, and we'll find a way out.

Her fingers trace a barely perceptible seam in the stonework. "It's too uniform to be natural. This has to be man made." Our wits are our best weapons in this dire situation. Hope surges within me as I examine her discovery. "You may be right. Let's see if we can activate it somehow."

Together, we press and prod at the stone, searching for any clue.

The chamber seems to hold its breath, the air thick with anticipation. Our freedom—and perhaps our lives—hang in the balance of this desperate gambit.

My analytical mind shifts into overdrive as I study the chamber's architecture, piecing together its sinister purpose. The arcane symbols etched into the walls and the eerie placement of ancient artifacts speak to a darker design.

"Evelyn," I murmur, my voice low and tense, "I believe this chamber was built for ceremonial purposes. The positioning of these artifacts... they form a pattern, almost like a summoning circle."

Her eyes widen, a mix of fear and fascination crossing her delicate features. "You don't think Thorne intends to—"

"Unleash something beyond our comprehension? I'm afraid that's exactly what I think." The realization chills me, but I force myself to continue. "These symbols, they're not just decorative. They're words, containment sigils. Whatever Thorne plans to bring forth, he means to control it."

Evelyn's brow furrows as she processes this information. "But why trap us here? Surely, we're not meant to be... sacrifices?"

I'm about to respond when a glint catches my eye. Evelyn notices it, too, her keen gaze zeroing in on the spot near the chamber's far corner.

"Arthur, look!" she exclaims, pointing to a small, hidden keyhole barely visible in the flickering torchlight.

My heart leaps. "Brilliant eye, Evelyn. That could be our salvation."

As we approach the keyhole, hope and trepidation war within me. Could this be our escape or another facet of Thorne's intricate trap?

The chamber seems to constrict around us as we frantically search for the key, our movements frenzied yet purposeful. Every second feels like an eternity, the weight of our predicament pressing down upon us with suffocating intensity.

"It must be here somewhere," I mutter, more to myself than to Evelyn. I meticulously explore dusty shelves and old books, examining everything. "Thorne wouldn't have left us without a chance, however slim. It's all part of his twisted game."

Evelyn's voice trembles slightly as she responds, "But what if we're wrong, Arthur? What if there is no key?"

I pause, turning to face her. The flickering torchlight casts dancing shadows across her face, accentuating the fear in her eyes. "We can't afford to think that way," I say firmly, confident. "We must believe in our abilities, in our chance to outsmart him."

As we continue our search, my mind races. What if we're overlooking something obvious? What if the key isn't physical but a riddle or a code?

Suddenly, a glint of metal catches my eye amidst a pile of crumbling scrolls. My heart leaps into my throat. "Evelyn!" I call out, my voice echoing off the chamber walls. "I think I've found it!"

With trembling fingers, I grasp the small, ornate key. It's cool, and its intricate design speaks of an age long past. As I hold it up, triumph and trepidation course through me.

"We've no time to waste," I say, striding towards the keyhole. "Let's pray this is our ticket out of this infernal trap."

My hands tremble as I insert the key into the ancient lock, its intricate teeth scraping against the mechanism. I hold my breath, acutely aware of Evelyn's presence beside me, her muted anticipation palpable in the stale air. With a silent prayer to whatever forces might be listening, I turn the key.

The sound of grinding stones fills the chamber as the heavy door creaks open. A surge of relief washes over me, so powerful it nearly brings me to my knees.

"It's working," I whisper, hardly daring to believe our fortune. "Evelyn, it's working."

She grasps my arm, her fingers digging into my sleeve. "Arthur, what if it's another trap? What if Thorne is waiting on the other side?"

I turn to face her, meeting her gaze in the dim light. The fear in her eyes is tempered by a steely resolve I admire. "Then we face it together," I say, my voice low and determined. "Whatever lies beyond, we've no choice but to confront it."

Evelyn nods, squaring her shoulders. "You're right, of course. We've come too far to falter now."

As the door grinds to a halt, fully open, we exchange a last glance.

At that moment, I see a reflection of my determination mirrored in Evelyn's face. This shared ordeal binds us, our fates intertwined in ways I'm only beginning to understand.

"Ready?" I ask though I know the answer.

"As I'll ever be," she replies, a hint of her usual dry wit returning.

Together, we step towards the threshold, bracing ourselves for whatever horrors or challenges await us on the other side: the unknown looms, a yawning void of terrifying and exhilarating possibilities. As we cross into the next chamber, I can't shake the feeling that we're walking into the belly of the beast itself.

The air shifts as we step through the doorway, a damp chill seeping into my bones. The musty scent of decay and age-old stone assaults my senses, and I fight the urge to cough. Beside me, Evelyn draws a sharp breath.

"Lord," she whispers, her voice barely audible.

Before us stretches a labyrinth of tunnels, twisting and turning into the darkness like the veins of some monstrous creature. The walls glisten with moisture, and the flickering light of our single lantern casts grotesque shadows that dance and writhe along the curved ceilings.

I take a tentative step forward, the sound of my shoe against the stone floor echoing ominously through the passageways. "Stay close," I murmur to Evelyn. "We mustn't lose sight of each other in this maze."

As we begin to navigate the winding tunnels, my mind races. What purpose could these passages serve? Are they remnants of some ancient civilization or a more recent construction? And more pressingly, how deep do they go?

"Arthur," Evelyn's voice breaks through my reverie, "do you hear that?"

I pause, straining my ears. At first, there's nothing but breathing and the distant water drip. Then, I catch a faint whisper of movement, so slight it might be my imagination.

"It could be the wind," I say, not believing it myself. "Or..."

"Or Thorne's men," Evelyn finishes, her voice tense.

We press on, our senses heightened to a knife's edge. Every shadow seems to conceal a potential threat, every sound a harbinger of danger. The tunnels twist and turn, leading us deeper into the earth's embrace.

"We need to find a way out," I mutter, more to myself than to Evelyn. "There must be a pattern to these passages, some logic we can discern."

Evelyn's hand brushes my arm. "Look there," she says, pointing to strange markings on the wall. "Could these be a guide of some sort?"

I lean in, studying the cryptic symbols. "Brilliant observation, my dear. These could indeed be our key to escaping this labyrinth. But what do they mean?"

As we ponder the markings, the distant sound grows louder. My heart races, knowing that our time is running short. We must decipher this puzzle quickly or risk being trapped in this underground nightmare forever.

The echoing footsteps grow louder, each rhythmic tap sending a jolt of adrenaline through my veins. I grab Evelyn's arm, pulling her closer as we quicken our pace.

"They're gaining on us," I whisper, my voice hoarse with urgency.

Evelyn's eyes widen, but she maintains her composure. "We mustn't panic, Arthur. Clear thinking is our greatest asset now."

We round a corner, our footfalls muffled by the damp earth beneath us. The tunnel splits into two diverging paths, each as dark and foreboding as the other. I feel a moment of paralysis, my analytical mind racing to deduce the correct choice.

Evelyn turns to me, her face pale in the dim light. "Which way?" she mouths silently.

I close my eyes briefly, trying to recall every detail of our journey thus far. The markings we saw earlier flash in my mind, a jumble of arcane symbols that suddenly coalesce into a pattern.

"Left," I whisper, pointing to the tunnel. "The symbols showed a leftward trajectory."

Evelyn nods, trusting my judgment implicitly. As we prepare to plunge into the darkness, I can't help but wonder if I've made the right choice. The weight of our lives hangs on this decision, and the echoing footsteps behind us leave no room for doubt or hesitation.

"Whatever happens," I say, squeezing Evelyn's hand, "we face it together."

Her fingers tighten around mine, a silent affirmation of our bond.

With one last shared glance, we enter the unknown, our hearts pounding in unison with the approaching threat.

We plunge into the left tunnel, our feet slipping on the slick stone as we push ourselves to our limits. The air grows thicker, a haze of decay and ancient secrets that clings to our skin.

"Arthur," Evelyn gasps between labored breaths, "I don't know how much longer I can—"

"You can," I interrupt, my voice low but firm. "You must."

The distant echo of pursuit spurs us onward, each step a defiance against the encroaching darkness. My mind races, cataloging every twist and turn, searching for any advantage we might exploit.

"Do you think Thorne knew about these tunnels?" Evelyn asks, her voice barely above a whisper.

I consider her question, my brow furrowing. "It's possible. The man's resources seem... unnaturally vast."

As we round another bend, I catch sight of a faint glimmer ahead.

Hope surges within me, tempered by caution. "There," I point, "Do you see it?"

Evelyn nods, her eyes wide. "What is it?"

"I'm uncertain," I admit, "but it may be our salvation... or our downfall."

We press on, the mysterious light growing stronger with each step.

The sounds of pursuit seem to fade, replaced by an eerie stillness that sets my nerves on edge.

"Arthur," Evelyn whispers, her hand gripping my arm, "I have a terrible feeling about this."

I place my hand over hers, offering what comfort I can. "As do I, my dear. But we've no choice but to press forward. Whatever awaits us, we'll face it together."

The light beckons us onward, a siren's call in this labyrinth of shadows. With hearts pounding and breaths shallow, we step towards the unknown, praying it leads to safety and not into Thorne's sinister trap.

Chapter 13 Dark Night

The flickering candlelight casts long shadows across my study, dancing over towering stacks of leather-bound books and scattered case files. I stand motionless, my weary gaze fixed on the wall before me, yet seeing nothing. The weight of recent events presses down, threatening to crush what remains of my resolve.

"How much longer can I go on?" I muttered, running a hand through my disheveled hair. The scent of stale tobacco and dust hangs heavy in the air, a fitting atmosphere for my brooding thoughts.

I turn, intending to pour myself a much-needed brandy when a chill races down my spine. The temperature in the room plummets, and my breath is visible in wispy tendrils. Before my eyes, a shimmering figure begins to materialize.

"Impossible," I whisper, frozen in place as Lady Ravenscroft's ghostly form takes shape. Her ethereal beauty is tinged with otherworldly sorrow, and her eyes pool with longing and regret.

She reaches towards me, spectral fingers passing through my chest.

"Arthur," she breathes, her voice echoing as if from a successful distance. "You mustn't give up."

I struggle to find words, my analytical mind reeling from this supernatural phenomenon. "Lady Ravenscroft, how—why are you here?"

Her translucent form shimmers, threatening to dissipate like morning mist. "The darkness grows stronger. You alone can uncover the truth."

My heart races, a maelstrom of emotions threatening to overwhelm me. Part of me wants to dismiss this as a hallucination born of exhaustion, yet I cannot deny the evidence before my eyes.

"I'm at my wit's end," I confess, the admission tasting bitter on my tongue. "Every lead turns cold, every clue a dead end. Perhaps I'm not the man for this task after all."

Lady Ravenscroft's spectral visage softens, a ghostly hand caressing my cheek without contact. "You underestimate yourself, Detective. Your intellect and determination are precisely what's needed to pierce the veil of secrecy surrounding these horrors."

I close my eyes, inhaling deeply. When I open them again, I'm met with her unwavering gaze. "And if I fail? If the Order's evil persists despite my efforts?"

"Then you will have fought with honor," she replies, her form beginning to fade. "But I have faith in you, Arthur Blackwood. The city needs you now more than ever." Her unwavering belief in me is a heavy burden and a source of strength.

As suddenly as she appeared, Lady Ravenscroft vanished, leaving me alone again in my study. The chill lingers, as does the faint scent of roses—a reminder that what I witnessed was no mere trick of an overworked mind.

I move to my desk, rifling through the case files with renewed purpose. The weight of responsibility settles on my shoulders, but it no longer threatens to break me. I vow to bring any dark forces at work in London's shadowy underbelly into the light.

"For you, Lady Ravenscroft," I murmur to the empty room, my voice filled doggedly. "And for all those who have suffered at the hands of evil. I will not rest until justice is served. I will fight this darkness with every fiber of my being."

I stumble backward, my heart thundering against my ribs as if trying to escape the confines of my chest. The room grows impossibly cold, my breath coming out in visible puffs of vapor.

Shadows dance across the walls, elongating and twisting into grotesque shapes that mock my disbelief. The supernatural is no longer a mere possibility but a chilling reality.

"This... this can't be real," I whisper, my analytical mind desperately grasping for a logical explanation.

Lady Ravenscroft's ethereal form remains before me, her sorrowful eyes fixed upon my face. The candlelight flickers violently, casting an otherworldly glow upon her spectral visage.

"Oh, but it is, Detective Blackwood," her voice echoes in my mind, a haunting melody that sends shivers down my spine. "The veil between worlds has grown thin, and the darkness that plagues our city bleeds through."

I struggle to compose myself, years of investigative training warring with the impossible sight before me. "Lady Ravenscroft, I... I don't understand. What darkness do you speak of?"

Her ghostly form wavers like a reflection in troubled water. "The Order's influence spreads like a cancer, Arthur. Their tendrils reach deeper than you know, corrupting the very soul of London."

I feel my resolve strengthening, curiosity overcoming fear. "Tell me more. How can I hope to combat such a force?"

"With the same determination that has guided you thus far," she replies, her voice a soothing balm to my frayed nerves. "Do not let despair cloud your judgment or weaken your spirit. If only you dare to seize the truth lies within your grasp."

I nod slowly, my mind racing with possibilities. "I won't give up, Lady Ravenscroft. I swear it."

A sad smile graces her spectral lips. "I know, dear Arthur. That is why I came to you. The city needs its protector now more than ever."

Her words linger in the air, a fragile thread of hope in the tapestry of darkness surrounding me. But as I reach out, desperate to grasp that thread, doubt seeps into my mind like a noxious fog.

"Am I truly the protector London needs?" I whisper, my voice barely audible in the oppressive silence of my study. "Or am I just a man fumbling in the dark, chasing shadows?"

Memories flood my consciousness, unbidden and unwelcome. One is the Whitechapel case, in which I arrived too late to save the last victim.

The mysterious disappearances in Kensington remain unsolved despite months of sleepless nights. Each failure weighs on me, a leaden burden that threatens to drag me into despair.

"I've failed before," I murmur, running a trembling hand through my hair. "What makes this time any different?"

Lady Ravenscroft's form begins to fade, her ethereal presence diminishing with each passing moment. "The difference, Arthur," she whispers, her voice growing fainter, "is that now you know the true nature of what you face. Knowledge is power, and you possess more than you realize."

A chill settles over the room as her spirit dissipates, causing the candle flames to flicker and dance. The air grows heavy with the scent of roses, a delicate fragrance that seems at odds with the somber atmosphere. It's as if Lady Ravenscroft has left an indelible mark on my study, a reminder of her otherworldly visit.

I inhale deeply, letting the floral aroma fill my lungs. "Knowledge is power," I repeat, clinging to her words like a lifeline. "But is it enough to unravel this infernal mystery?"

I pace the length of my study, my footsteps echoing in the oppressive silence. Each stride carries the weight of my decision, the floorboards creaking beneath me like a judgmental chorus.

"If I abandon this case," I mutter, fingers tracing the spines of dusty tomes as I pass, "how many more will suffer? How many souls will be lost in the darkness?"

The magnitude of the choice before me is paralyzing. My desire for justice burns fiercely, a flame that has guided me through countless investigations. Yet, the shadow of my limitations looms large, threatening to extinguish that fire.

"Am I truly equipped to face such malevolence?" I wonder aloud, my voice barely above a whisper. "Or am I merely tilting at windmills, destined to fail?"

A sharp rap at the door interrupts my spiraling thoughts. Before I can respond, it swings open, revealing the sturdy figure of Inspector Tobias Collins.

"Blackwood," he greets, his gruff voice tinged with concern. "You look like you've seen a ghost."

I force a wry smile. "Perhaps I have, old friend."

Collins' eyes narrow as he surveys the room, his mustache twitching. "What's troubling you? And don't tell me it's nothing—I've known you too long for that nonsense."

I slump into my chair, suddenly feeling every one of my years.

"Tobias, I... I'm wondering if this case is beyond me. The depths of depravity we're facing, the supernatural elements at play, are unlike anything we've encountered before."

"Aye, it's a right mess," Collins agrees, leaning against my desk. "But if anyone can unravel it, it's you, Arthur. You've got a knack for seeing what others miss."

I shake my head, memories of past failures flooding back. "And what if that's not enough this time? What if I'm simply prolonging the inevitable, giving false hope to those who deserve better?"

I take a deep breath, steeling myself for what I will reveal. "Tobias, there's something I haven't told you. Lady Ravenscroft, I've seen her. Not just in my dreams or imagination, but in this very room."

Collins' eyebrows shoot up, and his skepticism is evident. "You mean to say you've seen her ghost?"

"I know how it sounds," I reply, running a hand through my disheveled hair. "But she was here, as real as you are now. Her presence, her words, they haunt me still."

"Arthur," Collins says gently, his voice gruff but kind, "I've known you to be many things but never a fanciful man. Are you certain it wasn't just a trick of the light, or perhaps exhaustion playing tricks on your mind?"

I shake my head vehemently. "No, Tobias. She was here. And her message spoke of a darkness beyond our comprehension."

Collins is silent for a moment, his sharp eyes studying me. Then he speaks, his words measured. "I may not believe in ghosts, Arthur, but I believe in you. You've solved cases that baffled the entire force. Remember the Whitechapel Strangler? The Dockside Poisoner? You saw patterns where others saw chaos."

His words stir something within me, a flicker of the determination that once burned so brightly. "But this... this is different, Tobias. The stakes are higher, the enemy more elusive."

"Aye, and that's precisely why we need you," Collins insists.

"Think of the victims, Arthur. The innocent lives are at stake. If not you, then who?"

I close my eyes, seeing the faces of those we've lost, those we've yet to save. When I open them again, there's a new resolve in my gaze. "You're right, of course. I can't abandon them now, not when we nearly unravel this infernal mystery."

"There's the Blackwood I know," Collins says with approval. "So, what's our next move?"

I stand, my voice gaining strength as I speak. "We follow the trail, no matter how dark or twisted it becomes. The Order may think they're beyond the reach of justice, but we'll prove them wrong.

We'll shine a light into their shadows for every victim, every life touched by their evil."

Collins grins, a fierce glint in his eye. "Now that's a plan I can get behind. Lead on, Detective. The game's afoot."

I stride towards my desk with renewed purpose, my footsteps echoing in the study's silence. Once trembling with doubt, my hands move with practiced efficiency as I gather my belongings.

The weight of my revolver as I holster it is a grim reminder of the dangers that lie ahead.

"What are you thinking, Arthur?" Collins asks, watching me intently.

I pause, my fingers brushing over the worn leather of my notebook.

"I think we've been looking at this all wrong, Tobias. The Order isn't just a group of occultists—they're a cancer, spreading through London's very veins."

As I speak, I'm already mapping out our next moves. I snatch up a stack of case files, cramming them into my satchel. "We need to revisit every crime scene, every witness statement. There's a pattern here, I'm certain of it."

Collins nods, his brow furrowed. "And what of Lady Ravenscroft's... visitation? Do you truly believe it was her spirit?"

I meet his gaze, a chill running down my spine as I recall her ethereal presence. "I don't know what to believe anymore, old friend. But I can't ignore the possibility that forces are at work beyond our understanding."

My coat settles around my shoulders like armor as I shrug it on. I turn to face the room, eyes sweeping over the familiar surroundings. The flickering candlelight seems brighter now, the shadows less oppressive.

"Whatever comes," I say, more to myself than to Collins, "we face it head-on. No more hiding in the safety of these walls, poring over dusty tomes and hoping for answers to fall into our laps."

As I move towards the door, the air in the study seems to shift. The oppressive weight that had settled over the room during my moment of despair lifts as if the space itself is exhaling a sigh of relief. The shadows that once clung to the corners now retreat, shrinking back from the newfound determination radiating from my very being.

I pause at the threshold, my hand on the doorknob. "Tobias," I say, turning back to my friend and colleague, "thank you for reminding me of who I am and why we do this."

Collins offers a small smile. "That's what partners are for, Arthur. Shall we make London's underworld quake in their boots?"

With a nod, I open the door, ready to step out into the fog-shrouded streets of our beloved, beleaguered city. The mysteries that await us are daunting, but I feel equal to the task for the first time in what feels like an age. Whatever darkness lies ahead, we will face it—together.

I step out onto the cobblestone street, the heavy oak door of my study closing behind me with a dull thud. The fog engulfs me immediately, a thick, living thing that seems to breathe with evil intent. Gaslight from nearby streetlamps struggles to penetrate the murk, casting eerie, shifting shadows.

"Well, into the breach we go," I mutter, pulling my coat tighter.

The chill seeps through the wool, settling into my bones. It's not just the cold of a London night; there's something more sinister in this air.

As I walk, my footsteps echoing hollowly on the damp stones, I can't shake the feeling of being watched. Eyes in the mist, perhaps?

Or is it merely my imagination, overwrought from our recent supernatural encounters?

"Get a grip, Blackwood," I scold myself. "You've faced worse than a bit of fog."

But have I? The weight of Lady Ravenscroft's ghostly visitation still presses upon me. Her words echo: "The darkness surrounds us all, Detective. But you must not falter."

I pause at a crossroads, peering down each foggy avenue. Which way leads to the truth? To justice? To salvation for this city, I've sworn to protect.

"When in doubt," I murmur, "follow the scent of danger." I turn left towards the seedier districts where secrets fester like open wounds.

As I walk, my silhouette fading into the mist, I can't help but feel that this is merely the beginning. The real challenges, the tests of my resolve and abilities, lie ahead in the murky unknown. But I feel a flicker of hope for the first time in weeks. Whatever awaits me in London's shadowy underbelly, I'll face it head-on.

The fog swallows me, and I disappear into the night, ready to unravel the following thread in this infernal mystery.

Chapter 14 Resurrection

The gaslight flickers, casting monstrous shadows across the towering stacks of case files surrounding me. Once a sanctuary of Order and reason, my office now feels like a prison of futility. I bury my face in my hands, my fingers digging into my temples as if I could physically extract the tumultuous thoughts plaguing my mind.

"It's impossible," I mutter to the empty room. "There's no logical explanation for any of this."

The weight of failure presses down upon me, heavier than the mountains of evidence that mock my inadequacy. I've faced countless perplexing cases in my career, but this defies all rational understanding. How can I, Arthur Blackwood, renowned detective of Scotland Yard, hope to unravel a mystery that seems to transcend the very laws of nature?

My eyes drift to the photograph of my late wife, her smile frozen in time. "I'm sorry, Eleanor," I whisper. "I fear I've finally met my match."

The creak of the door interrupts my spiral of despair. Soft footsteps echo in the silence, a familiar rhythm that quickens my pulse despite my melancholy. I don't need to look up to know it's her.

"Detective Blackwood?" Lady Evelyn's melodic voice carries a note of concern.

I straighten, attempting to compose myself, but I know it's futile.

She's far too perceptive to be fooled by such a feeble facade.

"Lady Worthington," I manage, my voice hoarse. "I apologize, I wasn't expecting—"

Her hand lands gently on my shoulder, and I feel a tremor pass through me at the unexpected contact. "Arthur," she says softly, dispensing with formalities. "What's troubling you?"

I meet her gaze, those expressive eyes filled with worry and determination. For a moment, I consider deflecting, maintaining the professional distance I've cultivated for so long. But something in her steady presence compels honesty.

"I fear we've reached an impasse, Lady Evelyn," I admit. "The evidence before us... it defies all logical explanation. I'm wondering if we're chasing shadows and phantoms."

She moves to perch on the edge of my desk, her skirts rustling.

"And since when has Arthur Blackwood balked at the impossible?" she asks a hint of challenge in her tone.

I can't help but smile ruefully. "Since the impossible began to look distressingly real."

"Then perhaps," she says, leaning forward slightly, "it's time we embrace the impossible. Remember why we started this, Arthur.

Their lives are at stake, and evil must be stopped. We can't afford to falter now."

Her words stir something within me, a flicker of the resolve that brought me this far. I study her face, marveling at the muted strength radiating from her. Lady Evelyn Worthington has faced her brush with the inexplicable and emerged not broken but transformed.

"You're right, of course," I concede, straightening in my chair.

"Forgive my moment of weakness. It seems even the successful Detective Blackwood is not immune to doubt."

She smiles a warm gesture that chases away some shadows in the room. "Doubt is natural, Arthur. It's what we do despite it that defines us."

I nod, feeling a renewed sense of purpose coursing through me.

"Then let us define ourselves by our actions, Lady Evelyn. We have a mystery to solve and a city to save."

As I rise from my chair, the gaslight burns slightly brighter, illuminating the path forward. Whatever darkness awaits us, I know now that I don't face it alone.

The door creaks open, and Dr. Amelia Lancaster strides in, her fiery red hair catching the gaslight like a halo of flame. Her presence fills the room, commanding yet comforting.

"I hope I'm not interrupting," she says, her keen eyes darting between Evelyn and me.

"Not at all," I reply, gesturing for her to join us. "Your timing is impeccable, as always."

Lancaster's lips quirk into a half-smile. "I've always had a knack for arriving when I'm most needed." She pauses, her expression growing serious. "Arthur, I couldn't help but overhear your moment of doubt. It reminded me of something..."

She takes a deep breath, and I lean in, captivated by the sudden vulnerability in her usually confident demeanor.

"Years ago, when I was still a medical student, I faced a case that seemed utterly hopeless. A young girl is wasting away from an unknown ailment. Every test, every treatment failed. I was ready to give up, to admit defeat."

I watch Lancaster's eyes grow distant, lost in the memory. "But then, I noticed something about what we thought would be her last night. A pattern in her symptoms that shouldn't have been there. It led me down a path of research I'd never considered before, and in the end..."

"You saved her," Evelyn breathes, enthralled.

Lancaster nods. "Against all odds, yes. It taught me that even in our darkest moments when all seems lost, there's always a glimmer of hope. We just have to be stubborn enough to keep looking for it."

Her words resonate deeply, stirring memories of my past triumphs against impossible odds. I feel my resolve strengthening, my earlier despair melting like a morning mist.

"Thank you, Amelia," I say softly. "I needed that reminder."

She smiles, reaching out to squeeze my arm. "We all do, from time to time. Now, shall we get to work?"

I nod, gesturing toward the table in the center of the room. "Indeed. We have a puzzle to solve."

We gather around the table, its surface a chaotic sea of maps, photographs, and hastily scribbled notes. The flickering gaslight casts dancing shadows across the evidence of our investigation, lending an otherworldly air to our task.

"What do we know for certain?" I ask, my analytical mind already cataloging and connecting disparate pieces of information.

Evelyn leans in, her brow furrowed in concentration. "Thorne's activities have been centered on these five locations," she says, pointing to marked spots on the map. "But why these specific places?"

I study the map, tracing imaginary lines between the points.

"There's a pattern here, but I can't quite grasp it..."

Lancaster's eyes light up suddenly. "Wait, Arthur. Those markings on the corner of that photograph—I've seen something similar before, in an old text on occult symbolism."

As we delve deeper into the evidence, I feel the familiar thrill of the hunt coursing through my veins. Blackwood, the detective, is back, ready to face whatever darkness Thorne and his Order can muster.

I tap my finger on the map, my mind racing with possibilities. "We need a plan of action," I declare, my voice cutting through the tense silence. "We've uncovered enough to make our move, but we must be strategic."

Evelyn nods, her auburn hair gleaming in the flickering light.

"What do you propose, Arthur?"

I straighten, feeling the weight of responsibility settling on my shoulders. "We'll divide our efforts. Each of us has unique strengths that we must leverage to have any hope of stopping Thorne."

Lancaster leans forward, her eyes sharp with interest. "Go on."

"Evelyn," I turn to her, noting the determination in her posture.

"Your connections in high society are invaluable. We need you to gather more information, particularly about Thorne's recent movements and any unusual gatherings he might have attended."

A slight smile plays on Evelyn's lips. "Consider it done. I have a soirée to attend tomorrow evening, where several Thorne associates will be present. I'll put my charm to use."

I can't help but feel a twinge of concern. "Be careful, Evelyn. Thorne's influence runs deep."

"I always am, Arthur," she responds, her voice tinged with amusement. "You forget, I've navigated these treacherous social waters my entire life."

I nod, acknowledging her capability. "Very well. Use your intuition. Extract yourself from the situation if anything feels amiss."

As I outline the rest of our plan, I can't shake the feeling that we're stepping into the lion's den. But what choice do we have? The fate of London—perhaps the world—hangs in the balance.

I turn to Lancaster, her fiery hair catching the flickering lamplight.

"Amelia, your expertise in the occult will be crucial. We need to understand what we're up against."

Lancaster's eyes gleam with excitement. "I've been itching to delve deeper into this, Arthur. There are ancient texts at the British Museum that might hold the key to Thorne's weaknesses. I have a colleague there who owes me a favor."

"Excellent," I nod, feeling a glimmer of hope. "Focus on any rituals or artifacts connected to Thorne's Order. We need to find their weakness."

Lancaster's brow furrows in concentration. "I'll start with the Etruscan scrolls. There are whispers of a binding ritual that might neutralize supernatural entities. It's a long shot, but..."

"Any lead is worth pursuing," I interject. The weight of our task presses down on me, but I force myself to remain focused. "Be discreet, Amelia. We can't risk alerting Thorne to our intentions."

She nods solemnly. "Of course. I'll be as silent as the grave."

I suppress a shudder at her choice of words, my mind flickering to the horrors we've already witnessed. Shaking off the feeling, I move to my desk and reach for the telephone. "I'll coordinate our efforts and ensure we're all working together. We can't afford any missteps."

As I dial, my fingers trembling slightly, I can't help but wonder if we're truly prepared for what lies ahead. The familiar voice of Inspector Collins answers, gruff but reassuring.

"Collins," I say, my voice low. "We're moving forward with the plan. I need your support for this. Can you assemble a team you trust implicitly? We may need backup when we confront Thorne."

There's a pause on the other end of the line, and I can almost see Collins' weathered face creasing with concern. "Are you certain about this, Blackwood? We're treading on dangerous ground."

I close my eyes, and memories of our encounters with the supernatural flash through my mind. "We don't have a choice, old friend. The darkness is spreading, and we're the only ones who can stop it."

The grandfather clock in the corner chimes nine, resonant tones echoing through the room as we reconvene. The flickering gas lamps cast shadows on the walls, creating an atmosphere of foreboding that matches our grim expressions.

"What have we uncovered?" I ask, my eyes darting between Evelyn and Lancaster.

Evelyn steps forward, her auburn hair glowing like embers in the dim light. "My contacts in the upper echelons have been... reluctant to speak openly. But there are whispers, Arthur. Whispers of a gathering at Lord Thorne's estate on the night of the new moon."

I nod, processing this information. "That gives us three days. Lancaster?"

The doctor's fiery hair seems to crackle with intensity as she speaks. "I've found references to an ancient ritual in the Codex Umbra. It speaks of harnessing the power of the void between worlds. If Thorne is planning what I think he is..."

Her words trail off, and I feel a chill run down my spine. "We can't let that happen," I say, my voice barely above a whisper.

"The challenge will be getting close enough to disrupt the ritual," Evelyn interjects, her brow furrowed in concentration.

I pace the room, my mind racing. "We'll need a distraction. Something to draw Thorne's attention while we infiltrate."

Lancaster's eyes light up. "What if we used his hubris against him? A false tip about a rival occultist could lure some of his forces away."

"Brilliant," I breathe, a spark of hope igniting in my chest. "Evelyn, can you plant such a rumor through your social connections?"

She nods, a determined glint in her eye. "Consider it done."

As we complete our strategy, I can't shake the feeling that we're missing something crucial. But there's no time for doubt now. We move to gather our equipment, the weight of our task pressing down on us like a physical force.

I checked my revolver, and the cold metal was comforting in my hand. "Remember," I caution, "firearms may be of limited use against supernatural threats. Don't rely on them only."

Evelyn produces a small velvet pouch, carefully withdrawing a collection of intricately carved stones. "These protective runes should offer some defense against dark magic," she explains, distributing them among us.

Lancaster adds her contribution, a set of vials filled with various liquids. "Holy water, silver nitrate, and a concoction of my design," she says, her voice tense. "Use them wisely."

As we arm ourselves, I can't help but wonder if it will be enough.

The fate of London—perhaps the world—rests on our shoulders.

As I look at my companions, I see my determination and fear reflected in their eyes.

The air in the room grows thick with anticipation. Each of us is lost in our own thoughts as we make our final preparations. I run my fingers over the protective rune Evelyn gave me, feeling its rough edges and willing it to grant us the strength we'll need.

"Before we go," I say, breaking the tense silence, "I want you both to know how grateful I am. This isn't your fight, and yet—"

"Don't you dare finish that sentence, Blackwood," Lancaster interrupts, her eyes flashing. "This is every bit our fight as it is yours. The Order threatens us all."

Evelyn nods in agreement. "We're in this together until the end."

Their words warm me, chasing away some dread gnawing at my insides. "Then let's agree," I suggest, extending my hand.

"Whatever happens tonight, we face it as one."

They join their hands with mine, and for a moment, I feel an almost palpable connection between us. It's as if our shared purpose has forged an unbreakable bond.

"For London," Evelyn whispers.

"For truth," Lancaster adds.

"For justice," I finish.

We break apart, and I take a deep breath, steeling myself for what's to come. "Right then," I say, my voice steadier than I feel. "Let's go remind Quentin Thorne why it's unwise to meddle with forces beyond his control."

As we move towards the door, I catch sight of our reflection in a nearby mirror. Three figures, shadows in the dim light, united against the darkness threatening to engulf our city. I meet my gaze, seeing the fire of determination burning behind the fear in my eyes.

With a last nod to my companions, I reach for the door handle. The cool metal sends a shiver through me, a last reminder of the comfort and safety we're leaving behind. But as I turn the knob and step out into the fog-shrouded night, I know there's no turning back.

The streets of London await us, cloaked in mist and mystery.

Somewhere out there, Thorne and his Order are moving forward with their nefarious plans. But we're coming for them, armed with knowledge, determination, and a shared resolve that will be enough to see us through.

Chapter 15 Showcasing Skills

The flickering gaslight casts long shadows across my study, a testament to our team's skills and dedication. Scattered before me lie the fragments of our investigation—cryptic notes, arcane symbols, and haunting sketches that seem to writhe in the wavering light.

I trace my finger along a faded parchment, connecting disparate pieces of evidence as my mind races. "What are you planning, Thorne?" I mutter, the words barely audible even in the oppressive silence.

A soft knock at the door shatters the silence, a stark reminder of the urgency of our mission. "Enter," I call out, my voice betraying the tension in the room.

The door creaks open, admitting Lady Evelyn and Dr. Lancaster.

Their footsteps echo on the worn floorboards as they approach.

"Any progress, Detective Blackwood?" Lady Evelyn inquires, her melodic voice tinged with concern.

I gesture to the chaotic array before me. "Pieces of the puzzle, my lady, but the full picture eludes me still."

Dr. Lancaster leans in, her keen eyes scanning the documents.

"These symbols," she says, pointing to intricate glyphs, "I've seen similar markings in ancient medical texts. They speak of life force and spiritual energy."

I nod, a chill running down my spine. "Precisely. Thorne seems intent on harnessing such energies for his ritual. But to what end?"

Lady Evelyn's brow furrows as she examines a map of London I've annotated. "The locations of the previous incidents form a pattern," she observes. "Almost like... a summoning circle?"

My heart quickens at her insight. "Astute as ever, Lady Evelyn. If Thorne completes this circle..."

"The consequences could be catastrophic," Dr. Lancaster interjects, her voice grave. "We're dealing with forces beyond our comprehension."

I rise, pacing the room as my mind churns. The floorboards creak beneath my feet, a discordant melody accompanying my troubled thoughts. "We must expect his next move," I say, more to myself than my companions. "Intercept him before he can complete whatever infernal ritual he's concocted."

Lady Evelyn's eyes meet mine, determination shining in their depths. "How can we prepare for such an encounter? We're dealing with the supernatural, after all."

Dr. Lancaster reaches into her medical bag and produces a small vial of clear liquid. "I've been working on a formula," she explains.

Based on my research into psychic phenomena and spiritual energy, it might offer some protection against otherworldly influences.

I nod appreciatively. "Excellent work, doctor. Every advantage will be crucial."

As we discuss strategies and theories, I can't shake the feeling that time is slipping away. The air in the study grows heavy as if the atmosphere senses the impending confrontation. Outside, a thick fog rolls through the streets of London, muffling the sounds of the city and adding to the sense of isolation.

I turn back to the evidence, my resolve hardening. "We're close," I mutter, more to myself than my companions. "So close to unraveling this mystery. But will we be in time to stop Thorne's machinations?"

The question hangs in the air, unanswered, as we prepare for the battle.

My fingers trace the intricate engravings on the artifact's surface, a chill running down my spine as the pieces suddenly fall into place.

"God," I breathe, my heart racing. "It's here, hidden in plain sight."

Lady Evelyn leans in, her brow furrowed. "What is it, Arthur?"

"A message," I explain, my voice trembling with excitement and dread. "Cleverly concealed within these symbols. Thorne plans to perform the ritual beneath St. Bartholomew's—the abandoned church in Smithfield."

Dr. Lancaster's eyes widen. "But that's barely an hour from now! We must hurry!"

The urgency of the situation hits us like a physical force. We spring into action as we gather our equipment, a whirlwind of movement.

I snatch my revolver from the desk drawer, checking its chambers with practiced ease.

"Lady Evelyn, your occult texts—bring anything that might help us counter the ritual," I instruct, my mind racing through possibilities.

"Dr. Lancaster, your formula could be our ace in the hole."

As I don my coat, I glimpse myself in the mirror. The man staring back at me looks haunted and determined—a far cry from the detached investigator I once prided myself on being. This case has changed me, I realize. There's no going back now.

"Are we truly prepared for what we might face?" Lady Evelyn asks, her voice barely above a whisper.

I meet her gaze, the gravity of our situation weighing heavily on me. "Prepared or not, the fate of London rests in our hands. We cannot afford to falter now."

With a nod of agreement, we hurry out into the fog-shrouded night, the weight of our mission heavy upon our shoulders. The game is afoot, and the stakes have never been higher.

The gas lamps flicker, casting long shadows as we hurry through London's labyrinthine streets. My senses are heightened, and every nerve is on edge. The fog curls around our ankles as if trying to impede our progress.

"Wait," I hissed, holding a hand to halt our group. My eyes narrow, scanning the darkness behind us. "We're being followed."

Lady Evelyn's breath catches. "Are you certain, Arthur?"

I nod grimly. "There, in the alley. A figure, keeping pace with us."

Dr. Lancaster grips her medical bag tighter. "Thorne's men?"

"Possibly," I mutter, my mind racing. "We can't risk leading them straight to the ritual site. We need to lose them."

I guide us down a narrow side street, the cobblestones slick beneath our feet—the sense of being watched prickles at the back of my neck, raising gooseflesh.

"This way," I whisper, ducking into a hidden alcove. We press ourselves against the damp stone, barely daring to breathe.

Footsteps approach, then fade into the distance.

"That was too close," Lady Evelyn murmurs.

I nod, my jaw tight. "We're running out of time. The church isn't far now."

We emerge from our hiding spot, quickening our pace. The abandoned church looms before us, a crumbling testament to forgotten faith. I run my hands along the weathered stones, searching for the hidden mechanism I know must be there.

"Ah," I breathe as my fingers catch on a slight indentation. With a grinding of ancient gears, a section of wall slides away, revealing a dark passage.

"Remarkable," Dr. Lancaster whispers.

I produce a small lantern from my coat. "Stay close. These tunnels are a maze designed to confuse the uninitiated."

As we descend, the air grows thick and musty. The flickering lantern light barely penetrates the oppressive darkness. Our footsteps echo unnaturally as if the very stones are alive and listening.

"It feels as though we're leaving the world we know behind," Lady Evelyn observes, hushed.

I nod, a chill running down my spine. "In a way, we are. The boundary between our realm and something else grows thin here.

Be on your guard."

We press deeper into the earth, the weight of centuries bearing down upon us. Each step takes us further from the familiar streets of London and closer to a confrontation that, I fear, may change us all irrevocably.

The tunnel opens into a vast chamber, and I halt abruptly, my breath catching in my throat. A faint, pulsating glow emanates from the far side of the cavernous space, casting long shadows that dance across the ancient stone walls.

"God," I whisper, my eyes fixed on the source of the light. "We've found it."

Lady Evelyn steps forward, her face illuminated by the eerie glow.

"The artifact," she breathes, her voice a mixture of awe and trepidation.

I motion for caution as we approach. A perfect circle of candles surrounds a pedestal, upon which an object shrouded in shadow rests. The flames flicker in unison, as if moved by an unseen breath.

"Curious," I mutter, crouching to examine the candles. "These aren't ordinary tallow. The wax is black as pitch."

Lady Evelyn kneels beside me, her eyes narrowing as she studies the setup. "This arrangement," she says, her voice low and intense.

"It's reminiscent of the Ritual of Binding described in the Codex Umbra. But there are differences."

I glance at her, noting the furrowed brow that belies her calm demeanor. "What sort of differences?"

She traces a finger through the air, outlining invisible patterns.

"The positioning of the candles, the number... it's as if someone has taken the original ritual and twisted it. Amplified it, perhaps."

A chill runs down my spine as I consider the implications. "And the artifact itself?" I ask, gesturing toward the shadowed object at the center.

Lady Evelyn rises slowly, her eyes never leaving the pedestal. "I can't be certain of a closer look, but if I'm right..." She trails off, swallowing hard.

"Evelyn?" I prompt, unnerved by her hesitation.

She turns to me, her face pale in the flickering light. "Arthur, if this is what I think it is, we're dealing with power beyond mortal comprehension. The force that could tear the very fabric of reality."

I feel the weight of her words settles over me like a shroud. "Then we have no choice," I say, straightening my shoulders. "We must stop Thorne, whatever the cost."

As we stand there, the air thick with anticipation and dread, I can't shake the feeling that we're teetering on the edge of an abyss.

Whatever happens next, I know with grim certainty that our world will never be the same.

Dr. Lancaster steps forward, her fiery hair catching the candlelight as she leans over the artifact. Her delicate fingers hover just above its surface, tracing the intricate symbols without touching them. I watch her brow furrow, her usually warm eyes sharp with concentration.

"These markings," she murmurs, more to herself than to us. "I've seen nothing quite like them."

I move closer, drawn by the tension in her voice. "What do you make of them, Amelia?"

She looks up at me, her face a mask of concern. "They're a fusion of ancient alchemical symbols and something... else. Something older." She swallows hard. "If I'm interpreting this correctly, the ritual Thorne intends to perform isn't just about power or immortality. It's about breaking down the barriers between our world and something beyond."

The weight of her words settles in my chest like lead. "What sort of consequences are we talking about?"

Dr. Lancaster straightens, her voice steady but laced with urgency.

"If Thorne succeeds, it won't just be London at risk. The very fabric of our reality could unravel. We're talking about chaos on a scale beyond imagination—the dead walking, nightmares made flesh, the laws of nature twisting in on themselves."

I feel a chill run down my spine but force my voice to remain calm.

"Then we have no choice but to stop him, no matter the cost."

Turning to face my companions, I feel the mantle of leadership settle upon my shoulders. "We need a plan, and we need one now,"

I gesture to Lady Evelyn. Evelyn, your knowledge of rituals will be crucial. I need you to focus on disrupting the ceremony itself—identify the key elements and how we might interfere."

She nods, determination flashing in her eyes. "Consider it done, Arthur."

"Amelia," I continue, meeting Dr. Lancaster's gaze, "your medical expertise might be our saving grace if things turn violent. But more importantly, I need you to monitor that artifact closely. If Thorne activates it, you may be our best hope of reversing the effects."

"Understood," she responds, her voice steady despite the gravity of the situation.

I take a deep breath, squaring my shoulders. "I'll confront Thorne directly. He's clever, but he's also arrogant. If I can keep him talking and distracted, it may buy us the time we need."

As I lay out our strategy, I feel a surge of confidence. We may be facing forces beyond our comprehension, but we lack resources.

Together, we stand a chance of averting catastrophe.

"Remember," I add, my voice low and intense, "we're not just fighting for ourselves or London. The world's fate may well rest on what happens in this chamber tonight. Whatever comes, whatever horrors we face, we must not falter."

I meet each of their eyes, seeing my determination reflect on me.

"Are we ready?"

The air in the chamber feels electric, charged with anticipation and the weight of what's to come. As my companions nod their assent, I can't help but wonder if we truly understand the magnitude of what we're about to face. But there's no time for doubt now. The die is cast, and the last confrontation awaits.

I take my position behind a crumbling pillar, the cold stone pressing against my back as I strain my ears for any sign of Thorne's approach. Lady Evelyn crouches near the artifact, her nimble fingers hovering over the intricate symbols, ready to counteract the ritual at a moment's notice. Dr. Lancaster stands at the ready, her medical bag close at hand, a grim determination etched across her face.

The silence is oppressive, broken only by our shallow breathing and the occasional water drip from the chamber's vaulted ceiling.

My heart pounds in my chest, each beat a reminder of the precious seconds ticking away.

"Blackwood," Lady Evelyn whispers, her voice barely audible, "What if we're too late?"

I swallow hard, pushing down the fear that threatens to rise. "We're not. We can't be."

Suddenly, a faint tremor runs through the ground beneath our feet.

At first, it's barely perceptible, but it quickly intensifies. The walls begin to shake, and dust and small debris rain down from above.

"What's happening?" Dr. Lancaster cries out, struggling to maintain her footing.

I grip the pillar for support, my mind racing. "It's starting. Thorne must have already—"

My words are cut off as a deafening crack splits the air. A fissure opens in the chamber floor, pulsing with an otherworldly light. The tremors increase, and I can feel the very fabric of reality seeming to warp around us.

"Evelyn!" I shout over the din. "The artifact! Can you—"

But before I can finish, a wave of energy explodes from the fissure, knocking us all off our feet. As I struggle to rise, my vision blurring, I glimpse shadowy forms beginning to materialize at the edges of the chamber.

"God help us," I mutter, the taste of fear bitter in my mouth. "What have we unleashed?"

The shadows coalesce into writhing, humanoid figures, their forms flickering like candlelight. I force myself to my feet, my heart pounding in my ears.

"Stay together!" I shout, drawing my revolver. The weapon's weight is comforting, even if I doubt its efficacy against these otherworldly beings.

Lady Evelyn stands beside me, her face pale but determined. She clutches an ancient amulet, its surface glowing faintly. "The barrier, Blackwood! We must establish the barrier!"

I nod, remembering our plan. "Lancaster, the incantation!"

Dr. Lancaster's voice rises above the chaos, her words in a language long forgotten. The shadows recoil as if stung, but press forward again with renewed vigor.

I fire my revolver, the muzzle flash illuminating the chamber. The bullets pass through the entities harmlessly, but the sound momentarily disorients them.

"It's working!" I call out, reloading with practiced efficiency.

"Keep it up!"

Evelyn's amulet pulses with energy, creating a shimmering field around us. The shadows claw at it, their touch causing ripples in the protective barrier.

"I can't hold it much longer," Evelyn gasps, strain evident in her voice.

My mind races, searching for a solution. Then, through the chaos, I spot a familiar figure emerging from the shadows.

"Thorne," I snarl, my grip tightening on the revolver.

He approaches with measured steps, a cruel smile on his thin lips.

"Detective Blackwood," he purrs, his voice cutting through the din. "How kind of you to join us for this momentous occasion."

I step forward, positioning myself between Thorne and my companions. "This ends now, Thorne. Whatever you've started, we'll stop it."

He laughs, the sound chilling my blood. "Oh, my dear detective.

You can no more stop this than you can halt the tide. The wheels are already in motion."

"You do not know what forces you're dealing with," I retort, struggling to keep my voice steady. "The cost—"

"Cost?" Thorne interrupts, his eyes flashing. "I am intimately aware of the cost, Blackwood. The question is, are you prepared to pay it?"

I feel a cold dread settle in my stomach. What does he know? What has he seen?

"You speak of things you don't understand," I say, buying time as I search for a weakness, any vulnerability in his demeanor.

Thorne's smile widens. Detective. It is you who are fumbling in the dark. Tell me, have you deciphered the true nature of the artifact?

Do you comprehend the power it holds?"

I hesitate, and at that moment, I see a flicker of triumph in Thorne's eyes. He knows I'm grasping at straws, and we both know it.

"It doesn't matter," I say, steeling myself. "Whatever your plan, whatever dark forces you've allied yourself with, we will stop you."

Thorne's laughter echoes through the chamber, sending chills down my spine. "Oh, Blackwood. Your determination is admirable, if misguided. You're not here to stop anything. You're here to bear witness."

As he speaks, the surrounding shadows grow more frenzied, their forms becoming more solid with each passing second. I can feel the weight of the moment pressing down on me, the realization that we may be out of our depth settling like lead in my gut.

But I push the doubt aside. We've come too far to falter now.

"You're mistaken, Thorne," I say, my voice steady despite the fear coursing through me. "We're here to end this madness, whatever the cost."

Thorne's eyes flash with evil glee. "The cost, detective? I'm afraid it's far higher than you can imagine."

With a swift motion, he raises his hands, and the artifact at the center of the chamber begins to pulse with an otherworldly light.

The air grows thick and oppressive as if reality itself is bending to Thorne's will.

I turn to Lady Evelyn and Dr. Lancaster, their faces etched with horror and determination. "Now!" I shout, hoping our hastily concocted plan will be enough.

But her words falter as Lady Evelyn recites the counter-incantation we'd prepared. The shadows coalesce, wrapping around her throat like tendrils of smoke. Dr. Lancaster rushes to her aid but is thrown back by an unseen force.

"Did you think your feeble attempts at thwarting me would succeed?" Thorne's voice booms, filled with dark triumph. "You've played your part perfectly, Blackwood. Your presence here, your futile struggle—it's all part of the ritual."

My mind races, desperately seeking a way out of this trap. But with each passing second, I feel my strength ebbing as if the very life is being drained from my body.

"What have you done?" I croak, my vision blurring.

Thorne approaches, his figure seeming to grow larger, more imposing. "I've opened the door, detective. And you, my unwitting pawn, have provided the key."

As darkness encroaches on the edges of my consciousness, I see the artifact begin to crack, a blinding light spilling forth. The last thing I hear before succumbing to the overwhelming force is Thorne's chilling whisper:

"Welcome to a new age of darkness, Blackwood. Your world ends here."

Chapter 16 Battle or Showdown

The heavy oak doors explode inward, shards of splintered wood cascading through the stale air as I burst into the grand hall, my trusted allies, the fierce warrior Elara and the cunning mage Alastair, at my heels. The scent of decay and something far more sinister assaults my nostrils. My eyes dart around the cavernous space, taking in the crumbling stone walls adorned with tattered tapestries and the flickering shadows cast by guttering candelabras.

At the far end of the hall stands Quentin Thorne, his gaunt figure silhouetted against a massive stained-glass window. The Order of the Eternal Flame, a secretive cult known for its mastery of dark magic and fanatical devotion to Thorne, flanks him, its dark robes billowing in an unfelt breeze. My heart pounds in my chest, a primal fear threatening to overwhelm my carefully honed instincts.

"Ah, Detective Blackwood," Thorne's silky voice slithers across the room. "How kind of you to join us for this momentous occasion."

I clench my fists, willing my voice to remain steady. "Whatever you're planning, Thorne, it ends here."

A chuckle escapes his thin lips, sending a chill down my spine.

"Oh, my dear Arthur, it's only just beginning."

Thorne gestures to an intricate symbol etched into the floor with a graceful wave of his hand, a swirling vortex of arcane runes that seems to pulse with otherworldly energy. My mind races, recalling fragments of ancient texts and whispered legends. What infernal power has he tapped into?

"You see," Thorne continues, his eyes gleaming with a maniacal light, "tonight, we stand on the precipice of a new world order. One where the very fabric of reality bends to our will."

I take a step forward, my fingers itching to reach for the revolver concealed beneath my coat. "You're mad, Thorne. You can't possibly control such forces."

His laughter echoes off the stone walls, a sound of pure spite.

"Control? No, my simple-minded friend. We will become one with these forces, reshaping existence itself!"

As Thorne speaks, the air grows heavy, charged with an electric tension that makes the hairs on the back of my neck stand on end. I can feel the raw power building, threatening to tear through the very fabric of our world. Time seems to slow as I weigh my options, knowing that my next move could determine the fate of all we hold dear.

"You've gone too far this time," I growl, my voice barely above a whisper. "I won't let you unleash this chaos on the world."

Thorne's sinister smile widens, revealing teeth that seem unnaturally sharp in the flickering candlelight. "Oh, but you're too late, Detective. The wheels are already in motion. Soon, you'll witness the dawn of a new age where the Order of the Eternal Flame reigns supreme."

As his words hang in the air, I steel myself for the battle to come, feeling the weight of reality's fate hanging in the balance. Whatever dark forces Thorne has summoned, I vow to stop him, even if it costs me everything. The urgency of the situation is palpable, driving me forward.

I turn to my allies, my voice cutting through the tension like a knife. "Spread out! Engage the Order members. I'll handle Thorne."

My words are clipped and urgent, each syllable carrying the weight of our mission.

As my companions fan out across the grand hall, I gaze at Thorne.

His eyes, black as pitch, gleam with vicious anticipation. I step forward, my fingers curling into fists at my sides.

"It's just you and me now, Thorne," I say, my voice low and steady despite the hammering of my heart. My unwavering resolve is a stark contrast to Thorne's malevolent anticipation. "Let's end this madness."

Thorne's laughter fills the air, sending chills down my spine. "Oh, Arthur," he purrs, "you do not know what you're up against."

Before I could react, Thorne raised his arms, his fingers splayed wide. The surrounding air began to shimmer and distort, as if reality itself were bending to his will. A low hum filled my ears, growing louder with each passing second.

"What in God's name—" I start, but my words are cut short as a swirling vortex of dark energy erupts from Thorne's outstretched hands. It expands rapidly, forming a barrier between us, crackling with eldritch power.

I stumble back, shielding my eyes from the intense light. The vortex pulses with an otherworldly rhythm, its edges sharp and jagged like broken glass. Through the swirling chaos, I can see Thorne's triumphant grin.

"Do you see now, Detective?" he calls out, his voice distorted by the magical barrier. "This is but a taste of the power I will wield. The power to reshape the very fabric of existence!"

I grit my teeth, my mind racing to find a solution. How can I penetrate this barrier? What weakness can I exploit? As I search for answers, the sounds of battle echo around me—my allies locked in combat with the Order. Time is running out, and I know I must reach Thorne before it's too late.

Suddenly, Alastair Grey's cryptic words from our last encounter echo in my mind: "When darkness rises, seek the light that lies hidden in shadow." The realization hits me like a bolt of lightning. An artifact must be concealed within this decrepit mansion—powerful enough to break Thorne's barrier.

I spin on my heel, scanning the cavernous hall. "Where would they hide such a thing?" I mutter, my eyes darting from shadowy corners to ornate fixtures. The sense of mystery and discovery is palpable as I search for the hidden artifact.

A blast of sickly green energy whizzes past my ear, singeing a few strands of hair. I duck instinctively, my heart pounding in my chest.

"Blackwood!" a member of the Order snarls, conjuring another spell. "You won't leave this place alive!"

I roll behind a crumbling pillar, my mind racing. "I don't intend to," I retort, "but neither will your master's plans come to fruition."

As I dash from my cover, weaving through the chaos of spell fire and clashing steel, I can't help but ponder. What form could this artifact take? A book? A relic? My eyes flit from object to object, searching for anything out of place.

"To your left, Arthur!" one of my allies shouts. I sidestep just in time to avoid a bolt of crackling energy.

"Much obliged," I call back, never breaking stride. The grand staircase looms before me, promising unexplored territory above.

My thoughts turn inward as I take the steps two at a time.

Grey's riddles always have multiple layers. 'Light in shadow'—could it be something that appears ordinary but holds successful power? Or perhaps...

My musings are cut short as a hooded figure materializes at the top of the stairs, hands glowing with eldritch energy. I skid to a halt, my hand instinctively reaching for my revolver.

"Going somewhere, Detective?" the figure hisses, voice dripping with malice.

I force a wry smile. "Just admiring the architecture. I don't suppose you'd care to give me a tour?"

The figure's response is a searing blast of energy. I dive to the side, feeling the heat singe my coat as I roll across the worn carpet. My eyes dart around the landing, searching for an escape route.

There—a partially open door. I sprint towards it, shouldering it open and slamming it shut behind me. The heavy oak trembles as another spell affects it.

"Blast," I mutter, surveying the room. It's a study, walls lined with bookshelves. My heart quickens. Could it be here?

I run my fingers along the spines, searching for anything out of place. "Come on, Grey," I whisper. "What am I missing?"

A tome catches my eye—it's binding newer than the rest. I pull it, and a satisfying click echoes through the room. The bookshelf beside me swings open, revealing a hidden chamber.

An amulet rests on a pedestal. Its silver surface seems to ripple like water, catching the dim light. As I approach, I feel a thrumming energy, as if the air is charged with potential.

My hand closes around the amulet, and suddenly, power surges through me. It's exhilarating and terrifying all at once, like grasping lightning itself.

"Found you," I breathe.

The door splinters behind me. There is no time to marvel. I pocket the amulet and dash back into the fray, my mind already planning my route back to the grand hall.

As I descend the stairs, dodging and weaving through the ongoing battle, I can't help but wonder: will this indeed be enough to break Thorne's barrier? The amulet's weight seems to pulse against my chest as if answering my unspoken question.

I burst into the grand hall, my eyes immediately locking onto Thorne's sneering face beyond his shimmering barrier. The amulet grows warm in my hand as I approach.

"It's over, Thorne," I call out, my voice steady despite the chaos. "Your plans end here."

Thorne's laughter echoes unnaturally. "You think trinket will save you, Blackwood? You do not know the power you're meddling with."

I stand firm, feeling the amulet's energy coursing through me.

"Perhaps not," I admit, "but I'm about to find out."

The amulet pulses in my hand as I focus its energy, willing the barrier to weaken. Translucent ripple courses through Thorne's magical shield, and his smug expression falters momentarily.

"Now!" I bellow, my voice carrying over the din of battle.

As if choreographed, my allies spring into action. Constable Jenkins launches a well-aimed shot at an Order member's shoulder.

Dr. Eliza Blackwood, my quick-witted sister, hurls a vial of alchemical concoction that explodes in a burst of blinding light.

The air fills with shouts and the acrid smell of gunpowder and arcane energy.

"Impressive coordination, Detective," Thorne sneers, his barrier finally shattering like glass. "But party tricks won't save you from what's to come."

I advance, my mind racing to expect Thorne's next move. "I've faced worse than your parlor magic, Thorne."

He raises a skeletal hand, dark energy crackling between his fingers. "Have you now?"

I dodge the bolt of darkness he hurls, feeling its cold rush past my cheek. I instinctively reach for the revolver at my hip, but I pause.

No, this isn't a battle to be won with bullets.

"Your Order has always depended on deception," I taunt, cautiously circling him. "But strip away the pageantry, and what's left? Just men, playing at being gods."

Thorne's eyes narrow, his thin lips curling into a snarl. "You understand nothing, Blackwood. The power we wield—"

I cut him off, seizing the opening his anger provides. "Is nothing compared to the weight of your sins. How many lives have you destroyed in your quest for power, Thorne?"

As we trade blows, both physical and verbal, I can't help but marvel at the dance we're locked in. Each of Thorne's spells is met with a counter-move, and my years of study and observation allow me to expect and react. It's exhilarating and terrifying in equal measure.

"You're more than you seem, Detective," Thorne pants, a hint of respect creeping into his voice. "Perhaps you would have made a worthy addition to our Order."

I laugh, short and sharp. "I've seen what your Order does to its members, Thorne. I'll pass, thank you."

As we continue our deadly waltz, I can't help but wonder: how long can I keep this up? And what price will victory demand?

Thorne's eyes flash with a manic gleam, his composure finally cracking. "Enough of this charade!" he snarls, his voice echoing unnaturally through the cavernous hall.

I watch, heart pounding, as he raises his arms skyward. The air crackles with otherworldly energy, making the hairs on my neck stand on end. Darkness seeps from his fingertips, viscous and alive, spreading outward like an oil slick.

"Witness true power, Blackwood!" Thorne cries, his face contorted in a rictus of triumph and desperation.

The encroaching darkness swallows the flickering gaslight, plunging the mansion into an unnatural twilight. My allies cry out in alarm, their voices muffled as if coming from underwater.

"This is madness, Thorne!" I shout, fighting against the oppressive weight of the shadows. "You'll destroy us all!"

He laughs, a chilling sound devoid of mirth. "If I can't have this world, Detective, no one shall!"

My fingers close around the amulet, its warmth a stark contrast to the creeping cold of Thorne's spell. I draw upon its power, feeling it pulse in time with my racing heartbeat.

"Light always finds a way," I murmur, more to bolster my courage than anything else. With a deep breath, I channel every ounce of my will through the artifact.

A brilliant surge of radiance erupts from the amulet, colliding with Thorne's darkness in a cacophony and fury. The conflicting energies spiral outward, creating a maelstrom that threatens to tear the very fabric of reality asunder.

In that moment of chaos, a single thought flashes: "What have we wrought?"

The collision reaches its zenith, and the world explodes in a blinding flash...

As the blinding light recedes, I blink rapidly, trying to clear the dancing spots from my vision. The grand hall materializes around me, its once-opulent furnishings now in tatters. My ears ring, but I hear muffled groans and the crackle of smoldering embers through the din.

I force myself to focus, scanning the debris-strewn room. There, amidst a pile of splintered wood and torn velvet, lies Thorne. His once-immaculate suit is in ruins and a thin trickle of blood runs from his nose. His eyes, usually cold and calculating, now dart wildly, unfocused.

"It's over, Thorne," I say, my voice hoarse from the acrid smoke hanging in the air. I take a step towards him, wincing as my battered body protests the movement.

Thorne tries to rise but collapses back with a pained gasp. "You... you don't understand what you've done, Blackwood," he snarls, desperation replacing his usual smooth charm.

I kneel beside him, adrenaline still coursing through my veins. "I understand perfectly. Your reign of terror ends here."

With a last surge of strength, I deliver a swift, precise blow to Thorne's temple. His eyes roll back, and he slumps unconscious.

Around us, the remaining members of the Order are in disarray. Some flee, stumbling over fallen comrades and debris. Others throw down their arcane implements, hands raised in surrender.

"Detective Blackwood!" calls out one of my allies, limping towards me. "We've secured the perimeter. It's done."

I nod, a wave of exhaustion threatening to overwhelm me. "Indeed, it is," I murmur, more to myself than anyone else. "But at what cost?"

I rise slowly, my muscles screaming in protest, and survey the wreckage of the once-grand hall. The opulent chandelier lies shattered on the floor, its crystals glinting like fallen stars amidst the debris. Wisps of acrid smoke curl around the tattered remains of priceless tapestries, their histories now lost to the ravages of our supernatural battle.

"Round up the survivors," I instruct my allies, my voice barely above a whisper. "And... tend to the fallen."

As they move to carry out my orders, I find myself drawn to a cracked mirror hanging precariously on the wall. The face staring back at me is barely recognizable—streaked with soot, a gash above my brow oozing blood. My piercing blue eyes, usually so sharp and observant, now reflect a haunted weariness.

"Was it worth it, Arthur?" I ask my reflection, the weight of our pyrrhic victory settling heavily on my shoulders.

A hand touches my arm, and I turn to find Inspector Holloway, her own face a map of cuts and bruises. "We couldn't have done this without you, Blackwood," she says softly.

I manage a grim smile. "Perhaps. But look around us, Catherine. How many men and women lie dead or dying because of our actions?"

Holloway's eyes harden. "And how many more would have suffered if we hadn't stopped Thorne? You know the stakes we were facing."

I nod, my gaze drifting to where Thorne lies unconscious, already bound by my allies. "Indeed. The fate of reality itself." I pause, a chill running down my spine as I recall the swirling vortex of dark energy Thorne had summoned. "And yet, I can't help but wonder if we've truly seen the last of whatever force he was attempting to unleash."

Chapter 17 Climax

The flickering candlelight casts long shadows across the chamber, their dance macabre on stone walls etched with arcane symbols. I stand facing Quentin Thorne, my breath visible in the chill air. The room thrums with an unseen power, making the hairs on my neck stand on end.

Thorne's lips curl into a cruel smile. "Ah, Detective Blackwood. How fitting our paths should cross here, in the Order's heart's sanctum." His voice drips with contempt. "Did you truly believe your meager intellect could unravel our grand design?"

I keep my expression neutral, though my mind races. What is his game? I must not let him goad me into rashness. "Your 'grand design' ends here, Thorne. I've seen enough of your handiwork to know it must be stopped."

He chuckles, a sound devoid of mirth. "Oh, but you've seen nothing yet, my dear Detective. The power at my command..." Thorne raises his hands, and the air around him shimmers with dark energy. "I could reshape this pitiful world. And you? You're but an insect before a god."

My fingers twitch, longing for the familiar weight of my revolver.

But I know conventional weapons are useless here. I must rely on my wits and the knowledge I've gathered. "You're no god, Thorne. Just a man corrupted by forces he can't control."

Thorne's eyes narrow, a flash of anger marring his composure.

"Control? I am the master of these forces, Blackwood. Let me show you." He gestures towards an ornate mirror on the far wall.

Its surface ripples like water, and I see visions of London wreathed in eldritch fire, screaming masses fleeing unspeakable horrors.

I force myself to look away, my stomach churning. Is this the future he seeks? Or was it merely an illusion to break my resolve? I take a steadying breath, centering myself. "Your parlor tricks don't impress me, Thorne. I've seen the rot at the core of your Order. You speak of power, but I see only fear and desperation."

Thorne's mask of civility slips, revealing the madness beneath.

"Fear? You know nothing of genuine fear, Detective. But you will. Oh, you will." The air grows heavy, charged with evil intent. I brace myself, knowing the true battle is about to begin.

The chamber erupts into chaos as Thorne unleashes a torrent of supernatural energy. Bolts of crackling darkness shoot from his fingertips, and I dive to the side, feeling their heat as they sear past my cheek.

"Is this all you've got, Thorne?" I taunt, my mind racing to analyze his attack pattern. "I expected more from the so-called master of the dark arts."

He snarls, his face contorting into something inhuman. "You'll rue your insolence, Blackwood!"

I duck behind a pillar, my heart pounding. Think, Arthur. There's always a weakness, always a pattern. I peer out, overseeing Thorne's movements. His left side, I realize. He favors his right hand for casting, leaving his left flank exposed.

"Come out and face your doom, detective!" Thorne bellows, his voice echoing off the ancient stones.

"I think I'll pass," I reply, my tone deceptively casual. "The view's quite nice from here."

As I speak, I'm plotting my next move. The chamber's layout and the placement of the artifacts could be an advantage or a death trap.

Thorne's patience wears thin. With a guttural incantation, he summons writhing tendrils of shadow that slither across the floor towards me.

"Bloody hell," I mutter, leaping atop a nearby altar. The shadows coil around its base, seeking purchase.

I can't help but marvel at the impossibility of it all, even as I scramble to stay ahead of the encroaching darkness. "Fascinating," I breathe, "but how does it work? What's the source?"

"Your scientific mind can't comprehend the depths of this power," Thorne sneers, directing the shadows with grand gestures.

I vault from the altar to a hanging tapestry, using it to swing to a far corner. "Understanding is the key to overcoming," I reply, slightly breathless.

As I land, I notice a pattern in the floor tiles that mirrors the sigils on Thorne's robes. A connection, perhaps? A conduit for his power? I file the observation away, dodging another tendril of shadow.

"You can't evade me forever, Blackwood," Thorne growls, frustration evident in his voice.

I allow myself a grim smile. "I don't intend to, old chap. I'm just getting started."

My eyes dart around the chamber, searching for anything to turn the tide. A glint catches my attention - an ornate mirror positioned high on the wall. Perfect.

"Getting started, you say?" Thorne scoffs. "Your arrogance will be your downfall, Detective."

I lock eyes with him, mustering every ounce of focus I possess.

"Arrogance? No, Thorne. This is confidence born of observation."

With a swift motion, I grab a nearby ceremonial dagger and hurl it at the mirror. The glass shatters, sending a cascade of reflected light directly into Thorne's eyes. He recoils, momentarily blinded, his concentration broken.

"Damn you, Blackwood!" he snarls, clawing at his face.

I seize the moment, closing the distance between us in three long strides. "You forget, Thorne," I say, my voice low and controlled, "I've spent my life studying the patterns of human behavior. Even occultists have tells."

My fist connects with his solar plexus, driving the air from his lungs. As he doubles over, I deliver a precise strike to his temple, exploiting the weakness I'd noticed earlier when he flinched at a sudden noise.

Thorne staggers but recovers quicker than I expected. His eyes, now adjusted, blaze with fury. "Enough of these parlor tricks!"

Before I can react, he unleashes raw energy that slams into my chest. The force hurls me backward, and I crash into the stone wall with a bone-jarring impact. Pain explodes through my body, and for a moment, the world goes dark.

As consciousness returns, I find myself crumpled on the floor, every breath an agony. But beneath the pain, a fire burns - the same relentless determination that's driven me through countless cases, through personal tragedy, through the very boundaries of what I once thought possible.

"Is this how it ends, Arthur?" I ask myself, struggling to push up onto my elbows. "No," I growl through gritted teeth. "Not while there's still a mystery to solve, a wrong to right."

Thorne's footsteps echo as he approaches, his laughter cold and triumphant. "Your determination is admirable, Detective. But ultimately futile."

I raise my head, meeting his gaze with unwavering resolve. "We shall see about that, Thorne. We shall see."

As Thorne's shadow looms over me, I feel energy coursing through my veins. It's as if the surrounding air is charged with an otherworldly power. I close my eyes, focusing on the arcane knowledge I've gained through my relentless pursuit of the truth.

"Your persistence is becoming tiresome, Blackwood," Thorne sneers, raising his hand for another attack.

I concentrate, channeling the energy within me. "Perhaps you'll find this less tiresome," I mutter, my voice barely above a whisper.

Suddenly, a shimmering barrier materializes around me, its iridescent surface pulsing with an ethereal light. Thorne's next volley of dark energy crashes against it, dissipating harmlessly.

His eyes widen in disbelief. "Impossible! How did you—"

"You're not the only one who's learned a few tricks," I interject, a wry smile on my lips. The shield absorbs another barrage, allowing me to catch my breath and assess the situation.

Thorne's face contorts with rage. "You think this changes anything? You do not know the depths of my power!"

As he speaks, I notice the shadows in the chamber begin to writhe and twist unnaturally. A chill runs down my spine as I realize what's coming.

"Oh, I have some idea," I retort, steeling myself. "But I also know that power often blinds one to their weaknesses."

With a guttural incantation, Thorne raises his arms. The shadows coalesce into grotesque, spectral forms—twisted apparitions that hover menacingly around us.

I take a deep breath, pushing aside the fear threatening to paralyze me. "Well, Arthur," I think to myself, "this is certainly one for the memoirs... if I survive to write them."

As the first specter lunges toward me, I let my protective barrier drop and spring into action. My movements are fluid, honed by years of both mental and physical discipline. I dodge the creature's ethereal claws, countering with a precise strike imbued with the same energy I'd used for the shield.

The specter dissipates with an unearthly shriek, but two more take place. I weave between them, my mind racing to recall every scrap of supernatural lore I glean in my investigations.

"You can't keep this up forever, Detective," Thorne taunts from the edge of the fray.

I dispatch another creature with a well-timed blow. "Neither can you, Thorne. The question is, which of us will falter first?"

As I continue to fight, a grim determination settles over me. Each creature I vanquish brings me one step closer to Thorne, one step closer to unraveling this infernal mystery once and for all.

Just as I feel my strength beginning to wane, a familiar voice rings out across the chamber.

"Arthur! Duck!"

I drop instinctively, and a burst of blinding light sears over my head. The spectral creatures nearest to me dissolve with agonized wails. Lady Evelyn stands in the doorway, her auburn hair wild and eyes blazing with fierce determination. Beside her, Dr. Lancaster hefts an ancient-looking tome, its pages glowing faintly.

"Cavalry's arrived," I mutter, a grim smile tugging at my lips.

Evelyn rushes to my side, her movements graceful despite the chaos. "We couldn't let you have all the fun, could we?"

Dr. Lancaster's voice cuts through the din, reciting an incantation that causes several more specters to disintegrate. "Focus on Thorne, Detective! We'll handle these abominations!"

With my allies providing crucial support, I focus on Thorne. He snarls, his gaunt face contorted with rage. "You think your little friends can save you?"

"No," I reply, my voice steady as I gather my strength. "But they've given me the opening I need."

I launch towards Thorne, channeling every ounce of supernatural energy I can muster. My fist connects with his jaw, enhanced by a surge of power that sends him reeling. I press my advantage, my analytical mind working in concert with my newfound abilities.

Each strike is calculated, targeting Thorne's vulnerabilities with unerring precision. I can feel the raw energy coursing through me, amplifying my strength and speed.

Thorne stumbles, clearly surprised by the ferocity of my assault.

"How?" he gasps, blood trickling from the corner of his mouth. "You're just a detective!"

I grab him by the collar, my eyes bored into his. "I'm the Detective who will end your reign of terror, Thorne. Here and now."

With one final, devastating blow, I send Thorne crashing. He lies there, momentarily incapacitated, as the chamber falls silent save for our ragged breathing.

I stand over Thorne's prone form, my chest heaving as I catch my breath. The acrid scent of ozone hangs heavy in the air, a testament to the supernatural energies we've unleashed. Thorne's eyes, once burning with malevolent confidence, now flicker with something I've never seen in them before uncertainty.

"It's over, Thorne," I say, echoing in the ancient chamber. "Your schemes, rituals, the lives you've destroyed—it all ends here."

Thorne coughs, a trickle of blood staining his pale lips. "You don't understand, Blackwood. The power I wield... it's beyond your comprehension."

I kneel beside him, my gaze unwavering. "No, Thorne. It's you who doesn't understand. Power without justice is nothing but tyranny. And tyranny always falls."

As I speak, I see doubt creeping into Thorne's eyes. For a moment, just a fleeting instant, I glimpse the man he might have been—before the Order of the Eternal Flame twisted him.

"All those people, Thorne," I continue, my voice softening. "All those lives snuffed out for your rituals. Did you ever stop to think about them? Their families? The void you left in the world with each sacrifice?"

Thorne's lips quiver, and for a second, I think I've reached him. But then his eyes harden, a cruel smile spreading across his face.

"Sentiment, Detective?" he snarls. "How... disappointing."

Before I can react, Thorne's hand shoots out, gripping my wrist.

Dark energy crackles between us, and I feel my muscles seize.

"You forget," Thorne hisses, rising to his feet as I struggle against his supernatural hold. "I am the master of the dark arts. And I will not be defeated by the likes of you!"

A vortex of shadows erupts around us, tendrils of darkness lashing out like whips. I grit my teeth, fighting against the onslaught with every fiber of my being.

This is it, I realize—the last confrontation. Everything I've learned, everything I've become, has led to this moment. And I will not falter.

With a roar from the depths of my soul, I push back against Thorne's assault. Light erupts from within me, a beacon in the darkness, fueled by my unwavering resolve.

"No more, Thorne," I growl, feeling the tide turn. "No more victims. No more rituals. This ends now!"

Our energies clash, light against dark, in a tumultuous surge that threatens to tear the very fabric of reality asunder.

The chamber shudders violently, ancient stones groaning in protest as the supernatural energy dissipates. Dust and debris rain down from the vaulted ceiling, and I know we have mere moments before the entire structure collapses.

"We need to move now!" I shout, my voice hoarse from exertion.

I grab Evelyn's arm, steadying her as she stumbles over the uneven floor. Her eyes, wide with relief and lingering fear, lock onto mine.

"Arthur, is it truly over?"

"For now," I say grimly, scanning the crumbling room for our exit. "But we're not out of danger yet."

Dr. Lancaster's voice cuts through the din of falling stone. "This way! I've found a passage!"

We sprint towards her, ducking under a massive beam as it crashes behind us. The acrid scent of smoke and dust fills my lungs, making each breath a struggle.

"Mind the gap!" I warn as we leap over a widening fissure on the floor. The rumbling intensifies, and I can feel the very foundations of the chamber giving way.

We burst through a narrow archway, the cool night air a shocking contrast to the oppressive heat of the collapsing room. My legs burn with exertion as we race up a winding staircase, taking the steps two at a time.

"Almost there," I pant, urging my companions forward. "Don't look back!"

With a final, desperate surge, we emerge onto the cobblestone street as an ear-splitting crack echoes behind us. The ground beneath our feet trembles, and I instinctively pull Evelyn and Lancaster close as we watch the entrance to the chamber disappear in a cloud of dust and debris.

We stand in stunned silence for a moment, our ragged breathing the only sound in the fog-shrouded night. Then, as the reality of our narrow escape sinks in, I feel a weight lift from my shoulders.

"We did it," Lancaster whispers, her voice filled with wonder. "We did it."

I nod, a mix of exhaustion and joy washing over me. "Indeed, we did, Doctor. Though I daresay the cost was nearly too high."

Evelyn's hand finds mine, her touch grounding me at the moment.

"But think of the lives we've saved, Arthur. The balance we've preserved."

I squeeze her hand gently, marveling at her strength. "You're right, of course. It's just... the weight of it all. The responsibility."

"A burden we share," Lancaster says firmly, her eyes studying my face. "You're not alone in this, Blackwood. Remember that."

I manage a tired smile, looking between my two stalwart companions. "I couldn't ask for finer allies. Or friends."

As we stand there, battered but unbroken, I can't help but feel a sense of pride. We've faced the darkness and emerged victorious.

Yet, as I gaze out over the fog-shrouded streets of London, I know our work is far from over.

"The question remains," I muse, my eyes scanning the misty horizon, "what consequences will our actions bring?"

Evelyn's brow furrows, her auburn hair glowing in the gaslight.

"Surely we've done what's right, Arthur. The ritual was stopped."

"Yes," I nod, "but nature abhors a vacuum. We've disrupted a powerful dark force. Something will inevitably rush to fill that void."

Lancaster's voice is steady, but I detect a tremor of concern. "You think there are other... entities... waiting to seize this opportunity?"

I turn to face them both, my coat billowing in the chill night air.

"I'm certain of it. Our victory tonight is monumental but merely the opening salvo in a larger war."

"Then we must be prepared," Evelyn says, her chin lifting doggedly.

I can't help but feel a swell of admiration for her courage. "Indeed, we must. Our actions have likely drawn attention—both welcome and unwelcome."

Lancaster's eyes narrow in thought. "We'll need to be vigilant. Perhaps expand our network of informants?"

"Precisely," I agree. "And we need to explore further into the mysterious knowledge that we have only just started to uncover."

As we stand there, planning our next moves, I'm struck by a realization. The fog swirling around us seems to mirror the uncertainty of our future, yet I've never felt more certain of my path.

"Whatever comes," I say softly, "we face it together."

Chapter 18 Plot Twist

The gas lamps flicker, casting long shadows across the study's mahogany paneling. I stand before the fireplace, my fingers drumming an anxious rhythm on the mantle as I survey my team.

Lady Evelyn perches on the edge of a wingback chair, her gloved hands clasped tightly in her lap. Dr. Lancaster paces by the window, pausing occasionally to peer into the fog-shrouded street below.

"Any sign of him?" I ask, my voice low.

Amelia shakes her head. "Not yet, Detective Blackwood. But he'll come. He always does."

A chill runs down my spine, unbidden. Alastair Grey. The man who seems to hover at the edges of our investigation like a specter, always present yet just beyond our grasp. What game is he playing?

The grandfather clock in the corner chimes the hour, startling us all. Lady Evelyn lets out a small gasp, then composes herself with a rueful smile. "My apologies. I'm afraid my nerves are rather frayed this evening."

I cross the room to her side, resting a hand on her shoulder. "No need for apologies, my lady. We're all on edge."

The door creaks open as if summoned by our unease. My hand instinctively moves to the revolver at my hip as a figure steps into the room. The flickering lamplight catches his silver hair, creating an otherworldly halo around his sharp features.

Alastair Grey.

His penetrating gaze sweeps the room, settling on each of us. I feel its weight is like a physical thing, probing and assessing. When those eyes meet mine, I'm struck by a disturbing mix of fascination and dread.

"Evening," Grey says, his cultured voice filling the room. "I trust I haven't kept you waiting long?"

I struggle to find my voice, caught between the urge to demand answers and a strange, exciting desire to hear what this enigmatic man has to say. The air in the room seems to thicken, charged with anticipation and an undercurrent of something else—something I can't quite name, but that sets every instinct on high alert.

What secrets does Alastair Grey hold? And more importantly, what price will we pay to uncover them?

I clear my throat, forcing my voice to remain steady. "Mr. Grey, your timing is impeccable. We were just discussing the latest developments in our investigation."

Grey's lips curl into a smile that doesn't quite reach his eyes. "Ah, yes. The curious case of the vanishing artifacts. I've been following your progress with successful interest, Detective Blackwood."

A chill runs down my spine. How many does he know? I choose the following words carefully. "Have you now? I wasn't aware our investigation had become public knowledge."

Grey chuckles, the sound low and unsettling. "My dear Detective, brief escapes my notice in this city. Especially when it concerns matters of... shall we say, a more arcane nature?"

I feel Lady Evelyn stiffen beside me, her breath catching. Dr. Lancaster shifts uneasily, the floorboards creaking beneath her feet.

"And what exactly do you mean by that, Mr. Grey?" I press, my heart racing.

He leans in, voice dropping to a near-whisper. "Let's just say I have a particular insight into the forces at work here. Forces that, perhaps, you've only begun to glimpse."

I study his face, searching for any sign of deception. But Grey's expression remains maddeningly impassive, a mask of polite interest betraying nothing.

The room feels smaller suddenly, the shadows deeper. I'm acutely aware of my team's growing discomfort. Lady Evelyn's fingers twitch towards the hidden pocket of her dress where I know she keeps a small derringer. Dr. Lancaster's brow furrows, her analytical mind racing to make sense of Grey's cryptic words.

I'm caught in a vortex of conflicting instincts. Part of me wants to trust this man, to believe he holds the key to unraveling this impossible mystery. But another part, honed by years of facing humanity's darkest impulses, screams a warning.

What game is Alastair Grey playing? And are we pawns or players in whatever grand design he's set in motion?

Grey's silver hair catches the dim lamplight as he takes a measured step forward, his eyes gleaming with an unsettling intensity. "You see, Detective Blackwood, the supernatural isn't merely a force to be feared or fought against. It's a wellspring of untapped potential, waiting for those with the vision to harness it."

I feel my jaw tighten. "And you believe you possess that vision?"

"I don't merely believe, my dear Arthur. I know." His voice is silk, wrapping around us like a spider's web. "Think of the good we could do, the advancements we could make. Disease, poverty, war—all could be eradicated with the right application of these... otherworldly energies."

The air in the room grows thick and oppressive. I struggle to draw a full breath as Grey's words sink in—my mind races, piecing together fragments of evidence and snippets of conversation. The realization hits me like a physical blow.

"You're not just studying these forces," I breathe, my voice barely above a whisper. "You're actively manipulating them. The incidents we've been investigating are what you're doing, aren't they?"

Grey's lips curl into a smile that doesn't reach his eyes. "A crude way of putting it, but not entirely inaccurate. I prefer to think of it as... guiding the inevitable."

Anger flares within me, hot and sudden. "You've put countless lives at risk!" I snarled, taking a step toward him. "People have died, Grey!"

"Regrettable but necessary sacrifices for the greater good," he counters, maddeningly calm. "You, of all people, should understand that progress comes at a cost."

I clench my fists, fighting the urge to grab him by his perfectly pressed lapels. How could I have been so blind? The pieces were there, and I'd failed to see the larger picture. Grey hasn't just been aiding our investigation—he's been orchestrating events from the shadows, manipulating us like puppets on strings.

My confusion gives way to a cold, hard determination. Whatever Grey's endgame is, whatever power he seeks to control, I know now that I must stop him. The weight of this realization settles on my shoulders, a grim resolve taking root in my chest.

"You're mistaken, Grey," I say, my voice low and steady. "And I'll prove it."

I feel the shift in the room as Lady Evelyn and Dr. Lancaster step forward, flanking me. Their presence bolsters my resolve, a united front against Grey's machinations.

"What exactly are you trying to achieve, Mr. Grey?" Lady Evelyn's voice cuts through the tension, sharp as a blade. Her auburn hair gleams in the dim light, her eyes narrowed with suspicion.

Grey's gaze flicks to her, then back to me. "My dear Lady Worthington, surely you can appreciate the allure of power. The ability to shape the world as we see fit."

Dr. Lancaster's voice trembles with barely contained fury. "By unleashing forces beyond our control? You're playing with fire, Grey."

I watch as Grey's composure wavers momentarily, a flicker of something—irritation? Concern? —crossing his face before his calm mask descends again.

"Control is precisely the point, Dr. Lancaster," he says smoothly.

"These forces have always existed. I merely seek to harness them, to bring order to chaos."

"At what cost?" I demand, stepping closer. The scent of Grey's expensive cologne mixes with the musty air of the room. "You speak of order, but I've seen destruction in your wake."

Grey's silver hair seems to catch an otherworldly gleam as he turns to face me fully. "Detective Blackwood is always so focused on the immediate consequences. Have you never considered the long game?"

I feel my jaw clench. "Enlighten me," I growl.

As Grey opens his mouth to respond, I catch a movement out of the corner of my eye. Lady Evelyn has inched towards the desk, her hand hovering near a drawer. What has she noticed that I've missed?

The air in the room grows thick with tension, like the fog that clings to London's streets. I can hear my heart pounding as I wait for Grey's next move, acutely aware that we're balancing between revelation and catastrophe on a knife's edge.

Grey's eyes narrow, his composure fracturing like ice under pressure. "You cannot begin to comprehend the magnitude of what's at stake," he hisses, a tremor in his voice betraying his desperation. "These forces are not toys to be locked away in your evidence room, Blackwood. They're the key to reshaping reality itself!"

I watch him intently, noting the beads of sweat forming on his brow. My mind races, piecing together fragments of evidence we've gathered. "And who appointed you the arbiter of reality, Grey?" I challenge myself, taking another step forward. "What gives you the right to play God in people's lives?"

Lady Evelyn's fingers close around something in the drawer. I hear the rustle of paper, but I dare not look away from Grey.

"Someone had to take control!" Grey's voice rises, echoing off the walls. "The veil between worlds is thinning, and if we don't act now—"

"We?" Dr. Lancaster interjects, her tone sharp. "Or just you, Mr. Grey?"

I seize on this moment of vulnerability. "You've been manipulating events from the start, haven't you? The missing artifacts and the strange occurrences at the museum lead back to you."

Grey's laugh is hollow, tinged with madness. "You do not know how deep this goes, Detective. I've seen things that would shatter your sanity. I've communed with beings beyond your comprehension!"

"Alastair," Lady Evelyn's voice cuts through the tension like a knife. She holds up a weathered journal, its pages yellowed with age. "Is this what you've been using to alter the fabric of reality?"

The blood drains from Grey's face as he lunges for the book. In that instant, I know. The final piece clicks into place, and a cold certainty settles in my gut. "It's not just theoretical," I breathe, the implications staggering. "You've done it. You've changed history."

The realization hits me like a physical blow. I can see the same shock reverberating through Lady Evelyn and Dr. Lancaster. Grey's actions have torn the fabric of our reality, and the consequences are unfathomable.

I clench my fists, feeling the weight of responsibility bearing down upon us. "We must end this madness," I declare, my voice steadier than I think. "Whatever the cost."

Lady Evelyn's eyes meet mine, a fierce determination burning within them. "Agreed. We cannot allow him to continue meddling with forces beyond our control."

Dr. Lancaster nods grimly, her fingers already reaching for her medical bag. "I fear we may need more than scientific intervention this time, Arthur."

Grey's lips curl into a sneer. "You're all so painfully short-sighted. Can't you see I'm trying to save us all?"

"By playing God?" I spit back, taking a step towards him. "By rewriting history to suit your whims?"

"Sometimes, Detective," Grey hisses, "one must make hard choices for the greater good."

I lunge forward, my patience finally snapping. My fist connects with Grey's jaw, sending him stumbling backward. The satisfaction is fleeting as he recovers quickly, his eyes wild with rage and something else—a hunger for power that chills me to the core.

Grey charges at me, his movements unnaturally swift. I barely deflect his first blow, feeling the air whoosh past my ear. We grapple, the room spinning around us as we crash into furniture.

"Arthur!" Lady Evelyn cries out, but I can't afford to look away from Grey.

His fingers claw at my throat, and I struggle to breathe. In that moment, I see the depths of his madness, the way the pursuit of knowledge has twisted him into something barely human.

"You can't stop what's coming," Grey growls, his face inches from mine. "The barriers between worlds are crumbling, and I alone have the power to—"

I drive my knee upward, catching him in the stomach. As he doubles over, gasping, I wonder how we'll undo the damage he's wrought. But I push the doubt aside. We must try for the sake of all we hold dear.

"It ends now, Alastair," I pant, readying myself for another assault.

"Whatever you've done, we'll set it right."

As Grey lunges at me again, I reach into my coat pocket, my fingers closing around the cold metal of the amulet I'd discovered in the British Museum's archives. Its etched surface pulses with an otherworldly energy, and I silently pray my hunch is correct.

"You're a fool, Blackwood," Grey snarls, his silver hair wild and unkempt. "You can't possibly comprehend the forces at play."

I stand my ground, heart pounding. "Perhaps not," I reply, my voice steadier than I feel. "But I understand enough that you've meddled with powers beyond your control."

In one fluid motion, I withdraw the amulet, its ancient symbols glowing faintly in the dim light. Grey's eyes widen in recognition, and I see a flicker of fear on his face for the first time.

"How did you—" he starts, but I cut him off.

"Your hubris was your undoing, Alastair. You left breadcrumbs for those who knew where to look."

I recite the incantation I'd painstakingly translated, my voice growing stronger with each unfamiliar syllable. The air around us crackles with unseen energy, and Grey's face contorts in anguish.

"No!" he screams, lunging for the amulet, but it's too late.

A blinding flash of light erupts from the artifact, enveloping Grey in its radiance. When it fades, he collapses to the floor, his body wracked with tremors.

I approach cautiously, my mind reeling from what I've just witnessed. Dr. Lancaster rushes to Grey's side, checking his vital signs.

"He's alive," she announces, her voice tinged with relief and apprehension. "But something's... different."

Lady Evelyn joins us, her face pale. "What have we done, Arthur?"

I stare down at Grey's unconscious form, the weight of our actions settling heavily upon my shoulders. "What was necessary," I reply, though the words taste bitter on my tongue.

As the fog outside thickens, casting long shadows across the room, I can't shake the feeling that this is only the beginning. We've stopped Grey, yes, but at what cost? And what darker forces might we have inadvertently set in motion?

I turn away from Grey's prone form, my gaze sweeping across the dimly lit room. The floorboards creak beneath my feet as I approach the window, peering out into the fog-shrouded streets of London. The gas lamps flicker weakly, their light barely penetrating the dense mist.

"We can't stay here," I say, my voice hoarse. "We need to move him before anyone discovers what's happened."

Lady Evelyn's silk skirts rustle as she moves to stand beside me.

"And then what, Arthur? Where do we go from here?"

I meet her eyes, seeing my uncertainty reflected in their depths. "I don't know," I admit, the words tasting of defeat. "Grey's betrayal... it changes everything."

Dr. Lancaster's voice cuts through the heavy silence. "He's stirring. We need to decide quickly."

I turn back to face the room, my mind racing. "The abandoned warehouse on Blackfriars Bridge. We'll take him there for now."

As we hurriedly prepare to move Grey, I can't help but wonder what other secrets he might have been keeping. The thought gnaws at me, a persistent itch I can't scratch.

"Do you think there are others?" Lady Evelyn asks, echoing my unspoken fears. "Other... collaborators?"

I pause, my hand resting on the door handle. "It's possible. We can't trust anyone outside this room."

Dr. Lancaster looks up from securing Grey's bonds. "What about the artifacts? The ones he was collecting?"

A chill runs down my spine. "God only knows what power they hold. Or what might happen if they fall into the wrong hands."

As we carry Grey's limp form down the creaking stairs, the weight of our uncertain future presses down upon us. The fog swallows us as we step outside, and for a moment, I'm struck by how fitting it seems—our path forward as murky and treacherous as the London streets we now navigate.

"Whatever comes next," I say, my breath misting in the cold air, "we face it together. The game has changed, but we're still players in it. And I intend to see it through to the end."

The distant chime of Big Ben echoes through the night, a solemn reminder of the relentless march of time. As we disappear into the shadows, I can't shake the feeling that this is merely the eye of the storm. What darkness awaits us on the other side, I dare not imagine.

Chapter 19 Resolution

The flickering gaslights cast long shadows across the room, their feeble glow barely illuminating the menacing array of occult symbols etched into the walls. My eyes lock with Grey's, and the air between us crackles with unspoken tension. Ancient artifacts loom around us like silent witnesses to our confrontation.

I take a measured step forward, willing my voice to remain steady despite the torrent of emotions threatening to break free. "Enough games, Grey. I want answers about your involvement in this conspiracy. Now."

Grey's lips curl into his infuriating, cryptic smile, silver hair gleaming in the dim light like freshly polished silverware. "My dear Blackwood, always so direct. But surely you know by now that answers are rarely given freely in our line of work."

My jaw clenches as I fight to maintain composure. This man's presence seems to mock everything I stand for—truth, justice, and the sanctity of the law. Yet, a part of me can't help but admire his unflappable demeanor, even as it fills me with frustration.

"This isn't one of your academic puzzles," I growl, gesturing to the arcane symbols surrounding us. "Lives are at stake. The very fabric of our society hangs in the balance. If you have any shred of decency left–"

"Decency?" Grey interrupts, his voice silky smooth yet laced with danger. "An interesting choice of words from a man who's spent the last fortnight delving into realms. Most would consider indecent, to say the least."

I feel my face flush with anger and, if I'm honest, a touch of shame.

He's not wrong—this investigation has led me down paths I never imagined treading. But I steel myself, remembering the faces of those who've suffered, those who still need my help.

"Don't deflect, Grey. Your fingerprints are all over this conspiracy.

The rare artifacts, the whispers in dark corners of the museum—it all leads back to you."

Grey's smile never wavers, but I catch a flicker of something in his eyes. Amusement? Respect? Or perhaps... fear?

"You've done your homework, Detective. I'd expect nothing less.

But tell me, in all your digging, have you considered that perhaps there are forces at work beyond your comprehension? Beyond any of our comprehension?"

At his words, a chill runs down my spine, and I flash back memories of the impossible things I've witnessed during this case.

But I push them aside, focusing on the man before me.

"What I comprehend," I say, taking another step closer, "is that you have blood on your hands, Grey. And I intend to see justice done, no matter what dark corners I have to shine a light into."

Grey's smile finally falters momentarily before returning with renewed intensity. "Oh, Blackwood," he says, his voice barely above a whisper. "You do not know just how dark those corners can be."

I study Grey's face intently, my eyes tracing every line and shadow.

His silver hair catches the dim light, creating an otherworldly aura around him. But I'm not here to be mesmerized but to unravel the truth.

"Those dark corners you speak of, Grey," I say, low and measured, "I've faced them before. They don't scare me."

A chuckle escapes his lips, but it doesn't reach his eyes. "Bravery or foolishness, Detective? Sometimes, it's hard to tell the difference."

I circle him slowly, like a predator stalking its prey—my mind races, analyzing every twitch, every breath. There's a slight tension in his shoulders, a barely perceptible tightening around his eyes.

He's hiding something; I intend to drag it into the light.

"Let's talk about the Crimson Codex," I say abruptly, watching his reaction. "An ancient text, supposedly lost to time. Yet whispers of its power have been central to this affair."

Grey's eyebrow arches slightly. "Ah, the Codex. A fascinating piece of history, wouldn't you agree? But surely you don't believe in such... supernatural nonsense?"

I can feel the weight of the room pressing down on us, the artifacts around us seeming to lean in, listening. "What I believe," I reply carefully, "is that men will commit terrible acts in pursuit of power, real or imagined."

Grey steps towards me, his voice dropping to a silky whisper. "And what terrible acts do you imagine I've committed, Detective?"

I hold my ground, refusing to be intimidated. "That's what I'm here to find out. But know this, Grey—whatever web of lies and half-truths you're spinning, I will unravel it. The truth can come to light, no matter how deep the shadows."

His smile widens, but there's a coldness behind it now. "Oh, Blackwood," he says, "you do not know how deep those shadows go."

I reach into my coat pocket, my fingers brushing against the cool metal of the locket I'd uncovered earlier that day. The tension in the room crackles like static electricity as I withdraw the item, holding it up between us. The flickering candlelight catches on its tarnished surface, illuminating the intricate engraving of a serpent devouring its tail.

"Recognize this, Mr. Grey?" I ask, my voice steady despite the pounding of my heart.

For a fraction of a second, Grey's composure shatters. His eyes widen with a flicker of fear crossing his face before he transforms his features into their usual mask of calm indifference. But it's enough. I've seen the crack in his armor.

"An interesting trinket," he says, his voice betraying the slightest tremor. "Though I cannot see its relevance."

I step closer, the locket dangling between us like a pendulum. "This was found in the possession of Lord Ashbury mere hours before his untimely demise. The same Lord Ashbury who was about to expose your involvement in the theft of certain... shall we say, sensitive artifacts from the British Museum."

Grey's silver hair seems to lose some of its luster as he stares at the locket, his jaw clenching. I press on, and my words are precise and cutting.

"You see, Mr. Grey, I've been piecing together this puzzle: the missing artifacts, the whispers of dark rituals, the string of unexplained deaths. And at the center of it all, I find you. A respected antiquarian with unparalleled access to the museum's most guarded secrets."

I begin to circle him slowly, my voice never wavering. "You've been using your position to orchestrate a conspiracy of monumental proportions. The Crimson Codex isn't just a myth, is it? You believe it holds actual power, and you're willing to do anything—even murder—to get it."

Grey's eyes narrow, a dangerous glint appearing in them. "You're treading on thin ice, Detective. Accusations without proof are a dangerous game."

"Oh, I have proof," I counter, my mind racing through the evidence I've gathered. "Eyewitness accounts placing you at the scene of multiple thefts. Financial records show sizeable sums transferred to known occultists. And this locket, bearing your family crest, was found clutched in the hand of a dead man."

I can see the realization dawning on Grey's face as his carefully constructed world crumbles around him. The mask of civility slips away, revealing something far more sinister beneath.

Grey's composure shatters like fine china. With a guttural roar, he lunges at me, his eyes wild with desperation. I barely have time to brace myself before his complete weight slams into my chest, driving us both backward. We crash into an ornate bookshelf, sending ancient tomes cascading around us.

"You understand nothing!" Grey snarls, his fingers clawing at my throat.

I gasp for air, my mind racing. This is no longer a battle of wits but a primal struggle for survival. As we grapple, the room becomes a whirlwind of chaos. Priceless artifacts topple from pedestals, shattering on the floor. The air grows thick with dust and the acrid scent of old parchment.

"I won't let you ruin everything!" Grey hisses, his face contorted with rage.

I break his grip, ducking under his arm and using his momentum against him. "The truth will come out, Grey," I pant, "one way or another."

My eyes dart around the room, searching for anything I can use to my advantage. That's when I spot an ancient Egyptian ankh hanging on the wall. My research floods back to me; in occult circles, it's believed to weaken malevolent supernatural forces.

I dive for it, my fingers closing around the cool metal as Grey tackles me again. We hit the ground hard, but I don't let go.

Instead, I press the ankh against his chest, uttering an incantation I'd uncovered during my investigation.

"No!" Grey screams, his body convulsing as if struck by lightning. "You don't know what you're doing!"

But I do. I have the upper hand for the first time since this confrontation began. The tide is turning, and with it, the fate of London itself.

The shadows in the room seem to writhe and coalesce, drawn to Grey like moths to a flame. His silver hair whips around his face, no longer elegant but wild and unkempt. I press the ankh harder against his chest, feeling the metal grow hot in my grip.

"You're meddling with forces beyond your comprehension, Blackwood," Grey snarls, his voice distorting into something inhuman.

I grit my teeth, pushing through the pain as the ankh sears my palm. "Perhaps," I reply, "but I've learned enough to stop you."

My mind races, recalling every clue, every whispered secret I've uncovered during this investigation. The pieces fall into place, revealing the tapestry of Grey's nefarious plot. I see now how he's manipulated events, using his knowledge of the occult to orchestrate a conspiracy that threatens the very fabric of our society.

Grey's eyes flash with an otherworldly light as he lunges for my throat. I barely roll away, my back slamming against an overturned bookcase. Ancient tomes spill across the floor, their pages fluttering like the wings of trapped birds.

"You can't possibly understand the greater good I'm working towards," Grey pants, struggling to his feet.

I rise as well, my muscles screaming in protest. "Greater good?" I scoff. "There's nothing good about what you've done, Alastair."

With a primal roar, Grey charges at me once more. But this time, I'm ready. I sidestep at the last moment, using his momentum to slam him into the wall. The impact dislodges a heavy iron sconce, which crashes down onto Grey's head with a sickening thud.

He crumples to the floor, his silver hair matted with blood. The room falls eerily silent, except for my ragged breathing.

I lean against a shattered display case, my chest heaving as I gulp in the musty air. My piercing blue eyes dart around the dim room, searching for any lingering threats among the wreckage of priceless artifacts. Shadows dance in the corners, cast by the flickering gaslight, but nothing stirs.

"It's over," I mutter, more to reassure myself than anything else.

Turning my attention to Grey's unconscious form, I can't help but feel a pang of regret. The man's brilliance could have changed the world for the better. Instead, he walked a darker path.

"What have you wrought, Alastair?" I whisper, kneeling beside him to check his pulse. It's there, faint but steady.

The sound of hurried footsteps echoes from the hallway outside. I tense, ready for another fight, but relax as familiar faces appear in my team's doorway—battered, bruised, but alive.

"Blackwood!" Inspector Hawthorne calls out, his usual gruff demeanor tinged with concern. "Are you alright, man?"

I nod, rising to my feet with a grimace. "I've had worse nights at the opera," I quip, though the humor falls flat even to my ears.

Dr. Elizabeth Fairfax rushes to Grey's side, her nimble fingers already assessing his condition. "He'll live," she announces, her voice tight. "Though I daresay he'll have a frightful headache when he wakes."

As the team secures Grey and begins to sift through the wreckage, I find myself drawn to the shattered remains of an ornate mirror. My reflection stares back at me, a stranger with haunted eyes and blood-spattered clothes.

"What have we done?" I murmur, the weight of our actions settling heavily upon my shoulders.

Hawthorne appears beside me, his weathered face etched with relief and exhaustion. "We've stopped a madman, Arthur. Saved countless lives."

I turn to face him, my voice low. "At what cost, old friend? The secrets we've unearthed, the forces we've meddled with... there's no going back from this."

"There never is," he replies softly. "But we made our choice. Now we live with the consequences."

As we stand there, surrounded by the remnants of our battle, I can't shake the feeling that this victory is merely the beginning of something far greater and more terrifying than we could ever have imagined.

I shake off my momentary introspection, my resolve hardening like steel. "Right then," I announce, my voice cutting through the tense silence. "We've work to do."

Striding to the center of the room, I issue orders, my analytical mind already piecing together our next steps. "Hawthorne, secure all entrances. Elizabeth, tend to Grey and ensure he's fit for transport. Jenkins, start cataloging every artifact in this room—I want detailed sketches and descriptions."

As my team springs into action, I pull out my notebook, its leather cover worn from countless investigations. With meticulous precision, I document every detail of our confrontation, my pen scratching across the paper in rapid strokes.

"What of the authorities, sir?" Jenkins asks, his voice tinged with apprehension.

I pause, considering. "We'll need to tread carefully. This goes beyond the scope of Scotland Yard. I have contacts in the Home Office who can be trusted—to a point."

My thoughts race as I weigh the implications of each potential move. The wrong word to the ear could unravel everything we've fought for.

"Arthur," Elizabeth calls, her tone urgent. "Grey's coming round."

I glide to her side, crouching beside our captive. Grey's eyes flutter open, focusing on me with a mix of hatred and... something else. Fear? Respect?

"It's over, Grey," I state firmly. "Your conspiracy ends here."

He chuckles weakly, a trickle of blood at the corner of his mouth.

"Oh, Blackwood. You do not know what you've set in motion. The wheels are already turning."

I lean in closer, my voice a low growl. "Then you'd best start talking. Because I promise you, I will uncover every secret, no matter how deep it's buried."

As Grey's cryptic words hang in the air, I can't help but feel a chill run down my spine. We might have found the answer to the mystery, but I believe there is still a much larger and unknown issue lurking beneath the surface.

I rise, my eyes scanning the room. The flickering gaslight casts long shadows across the walls, and for a moment, I swear I see them move of their own accord. A trick of the light, surely. Yet, after all we've witnessed, can I truly dismiss such things?

"We should flick," I announce, straightening my coat. "Jenkins, secure Grey. Elizabeth, gather any remaining evidence."

As they set to work, I find myself drawn to the window. The fog outside has thickened, obscuring the street below. London seems to have vanished, leaving us adrift in a sea of mist. My reflection stares back at me, blue eyes haunted by unresolved questions.

"What troubles you, Arthur?" Elizabeth's voice breaks through my reverie.

I turn, offering a tight smile. "It's the loose ends, my dear. They tug at my mind like errant threads."

She nods, understanding in her eyes. "The symbols we found in the crypt?"

"Among other things," I murmur. "The connection to the Royal Society, the missing pages from Sir Alastair's journal..."

Jenkins interrupts Grey, now securely bound. "Not to mention the blasted thing in the sewers, sir. Still gives me nightmares, that does."

I suppress a shudder, recalling the otherworldly horror we'd encountered beneath the city streets. Some mysteries, perhaps, are best left unsolved. And yet...

"We've closed this chapter," I say, my voice firm despite the doubt gnawing at my insides. "But I fear we've only read the prologue of a far greater tale."

ELIZABETH PLACES A comforting hand on my arm. "Whatever comes next, we'll face it together."

I nod, grateful for her unwavering support. As we prepare to leave this room of shadows and secrets, I can't shake the feeling that unseen eyes are watching us. The case may be closed, but the true adventure, I suspect, has only just begun.

Chapter 20 Returning Home

The familiar scent of old books and ink embraces me as I step into my office, a sanctuary of sorts amidst the chaos of Victorian London. I hang my coat on the worn hook by the door, the fabric still damp from the pervasive fog that clings to the city like a second skin. As I settle into my leather chair, it creaks a welcome chorus; I can't shake the feeling that something out there is waiting, watching.

"Another day, another mystery," I mutter, reaching for the stack of case files that threaten to topple from the corner of my desk. My fingers, calloused from years of meticulous note-taking, trace the edges of photographs spread before me. Each image fragments a giant puzzle that has plagued my thoughts since our last supernatural encounter.

I lean in closer, my eyes narrowing as I scrutinize a photograph.

"What are you hiding?" I whisper, tracing the outline of a shadowy figure lurking in the background. The image seems to pulse with otherworldly energy, a reminder that the veil between our world and the next is thinner than most would believe.

My mind races, connecting invisible threads between seemingly unrelated details. The symbol etched into the victim's palm, and the peculiar arrangement of objects at the crime scene speak to something greater beyond the realm of ordinary crime.

I reach for my notebook, jotting down observations with feverish intensity. "The symbol matches the one from the Whitechapel," I murmur, my pen scratching against the paper. "But why here? Why now?"

A chill runs down my spine as I recall the events of our last investigation. The things we saw and uncovered truths were enough to shake even the most steadfast beliefs in the natural order. And yet, here I am, diving headfirst into another mystery that threatens to unravel the very fabric of reality.

I lean back in my chair, running a hand through my hair. The weight of responsibility settles heavily on my shoulders. "What am I missing?" I ask the empty room, half-expecting the shadows to answer.

My gaze falls on a framed photograph on my desk—a reminder of what's at stake. The faces of those I've sworn to protect stare back at me, their eyes filled with trust and expectation. I can't let them down, and I won't.

With renewed determination, I turn back to the files. Each page turned, each photograph examined brings me one step closer to the truth. And in this game of cat and mouse, with forces beyond comprehension, the truth might be our only salvation.

"Whatever you are," I say to the unseen presence that seems to linger just beyond the edges of perception, "I will find you. And I will stop you."

The gas lamps flicker outside my window, casting long shadows across the room. As night descends upon London, I prepare myself for another long vigil in the pursuit of justice—both earthly and otherworldly.

The creak of floorboards outside my office door snaps me from my reverie. I glance up, my hand instinctively reaching for the drawer where I keep my revolver. The door bursts open, revealing the stocky figure of Inspector Tobias Collins, a long-time ally in the pursuit of justice, his face flushed and eyes wild with urgency.

"Blackwood!" he exclaims, barely catching his breath. "We've got a situation that requires your... unique expertise."

I lean forward, my interest piqued. "What is it, Collins? Another body in the Thames?" My heart quickens at the thought of another supernatural mystery to unravel.

He shakes his head, his mustache quivering. "Worse. An artifact's gone missing from the British Museum. And there's something... unnatural about the theft."

My pulse quickens. "Unnatural, you say? How so?"

Collins lowers his voice as if afraid the very walls might be listening. "The guards swear they saw shadows moving on their own. And there's a symbol left behind that's got the curator in a right state."

I rise from my chair, my mind already racing with possibilities. Could this be connected to our recent supernatural encounters? The timing is too convenient to be a mere coincidence.

"Tell me more about this artifact," I press, moving to grab my coat.

Collins runs a hand through his graying hair. "It's an ancient amulet, supposedly with mystical properties. The curator was tight-lipped about the details but seemed terrified of what might happen if it falls into the wrong hands."

I nod; my decision has already been made. "I'll take the case, Collins. This could be the break we've been waiting for."

As I don my coat, I can't help but feel a mix of excitement and trepidation. Another piece of the puzzle has fallen into place, but at what cost? The game is afoot, and the stakes have never been higher.

"Lead the way, Inspector," I say, gesturing towards the door. "The night is young, and the shadows are restless. It's time we shed some light on this mystery."

The British Museum looms before me, its Grecian columns casting long shadows across the fog-shrouded courtyard. As I ascend the steps, the weight of anticipation settles heavily upon my shoulders.

The massive doors creak open, revealing a dimly lit interior that seems to pulse with an otherworldly energy.

"This way, Detective Blackwood," a voice calls from the gloom.

I follow the sound, my footsteps echoing through cavernous halls filled with relics from bygone eras. Glass cases glint in the low light, their contents—ancient pottery, weathered statues, and cryptic inscriptions—seeming to watch my progress with unseeing eyes.

"I can't shake the feeling we're being observed," I mutter, my gaze darting from shadow to shadow.

The curator materializes from the darkness, his thin frame trembling slightly as he approaches. "Detective, I'm Dr. Thaddeus Winthrop. I... I'm grateful for your swift arrival."

I study the man before me, noting his pallid complexion and the dark circles beneath his eyes. "Dr. Winthrop, perhaps you could illuminate the situation for me. What exactly are we dealing with here?"

He wrings his hands, glancing nervously over his shoulder before responding. "The artifact in question is known as the Amulet of Nefertiti. It's said to possess... extraordinary capabilities."

"Such as?" I press, my curiosity piqued.

Winthrop's voice drops to a whisper. "Legend speaks of its power to bridge the gap between our world and the realm of spirits. In the wrong hands, it could unleash chaos beyond imagination."

A chill runs down my spine as I contemplate the implications.

"And you believe these legends to be true?"

"I've seen things, Detective," he replies, his eyes wide with barely contained fear. "Inexplicable occurrences since the amulet arrived.

Objects are moving of their own accord, whispers in empty rooms. And now... now it's gone."

I nod slowly, my mind racing to piece everything together. "Show me where it was last seen. Every detail could be crucial."

As we move deeper into the museum's labyrinthine corridors, I can't shake the sensation of unseen eyes upon us. The air grows thick, charged with an energy that sets my nerves on edge.

I'm worried that we've only scratched the surface regarding understanding the fundamental nature of what's happening here.

I kneel beside the empty display case, my fingers tracing the air just above its surface. The glass is intact, and there are no signs of forced entry. My eyes narrow, searching for the minutest detail that might unravel this enigma.

"Tell me, Mr. Winthrop," I murmur, not taking my gaze from the case, "were there any unusual disturbances in the days leading up to the disappearance?"

The curator shifts uneasily behind me. "Well, now that you mention it, this room has a peculiar chill. Even on the warmest days, it felt... unnaturally cold."

I nod, filing away the information. My hand moves to my coat pocket, retrieving a small magnifying glass. I scrutinize every inch of the display: the polished wood base and the velvet lining. Nothing seems amiss, and yet...

"There's always something," I mutter, a mantra that's served me well over the years.

A glint catches my eye as I pivot on my heel, ready to expand my search. Barely visible in the dim light, a faint etching on the museum's marble floor. My heart quickens as I crouch to examine it more closely.

"Mr. Winthrop, bring that lamp closer if you would."

The curator complies, and as the light falls upon the floor, I can't suppress a sharp intake of breath. There, etched with painstaking precision, is a symbol I've encountered before—a circle bisected by a wavy line, with three stars arranged in a triangle above it.

"God," I whisper, my mind reeling. "It can't be."

"What is it, Detective?" Winthrop asks, his voice tinged with both curiosity and fear.

I rise slowly, my eyes never leaving the symbol. "This, Mr. Winthrop, is a sign I've seen only once. In a case, that nearly cost me everything."

The implications flood my mind. If this symbol is connected to the missing amulet, we deal with forces far beyond mortal comprehension.

The hairs on the back of my neck stand on end as I recall the horrors of that previous encounter.

"Detective Blackwood?" Winthrop's voice breaks through my reverie. "What does this mean?"

I turn to face him, my expression grave. "It means, Mr. Winthrop, that we're standing on the precipice of something far more dangerous than a simple theft. This symbol confirms my worst suspicions—we deal with powers that defy natural law."

As the weight of my words settles over us, the air in the museum seems to grow even heavier. The shadows in the corners appear to deepen. For a moment, I swear I hear a faint, otherworldly whisper echoing through the halls.

"Heaven help us," I murmur, steeling myself for the challenges ahead. "For we may face forces that no earthly power can contend with."

I stride purposefully through the fog-shrouded streets of London, my mind racing with the implications of what I've discovered. The gaslights flicker, casting eerie shadows that dance with malevolent intent. I must reach out to my allies; this case has grown far beyond my ability to handle it alone.

At Lady Evelyn's townhouse, I rap sharply on the door. Her butler ushers me into the lavish drawing room where she sits, poised as ever.

"Arthur," she greets me, her auburn hair gleaming in the lamplight. "What brings you here at this hour?"

I lean in, my voice low and urgent. "Evelyn, I've uncovered something. The missing artifact—it's connected to the supernatural. I need your expertise."

Her eyes widen, a mix of intrigue and apprehension flickering across her face. "Tell me everything," she says, leaning forward.

As I recount the details, I can see her analytical mind piecing together the puzzle. "We must act quickly," she declares, rising doggedly. "I'll gather my resources."

Next, I make my way to Dr. Lancaster's clinic. The petite doctor greets me with a knowing look. "Another mystery, Detective?"

I nod grimly. "One that may require your unique insights, Amelia. We're dealing with forces beyond our understanding."

Her sharp eyes narrow. "I suspected as much. Count me in, Arthur. We can't let these dark powers run unchecked."

As we converge in my office, the sense of urgency is palpable.

Books and ancient texts litter every surface, their musty scent mingling with the ever-present London fog seeping through the windows.

"This symbol," I say, sketching it on a scrap of paper, "is our key. We need to decipher its meaning."

Lady Evelyn pores over a leather-bound tome, her brow furrowed in concentration. "I've seen something similar in occult literature," she murmurs. "It speaks of gateways between worlds."

Dr. Lancaster leans in, her fiery hair catching the lamplight. "And the missing artifact? Could it be a key to such a gateway?"

I feel a chill run down my spine at the thought. "If it is, we're racing against time. Who knows what horrors could be unleashed if it falls into the wrong hands?"

As we delve deeper into our research, the night wears on. The clock's ticking grows louder, a constant reminder of the impending danger. I can't shake the feeling that we're on the brink of uncovering something that could shake the very foundations of our reality.

"We must find this artifact," I declare, my voice filled with grim determination. "Before it's too late."

My eyes scan the pages of an ancient tome, its brittle parchment crackling beneath my fingertips. Suddenly, a passage leaps out at me, and my breath catches in my throat. "By God," I whisper, my voice barely audible over my heart pounding.

Lady Evelyn looks up sharply. "What is it, Arthur?"

"This symbol," I say, tapping the page with trembling fingers, "is linked to an entity known as the Shadow Weaver. It is a being of immense power, capable of bending reality to its will."

Dr. Lancaster leans in, her eyes widening. "And the artifact?"

I nod grimly. "A conduit. If wielded correctly, it could grant the user control over the Shadow weaver itself."

The weight of this revelation settles over us like a shroud. The stakes have risen beyond our wildest imaginations.

"We need to move," I declare, snapping the book shut. "Now."

As we prepare for our journey, I can't help but feel a mix of trepidation and exhilaration. The unknown beckons, dark and foreboding, yet tinged with the allure of adventure.

"Pack light," I instruct, holstering my revolver. "We don't know what we'll encounter."

Lady Evelyn nods, her face set doggedly. "I've arranged transportation. A carriage awaits us outside."

As we enter the fog-shrouded night, I feel a surge of resolve.

Whatever dangers lie, we face them together, united in our quest to unravel this supernatural mystery and protect the world from forces beyond mortal comprehension.

The carriage rattles to a stop, and I step out into the chill night air, my eyes immediately drawn to the looming silhouette before us.

The crumbling mansion rises from the mist like a specter, its dilapidated grandeur a testament to forgotten opulence.

"Lord," Dr. Lancaster breathes, her voice barely above a whisper. "It's as if the very stones are watching us."

I nod my senses on high alert. "Stay close," I murmur, leading our small group toward the grand entrance. The door creaks open at my touch as if inviting us into its maw.

The foyer unfolds before us, a cavernous space choked with shadows and decay. Tattered tapestries hang like spectral sentinels, and the air is thick with the musty scent of abandonment.

"Arthur," Lady Evelyn whispers, her hand brushing my arm. "Do you feel that? It's as if the air itself is... alive."

I pause, allowing my heightened senses to absorb our surroundings.

"Indeed," I reply, my voice low. "There's a palpable energy here—something... otherworldly."

As we venture deeper into the mansion's labyrinthine corridors, each step echoes ominously. Flickering candlelight casts grotesque shadows that dance and writhe on the walls.

"The artifact must be here somewhere," I muse, more to myself than my companions. "But where would one hide such a powerful object?"

Dr. Lancaster's voice trembles slightly as she responds, "Perhaps in a place where the veil between worlds is thinnest?"

I nod, my mind racing. "A sound theory. We should look for areas of particular mystical significance. A study, perhaps, or a hidden chamber."

As we round a corner, a gust of cold air extinguishes our candles, plunging us into darkness. I feel my heart rate quicken, adrenaline coursing through my veins.

"Stay calm," I instruct, fumbling for matches. "We're not alone here, but panic will only cloud our judgment."

The match flares to life, illuminating our tense faces. In that moment of light, I glimpse something moving in the shadows at the far end of the corridor.

"Did you see that?" Lady Evelyn gasps.

I nod grimly. "Whatever lives here, it's aware of our presence. We must tread carefully. The line between hunter and hunted has never been so thin."

With bated breath, we follow the shadowy movement to the end of the corridor. My hand brushes against a peculiar indentation in the wall, and I pause, running my fingers along its edges.

"Here," I whisper, "there's something..."

A soft click echoes through the hallway as a hidden door swings open, revealing a chamber bathed in an otherworldly blue glow.

We step inside, our eyes widening in collective awe.

"By Jove," Dr. Lancaster breathes, his scholarly composure momentarily shattered.

The room is a treasure trove of antiquities, each more fantastical than the last. Ancient tomes line floor-to-ceiling shelves, their spines adorned with arcane symbols. Glass cases house artifacts that seem to pulse with an inner light. And at the center of it all, atop a stone pedestal, sits an object that can only be our missing artifact.

"Incredible," I murmur, my analytical mind already cataloging every detail. "But we mustn't touch anything yet. The air itself feels charged with... something."

Lady Evelyn nods, her eyes gleaming with fear and fascination.

"It's as if we've stepped into another world entirely. Arthur, what do you make of these symbols?"

I approach a nearby wall covered in intricate carvings. My heart races as I recognize patterns similar to those we've encountered.

"These markings... they're connected to our previous case. But how?"

A sudden chill runs down my spine as I trace the symbols with my fingertips. The room seems to shift around us, the blue glow intensifying.

"We're on the precipice of something monumental," I say, barely above a whisper. "The truth we seek... it's here, woven into the very fabric of this place."

Dr. Lancaster approaches the pedestal, his hand hovering above the artifact. "Should we...?"

I shake my head, a warning on my lips. "Not yet. We need to understand what we're dealing with first. One wrong move, and we could unleash forces beyond our comprehension."

The air grows heavy with anticipation as we stand on the threshold of revelation, the supernatural world we've long pursued finally within our grasp.

Chapter 21 Epilogue

T he flickering gaslight casts long shadows across my cluttered desk, illuminating the myriad case files and arcane artifacts surrounding me like past sentinels. I lean back in my creaking chair, feeling the weight of years pressing down upon my shoulders. My fingers trace the edge of a worn leather journal, its pages filled with solved and unsolved mysteries.

"Another dead end," I mutter, tossing aside a yellowed newspaper clipping. The headline blares about a series of unexplained disappearances—a case that's haunted me for decades.

I rise, wincing at the stiffness in my joints, and make my way to the window. Outside, London's fog-shrouded streets stretch into the distance, a labyrinth of secrets and shadows. The city has changed so much, yet it remains the same—a place where darkness lurks behind every corner, waiting to be uncovered.

A knock at the door jolts me from my reverie. "Enter," I call, turning to face my visitor.

My assistant, a young lad named Timothy, steps in hesitantly.

"Begging your pardon, Detective Blackwood, but there's a telegram for you. It's marked urgent."

I take the proffered envelope, noting the familiar seal. "Thank you, Timothy. That will be all."

As the door closes behind him, I break the seal and unfurl the message. My eyes widen as I read its contents. "Well, well," I murmur, excitement igniting within me. "It seems the game is afoot once more."

I grab my coat and hat, gazing at the portrait of my late wife on the mantle. "Wish me luck, my dear," I whisper before stepping out into the night, ready to face whatever new mystery awaits.

The scene shifts, and I find myself seated in the back row of a packed lecture hall at Oxford University. The air thrums with anticipation as Lady Evelyn Worthington takes the stage, her presence commanding instant attention.

"Ladies and gentlemen," she begins, her voice clear and confident.

We gather here today to explore the shadows of our past—the mysteries that have shaped our world and continue to influence our present."

I lean forward, captivated by her words and the passion behind them. Lady Evelyn's eyes seem to gleam with an inner fire as she delves into her subject, weaving a tapestry of historical intrigue and supernatural speculation.

"Consider, if you will, the inexplicable events surrounding the disappearance of the Roanoke Colony," she continues, gesturing to a series of projected images behind her. "What forces were at play that could cause an entire settlement to vanish without a trace?"

A murmur ripples through the audience, and I can't help but smile. Lady Evelyn has always had a knack for stirring the imagination, for making people question the world around them.

As she speaks, I find my mind drifting back to our shared adventures and the dangers we faced together. She's changed and grown more assured in her expertise, but I can still see traces of the young woman who once stood by my side in the face of unimaginable horrors.

The lecture concludes with thunderous applause, and I watch Lady Evelyn graciously field questions from eager students and colleagues alike. Our eyes meet across the crowded room, and a flicker of recognition passes between us.

I approach her, my heart pounding with anticipation and trepidation. It's been years since we last spoke, and I can't help but wonder what new mysteries await us on the horizon.

The evening sun casts long shadows across my garden, painting the world in hues of amber and gold. I kneel on the soft earth, my weathered hands gently tending to a row of budding roses. The scent of freshly turned soil and blooming flowers fills my nostrils, a far cry from London's streets' acrid smoke and grime.

"You've outdone yourself this year, old boy," I mutter, a smile tugging at the corners of my mustache. The tranquility of this moment is a balm to my soul, soothing the restlessness that still stirs within me.

As I work, my mind wanders to days long past. The clatter of horse hooves on cobblestones echoes in my memory, mingling with the phantom sounds of urgent whistles and shouted orders. I see Blackwood's face, etched doggedly as we pursue a shadowy figure through fog-shrouded alleys.

"Penny, for your thoughts, Inspector?" I hear my wife call from the cottage doorway.

I chuckle, rising slowly to my feet. "Just reminiscing, my dear. The garden has a way of bringing out my reflective side."

She approaches, her eyes twinkling with mischief. "Ah, I know that look. You're thinking about your old cases again, aren't you?"

I nod, unable to deny it. "It's strange, isn't it? After all these years, the thrill of the chase still lingers."

"Do you miss it?" she asks, her voice soft and understanding.

I pause, considering her question. "Parts of it, yes. The camaraderie, the sense of purpose. But I wouldn't trade this peace for all the excitement in the world."

As we stand together in the fading light, I can't help but wonder what Blackwood and the others are up to now. Little do I know that another chapter in our shared story is about to unfold across the city.

The scene shifts to a grand auditorium, where Dr. Amelia Lancaster stands before a rapt audience of medical professionals.

Her fiery red hair catches the light as she gestures emphatically, her voice clear and confident.

"Ladies and gentlemen," she begins, her eyes scanning the crowd, "we stand on the precipice of a new era in medical science. An era where the boundaries between the explicable and the inexplicable blur, where the supernatural and the scientific intertwine in ways we've only begun to understand."

A murmur ripples through the audience, a mixture of skepticism and intrigue. Amelia allows herself a small smile, relishing the challenge.

"I know many of you have doubts," she continues, her tone measured. "I once shared those doubts. But the evidence I'm about to present will challenge everything you think you know about the limits of human physiology and the nature of reality itself."

As she speaks, images flash across the screen behind her—detailed medical scans juxtaposed with ancient symbols, case studies of seemingly miraculous healings alongside charts of unexplained energy patterns.

"What we're witnessing," Amelia says, her voice rising with passion, "is not the negation of science but its expansion. We're pushing the boundaries of what we thought possible, and in doing so, we're uncovering truths that have lain hidden for centuries."

She pauses, allowing her words to sink in. In that moment of silence, she feels the weight of her journey—from skeptic to believer, from outsider to respected expert. She thinks of Blackwood, Evelyn, and Collins and the adventures that led her to this stage.

"The intersection of science and the supernatural is not a crossroads," she declares, her voice ringing out. "It's a vast, uncharted territory waiting to be explored. And we, my esteemed colleagues, are the pioneers who will map its wonders."

As applause erupts, Amelia feels a familiar thrill course through her veins. She knows new mysteries are stirring, waiting to be unraveled. And she'll be ready when they come.

The package arrives as darkness settles over London, a city that never truly sleeps but merely slumbers fitfully, its dreams haunted by secrets old and new. I sit at my desk, the lone candle casting flickering shadows across the worn surface. The parcel, unremarkable in its brown paper wrapping, seems to pulse with its own energy.

My fingers, calloused from years of handling evidence and chasing phantoms, tremble slightly as I untie the twine. The scent of aged paper wafts up, stirring memories long dormant. As the wrapping falls away, I'm left staring at a leather-bound journal, its cover cracked and weathered by time.

"Impossible," I breathe, recognizing the intricate symbol embossed on the cover—Alastair Grey's personal seal.

I open the journal, and a wave of nostalgia washes over me as I see the familiar, elegant script. "My dear Blackwood," it begins, "if you are reading this, then the wheels I set in motion long ago have finally begun to turn."

My heart races as I scan the pages with cryptic references and half-formed theories. "What game are you playing now, old friend?" I muttered, running a hand through my graying hair.

A knock at the door startles me from my reverie. "Come in," I call, hastily closing the journal and slipping it into my desk drawer.

My assistant, a young man named Thomas, enters hesitantly.

"Pardon the interruption, sir, but there's a lady here to see you. Says it's urgent."

I sigh, but the weight of Grey's journal is still heavy on my mind. "Very well, show her in."

As Thomas leaves, I can't shake the feeling that Grey's journal and this unexpected visitor are connected. The pieces of a new puzzle are falling into place, and I find myself both dreading and expecting the challenge ahead.

Across town, in her study at the British Museum, Lady Evelyn Worthington sits bathed in the warm glow of a gas lamp, her auburn hair gleaming like burnished copper. Her fingers, adorned with a single, ornate ring—a family heirloom—trace the embossed lettering on a cream-colored envelope.

"The Orphic Circle cordially invites you..." she reads aloud, her voice barely above a whisper.

A thrill runs through her, equal parts excitement and trepidation.

The Orphic Circle—a name whispered in shadowy corners, a group said to guard secrets that could reshape the very fabric of reality.

Evelyn sets the invitation down, her mind racing. "After all these years," she murmurs, "why now?"

She rises and moves to the window overlooking the museum's grand facade. The London fog swirls beyond the glass, concealing and revealing the city's secrets in equal measure.

"It's a trap," she tells herself, as her pulse quickens at the thought of unraveling this new mystery. "Or an opportunity."

Evelyn returns to her desk, where stacks of research papers and ancient texts await her attention. Her latest findings—breakthrough discoveries linking disparate mythologies—lie half-hidden beneath a map of ley lines crisscrossing Britain.

"What if they've found something?" she wonders aloud.

"Something that could change everything we thought we knew?"

The temptation is almost overwhelming. Yet caution, hard-won through years of perilous adventures, gives her pause.

Evelyn picks up a small silver bell, its chime cutting through the silence of her study. Moments later, her trusted assistant appears.

"Margaret," Evelyn says, her voice steady despite the excitement coursing through her veins, "I need you to send a message to Detective Blackwood. Tell him... tell him the game is afoot once more."

As Margaret hurries away, Evelyn turns to the window, her reflection ghostly in the glass. The woman staring back at her is no longer the wide-eyed adventurer of her youth, but a scholar tempered by experience and loss. Yet beneath that carefully cultivated exterior, the fire of curiosity still burns bright.

"One last adventure," she whispers, a smile playing at the corners of her mouth. "For old times' sake."

The cottage door creaks open, revealing Inspector Tobias Collins's weathered face. His once-dark hair has faded to steel gray, matching the bristles of his well-trimmed mustache. His piercing eyes, however, remain as sharp as ever, scanning the young man on his doorstep.

"Well, lad," Collins grunts, "you going to stand there gawking or come in?"

The young detective, barely out of his twenties, stumbles forward.

"Thank you, sir. I'm Detective Constable Henry Finch. I... I need your help."

I usher him into my sitting room, the scent of pipe tobacco and old leather mingling. "Sit," I command, lowering myself into my favorite armchair. "Now, what's got you so rattled you're bothering a retired inspector?"

Fitch perches on the edge of the settee, his hands fidgeting. "It's this case, sir. Bodies turned up drained of blood, strange symbols carved into their skin. The higher-ups are calling it the work of some deranged cult, but..."

"But you suspect something more," I finish for him, leaning forward. My joints creak in protest, reminding me of the years that have passed. "Something that doesn't quite fit the tidy explanation they're pushing."

The lad nods vigorously. "Exactly, sir! There's something... unnatural about it all. I remembered hearing stories about you and Detective Blackwood and how you solved cases that defied explanation."

I can't help but chuckle, though there's little mirth in it. "We saw things that would turn your hair white, boy. Things that lurk in the shadows of our so-called civilized world."

Fitch leans in, his eyes wide. "Then it's true? The supernatural... is it real?"

I fix him with a hard stare. "Real as you or me, lad. But knowledge comes at a price. Are you sure you're ready to pay it?"

As I wait for his answer, my mind drifts to the cases Blackwood and I solved, the horrors we faced. Part of me wants to send this bright-eyed youngster away to spare him the nightmares that still haunt my dreams. But I see the determination in his gaze, the same fire that once burned in me.

"I am, sir," Fitch says, his voice steady. "I became a detective to seek the truth, no matter where it leads."

I nod slowly, a mix of pride and trepidation washing over me.

"Very well, then. Let's hear the details of your case, and I'll tell you what I can. But remember, lad—once you step into this world, there's no going back."

As Fitch begins to recount his tale, I settle back in my chair, feeling the familiar thrill of the hunt stirring in my old bones. Perhaps there's one last mystery for this old detective to solve.

The scene shifts, the cozy confines of Collins's cottage fading away to reveal Dr. Amelia Lancaster's study. Sunlight streams through tall windows, illuminating shelves lined with medical texts and arcane tomes. Amelia holds a letter at her desk, her fingers tracing the heartfelt words penned by a grateful patient.

"My dear Dr. Lancaster," she reads aloud, her voice soft with emotion. I cannot express the depth of my gratitude for your help uncovering the truth behind my family's curse."

I set the letter down, a warm sense of satisfaction spreading through my chest. How many lives have been transformed by the work we do? How many families were freed from the shackles of supernatural afflictions that science alone could not explain?

My gaze falls on a framed photograph on my desk—Blackwood, Collins, Evelyn, and I, gathered after solving a harrowing case. We look younger, our faces etched with exhaustion but also triumph.

Those were dark days filled with terrors that still haunt my dreams and moments of profound connection and purpose.

A knock at the door pulls me from my reverie. "Come in," I call, straightening in my chair.

My assistant, a bright young woman named Emily, enters with a stack of patient files. "Your next appointment is here, Dr. Lancaster," she informs me. "And there's been another inquiry about your research on spectral manifestations and their effects on the human nervous system."

I nod, feeling a familiar spark of excitement. "Thank you, Emily. Show the patient in, and we'll discuss the research inquiry later."

As Emily departs, I take a deep breath, centering myself. The work continues, each day bringing new challenges and mysteries to unravel. But with every life touched, and every family freed from supernatural torment, I know our unconventional path has been exemplary.

"One patient at a time," I murmur to myself, a determined smile on my lips. "One mystery at a time. This is how we change the world."

The gas lamps flicker as I hurry down the fog-shrouded alley, my heart pounding against my ribs. The note burns in my pocket, its cryptic message seared into my mind: "Midnight. The Black Raven. Come alone." I've barely spoken to Blackwood, Collins, or Evelyn in months. Yet, here we are, drawn together once more by the tendrils of mystery.

The tavern looms before me, its weathered sign creaking in the night breeze. I push open the heavy wooden door, the scent of stale ale and tobacco smoke assaulting my senses. My eyes scan the dimly lit room, settling on three familiar figures huddled in a shadowy corner.

"Amelia," Blackwood greets me, his piercing blue eyes softening with a mix of relief and concern. "You made it."

I slide into the booth beside Evelyn, noting the tension in her posture. "What's this about?" I whisper, my gaze darting between their faces.

Collins leans forward, his grizzled features etched with worry.

"We've all received a similar summons. Anonymous, urgent. Something's brewing, mark my words."

Evelyn nods, her fingers tracing the rim of her untouched glass.

"I've heard whispers in certain circles. Old powers are stirring, ancient secrets resurfacing."

A chill runs down my spine. "You don't think—"

"We can't be certain," Blackwood interjects, his voice low and measured. "But we must be prepared for anything."

As we huddle closer, exchanging theories and fragments of information, I feel a familiar electricity in the air. Despite the years and distance between us, our bond remains unbroken, forged in the fires of shared peril and triumph.

Suddenly, the tavern door swings open, admitting a well-dressed gentleman who surveys the room with calculated nonchalance. His gaze locks onto our table, and he approaches with purposeful strides.

"Dr. Lancaster, Lady Worthington, gentlemen," he addresses us with a slight bow. "Your presence is requested at the Blackthorn Society's annual gala. Tonight."

My breath catches in my throat. The Blackthorn Society—a name whispered in hushed tones, synonymous with power and secrets. I exchange glances with my companions, seeing my curiosity and apprehension reflected in their eyes.

"And if we decline?" Collins challenges, his hand instinctively moving towards his coat pocket.

The messenger's smile doesn't reach his eyes. "That would be... most unwise. Your carriage awaits outside."

As we rise to follow him, I can't shake the feeling that we're stepping into the lion's den. But with Blackwood's unwavering resolve, Collins' steadfast loyalty, Evelyn's keen intellect, and my determination by my side, I know we're ready to face whatever darkness lies ahead.

"Into the breach once more," I murmur, squaring my shoulders as we step out into the misty London night.

The opulent ballroom glitters with crystal chandeliers and polished marble, but beneath the veneer of refinement, I sense a palpable undercurrent of malice. My eyes dart to a conspicuous seam in the ornate flooring as we mingle.

"Blackwood," I whisper, inclining my head subtly. His piercing blue eyes follow my gaze, narrowing with understanding.

"Well spotted, Amelia," he murmurs. "Shall we investigate?"

With practiced nonchalance, we drift toward the anomaly. Evelyn's melodious laugh provides cover as Collins deftly manipulates the hidden mechanism. A section of the floor slides away, revealing a steep, winding staircase descending into darkness.

"After you, old friend," Collins gestures to Blackwood, a wry smile beneath his greying mustache.

We descend, the air growing thick with the scent of age and secrets. The chamber that greets us steals the breath from my lungs.

Ancient artifacts line the walls, their surfaces etched with symbols that seem to writhe in the flickering torchlight.

"My God," Evelyn breathes, her eyes wide. "This is far beyond anything we imagined."

Blackwood's voice is grim. "The Blackthorn Society isn't merely influencing world events. They're harnessing forces beyond mortal ken."

A low chuckle echoes through the chamber. "How perceptive, Detective Blackwood."

We whirl to face a group of robed figures, their leader's eyes gleaming with dark triumph.

"You've meddled in affairs beyond your comprehension for the last time," he snarls, raising a gnarled staff crackling with eldritch energy.

I feel the hairs on my neck rise as the air thrums with supernatural power. "Whatever you're planning," I declare, my voice steadier than I feel, "we will stop you."

The battle erupts in a maelstrom of light and shadow. Blackwood's analytical mind works furiously to counter each arcane assault.

Collins' unwavering resolve manifests itself in a shield of shimmering energy. Evelyn's knowledge of ancient lore proves invaluable as she deciphers and disrupts their rituals.

I channel every ounce of my medical expertise and intuition into sensing the ebb and flow of the supernatural forces at play.

"There!" I shout, identifying a critical weakness in their defenses.

Together, we press our advantage, our determination a bulwark against the darkness threatening to engulf the world we've sworn to protect.

The chamber falls silent, save for our ragged breathing. I lean against a crumbling stone pillar, my legs trembling with exhaustion. The acrid scent of ozone lingers in the air, a testament to the clash of supernatural forces that has subsided.

Blackwood stands in the center of the room, his coat tattered and singed. His piercing blue eyes, ever vigilant, scan the fallen forms of the Blackthorn Society members. "Is everyone alright?" he asks, his voice hoarse but steady.

"Bit worse for wear," Collins grunts, dabbing at a gash on his forehead with a handkerchief. "But I'll live."

Evelyn brushes dust from her skirts, her auburn hair in disarray.

"We... we did it," she breathes, awe and disbelief mingling in her voice.

I nod, a wave of relief washing over me. "The balance is preserved," I say, my medical instincts kicking in as I move to check on my companions. "For now, at least."

Blackwood's shoulders relax infinitesimally. "Indeed, Dr. Lancaster. I fear this victory may be the first skirmish in a longer war."

We exchange glances, the weight of our shared ordeal evident in our eyes. Without a word, we make our way out of the underground chamber, emerging into the cool night air of London.

"I know a place," Collins murmurs, leading us through winding alleyways until we reach a secluded courtyard, hidden from prying eyes by overgrown ivy.

As we settle onto weathered stone benches, I can't help but marvel at the bond forged between us—four individuals from vastly different walks of life united by a shared purpose.

"What now?" Evelyn asks, breaking the contemplative silence.

Blackwood's gaze is distant. "We remain vigilant. The supernatural realm has always brushed against our world, but now..." He trails off, leaving the implications hanging in the air.

I lean forward, my voice low but determined. "Whatever comes next, we face it together."

A sudden gust of wind sweeps through the courtyard, rustling the ivy and sending a chill down my spine. The leaves whisper secrets in an ancient tongue, and I can't shake the feeling that unseen eyes are watching us from the shadows.

Blackwood's head snaps up, his piercing blue eyes scanning the darkness. "Did you hear that?" he asks, his voice barely above a whisper.

Evelyn leans in, her auburn hair catching the moonlight. "Hear what, Arthur?"

I strain my ears, trying to catch whatever has caught Blackwood's attention. The wind dies down, leaving an eerie stillness in its wake. Then, faintly, I hear a melodic whisper, words beyond comprehension.

"It's as if the city itself is trying to speak to us," Collins mutters, his weathered face creased with concern.

I feel a spark of excitement ignite within me despite the lingering exhaustion. "Perhaps it is," I say, my mind racing with possibilities.

"The veil between worlds has been disturbed. Who knows what other mysteries await us?"

Blackwood's eyes meet mine, a familiar glint of curiosity replacing the weariness. "Indeed, Amelia. Our work, it seems, is far from over."

Evelyn stands, brushing off her skirts. "Well then," she says, a hint of her old, adventurous spirit creeping into her voice, "I suppose we'd best prepare ourselves for whatever comes next."

As we rise to our feet, I can't help but notice the change in our demeanor. The weight of our recent battle still lingers—a new energy coursing through us—a mixture of anticipation and determination.

"Together," Collins affirms, his gruff voice carrying a note of warmth.

The wind picks up again, carrying the faintest scent of something otherworldly. As we step out of the courtyard and into the fog-laden streets of London, I feel a shiver of excitement. Whatever challenges and dark forces we may face, I know we are ready to confront the unknown with this unlikely team by my side.

Chapter 22 Reflection

The flickering candlelight casts long shadows across my study, dancing over artifacts from cases long past. I lean back in my leather chair, fingers steepled beneath my chin, contemplating the inexplicable events that have led me to this moment. The air feels heavy, charged with an unseen energy that sets my nerves on edge.

My gaze falls upon a peculiar amulet resting on my desk. Its ancient symbols seem to writhe in the dim light. Seeing it sends a chill down my spine, transporting me back to that fateful encounter in the secret room.

"It can't be real," I mutter, reaching out to trace the intricate engravings. "And yet..."

The memory floods back with startling clarity - the oppressive darkness, the suffocating silence broken only by my ragged breath.

And then, emerging from the shadows, a figure both there and not there, its form shifting and undulating like smoke given life.

I shake my head, trying to dispel the image. "Pull yourself together, Blackwood," I scold myself. "There must be a logical explanation."

But even as I say the words, doubt gnaws at me. The entity's otherworldly presence defied all rational thought, challenging everything I knew about the natural world.

Rising from my chair, I pace the room, and the thick Persian rug muffles my footsteps. The walls are lined with bookshelves, each tome a testament to mankind's pursuit of knowledge. Yet, at that moment, I felt acutely aware of how little we truly understand.

"What am I missing?" I wonder aloud, running a hand through my hair. "What connection am I failing to see?"

The case has consumed me, its tendrils reaching into every aspect of my life. Sleep eludes me, my mind constantly churning over clues and theories. Even now, in the sanctuary of my study, I cannot escape its grip.

I turn to my desk, scanning the scattered papers and hastily scribbled notes. Some overlooked details must contain an answer that will clarify this maddening puzzle.

As I settle back into my chair, a gust of wind rattles the windows, causing the candle flames to dance wildly. For a moment, I could swear I saw a familiar, shifting form reflected in the glass. My heart races, and I spin around, half-expecting to find the entity materializing in my study.

But there is nothing there—just shadows and silence.

I let out a shaky breath, acutely aware of how this case has frayed the edges of my sanity. But I refuse to be deterred. "Focus, Arthur," I tell myself firmly. "The truth is out there, waiting to be uncovered. And I will find it, no matter the cost." My determination is unwavering, and I can feel the readers' commitment to see this through with me.

With renewed determination, I pull a fresh sheet of paper towards me and dip my pen in ink. The night is young, and there are mysteries yet to be solved.

The scratching of my pen against paper is suddenly drowned out by the tolling of Big Ben in the distance. Its resonant chimes transport me back to another time, another place. Suddenly, I'm no longer in my study but standing on London Bridge, the weight of my grief as heavy as the fog that shrouds the city.

"Elizabeth!" I cry out, and my voice is hoarse with desperation.

The figure of my beloved sister flickers at the edge of my vision, always just out of reach. Her pale face turns towards me, eyes wide with terror before she vanishes into the mist.

I blink and I'm back in my study, my hands trembling. The memory of that fateful night still haunts me, fueling my relentless pursuit of justice. Elizabeth's unsolved disappearance was my first case, and it remains my most painful failure. But I refuse to give up. My dedication to justice is unwavering, and I can feel the readers' inspiration as they witness my determination.

"I should have been there," I muttered, running a hand through my messy hair. "I should have protected her."

The guilt gnaws at me, a constant companion in my darkest moments. I rise from my chair, pacing the room as I contemplate my sacrifices in my quest for truth. My struggle with guilt is palpable, and I can feel the readers' empathy as they witness my inner turmoil.

"Is it worth it, Arthur?" I ask myself, pausing before a mirror. The face that stares back at me is haggard, lined with worry and sleepless nights. "How many more nights will you spend chasing shadows?"

I turn away, unable to face my reflection. "As many as it takes," I answered grimly. "For Elizabeth. For all those who have no one else to speak for them."

Yet, doubt creeps in, insidious and persistent. How many relationships have I neglected? How many simple pleasures have I denied myself? The toll of my obsession is written in the greying of my temples and the deepening of the lines around my eyes.

"You're not getting any younger, old boy," I murmur, a hint of my usual dry humor surfacing. "Perhaps it's time to consider retirement. Take up gardening, perhaps?"

The very thought makes me chuckle, but it's a hollow sound. We both know I could never walk away, not while there are still mysteries to solve, still wrongs to right.

I return to my desk, determination to settle over me like a familiar cloak. "One more case," I promise myself, knowing it's a lie. "One more, and then I'll rest."

As I bend over my notes again, the candle flames flicker, casting long shadows across the room. In their dancing light, I see the ghosts of my past and the promise of future mysteries intertwined in an endless, haunting dance.

The candle flames dance, casting eerie shadows on the walls of my study. I lean back in my chair, fingers steepled beneath my chin, contemplating the tapestry of mysteries woven into the fabric of London's history.

"It's all connected," I mutter, eyes scanning the artifacts and case files scattered across my desk. "The past bleeds into the present, leaving echoes we can't ignore."

I reach for an ancient amulet, its tarnished surface glinting dully in the candlelight. "How many hands have held you?" I ask softly. "How many secrets do you keep?"

The weight of centuries presses down on me, a tangible force in the room's stillness. I've seen things that defy explanation and encountered entities that should not exist in our rational world. Yet they are, lurking in the shadows of our modern age, as accurate as the cobblestones beneath our feet.

"We're fooling ourselves," I say aloud, my voice barely above a whisper. "Thinking we've outgrown the old ways, the old beliefs. They're still here, just waiting for us to remember."

A chill runs down my spine as I recall the ghostly guardian of the secret room, its otherworldly presence a stark reminder of how little we truly understand.

Doubt creeps in, unbidden and unwelcome. I push back from the desk, pacing the length of the study. "Am I the right man for this?"

I ask about the empty room. "Can I truly unravel this web of history and the supernatural?"

My reflection in the window catches my eye—a man haunted by his past, burdened by the weight of mysteries. For a moment, I see not the decorated detective but a weary soul grasping at shadows.

"What if I'm not enough?" The words taste bitter on my tongue. "What if this case is beyond even my abilities?"

I pause, hand resting on the cold glass. Outside, fog swirls through gas-lit streets, concealing untold secrets in its misty embrace.

"No," I say firmly, squaring my shoulders. "I cannot falter now. Too much depends on this."

Yet even as I speak the words, a flicker of uncertainty lingers in my eyes, reflecting at me in the darkened window.

I turn from the window, my gaze falling upon the artifacts scattered across my desk. Each one is a testament to past cases, to mysteries unraveled. But I also realize with a pang that it is an obsession that has consumed me for far too long.

"You've let it become your entire world, Arthur," I muttered, running a finger along the edge of an ancient Egyptian scarab. "At what cost?"

The realization settles heavily upon my shoulders. My pursuit of justice, my need to uncover the truth, has often blinded me to the toll it takes on those around me and myself.

"I can't keep going like this," I say, my voice barely above a whisper. "There must be balance."

A knock at the door startles me from my reverie. "Come in," I call, straightening my posture.

Inspector Holloway enters, his weathered face creased with concern. "Blackwood, we've got a new lead on the Whitechapel.

Thought you'd want to know straight away."

I feel the familiar pull of curiosity, the thrill of the chase. But this time, I pause. "Thank you, Holloway. I'll review the details in the morning. For now, I believe I need some rest."

The inspector's eyebrows rise in surprise. "Are you feeling alright, sir?"

A small smile tugs at my lips. "Never better, old friend. I'm simply learning that even the sharpest minds need respite."

As Holloway takes his leave, I turn back to my desk. My eyes settle on a framed photograph—my late wife, smiling on our wedding day. "I won't forget what truly matters," I promise her.

"Not again."

With renewed purpose, I gather my coat and hat. The mysteries of London can wait for one night. I'll seek balance tonight, knowing it will only sharpen my resolve on the challenges ahead.

As I exited the fog-laden streets, my mind raced with possibilities. The unsolved cases, supernatural entities, and dark corners of history call me as strongly as ever. But now, I feel better equipped to face them.

"Come what may," I murmur, my breath visible in the chill air, "I'll meet it with a clear head and an open mind."

The gas lamps flicker, casting long shadows as I go home. For once, I'm not chasing ghosts through the night. Instead, I'm preparing myself for the battles to come, knowing that true strength lies in acknowledging one's limitations as much as one's abilities.

London's secrets will still be there tomorrow, waiting for me to unravel them. And I'll be ready, more determined than ever, to seek the truth—without losing myself.

The fog thickens as I wind through London's labyrinthine streets, each step echoing off the damp cobblestones. A shiver runs down my spine, not from the cold but from the weight of unseen eyes. I can't shake the feeling that the city itself is watching, waiting.

"What mysteries do you hold for me next?" I whisper into the shadows.

As if in answer, a gust of wind carries the faint scent of incense—the same scent I encountered in the secret room guarded by that otherworldly entity—my mind races, connecting invisible threads.

"The Order of the Eternal Flame," I mutter, my voice barely audible above the distant clatter of a carriage. "What are you planning?"

I pause beneath a flickering gas lamp, its light creating a small island in the encroaching darkness. My hand instinctively reaches for the pocket watch that once belonged to my father, its familiar weight grounding me.

"Whatever it is, I'll find out," I vow, my resolve hardening. "And I'll put an end to it."

A passing constable tips his hat. "Evening, Detective Blackwood. All muted tonight?"

I force a smile. "So it seems, Constable. But appearances can be deceiving."

As he moves on, I make my decision. The Order of the Eternal Flame has evaded justice for too long. Their tendrils reach into the very heart of London, entwining with both the mundane and the supernatural. It's time to cut them out, root and stem.

"No more half-measures," I say, clenching my fist. "I'll uncover every secret, face every horror. Whatever the cost."

The chimes of Big Ben echo in the distance as if sealing my oath. I turn towards home, my mind already mapping out the investigation to come. The game is afoot, and London's shadows have never felt more alive.

I stride back to my study, my footsteps echoing with newfound purpose. The familiar scent of leather-bound books and aged parchment greets me as I enter, but tonight, it feels different—empowered.

"I've faced ghosts and ghouls," I muttered, running my fingers along the spines of tomes that have guided me through countless cases. "Unmasked charlatans and confronted genuine horrors. The Order is just another mystery to unravel."

I settle into my chair, its worn leather creaking softly. My gaze falls upon the artifacts scattered across my desk—reminders of past triumphs and near-misses. Each one holds a lesson, a piece of the puzzle that has shaped me into the detective I am today.

"You've come a long way, Arthur," I chuckle darkly. "Remember when you thought that banshee in Whitechapel was just a clever trick of acoustics?"

The memory of that case—my first brush with the genuinely supernatural—floods back. I'd been so sure, so arrogantly logical. And yet, when faced with the undeniable truth, I'd adapted. Learned. Grown.

I lean back, steepling my fingers. "Every case, every confrontation... they've all led to this moment."

My eyes drift to a small, framed daguerreotype on my desk. Sarah's smile, frozen in time, stares back at me. The familiar pang of loss tightens my chest, but it no longer paralyzes me as it once did.

"I couldn't save you," I whisper to her image. "But I can save others. I can stop this darkness from spreading."

With a deep breath, I rise from my chair. My coat, draped over a nearby chair, seems to beckon. I shrug it on, feeling its familiar weight settle on my shoulders like armor.

"No more hesitation," I declare to the empty room, my voice steady and persistent. "No more doubts. The Order of the Eternal Flame thinks they can hide in the shadows. They're about to learn that shadows are where I thrive."

I gather my notebook, magnifying glass, and a small vial of holy water—a precaution I've learned never to neglect. As I move towards the door, I glimpse myself in the mirror. The man staring back at me is no longer haunted by uncertainty. His eyes burn doggedly, and his posture radiates confidence.

"London's fate hangs in the balance," I murmur, adjusting my collar. "And I'll be damned if I let it fall."

With one last sweeping glance around my study, I extinguish the lamp and enter the night. The fog swirls around my feet, but it no longer feels ominous. Instead, it's a veil I'm ready to tear away, revealing the truth that lies beneath.

The game is on foot, and I've never been more prepared to play it.

Don't miss out!

Visit the website below and you can sign up to receive emails whenever David L. Waters publishes a new book. There's no charge and no obligation.

https://books2read.com/r/B-A-JCBLC-ZQKDF

BOOKS 2 READ

Connecting independent readers to independent writers.

Also by David L. Waters

Mystery in the Harbor
Echoes of the Past: Detective Arthur Blackwood's Haunting Case in
Victorian London
Veil of Shadows: The Case of the Order of the Eternal Flame
Whispers from the Docks

About the Author

David Waters, a 67-year-old retired Navy veteran, has lived a life marked by dedication, bravery, and service to his country. Born in 1957 in Charleston, South Carolina, David grew up with an intense patriotism and a desire to serve. This calling led him to enlist in the United States Navy at 21.

After six years of honorable service, David was discharged from the Navy in 1984. His retirement did not mark the end of his contributions, however. David became an active member of veteran organizations, advocating for the rights and welfare of fellow veterans. He also dedicated time to mentoring young sailors and sharing his knowledge and experience.

Now, at 67, David is embarking on a new adventure: a writing career he has long dreamed of. With a passion for storytelling and a wealth of experiences to draw from, David is excited to share his stories with the world. His writing focuses on naval history, personal memoirs, and fictional tales inspired by his adventures at sea.